A SPELL OF TIME

A Shade of Vampire, Book 10

Bella Forrest

Also by Bella Forrest:

A SHADE OF VAMPIRE SERIES:
A Shade of Vampire (Book 1)
A Shade of Blood (Book 2)
A Castle of Sand (Book 3)
A Shadow of Light (Book 4)
A Blaze of Sun (Book 5)
A Gate of Night (Book 6)
A Break of Day (Book 7)
A Shade of Novak (Book 8)
A Bond of Blood (Book 9)
A Spell of Time (Book 10)

A SHADE OF KIEV TRILOGY:
A Shade of Kiev 1
A Shade of Kiev 2
A Shade of Kiev 3

BEAUTIFUL MONSTER DUOLOGY:
Beautiful Monster 1
Beautiful Monster 2

For an updated list of Bella's books,
please visit www.bellaforrest.net

Contents

PROLOGUE: CALEB

Tick, tock.

Tick, tock.

I sat in my armchair, staring up at the clock in the corner of the room. The hours seemed to drag by, the time between Annora's nightly visits growing longer. Or perhaps it was just the absence of music.

Nobody knew what the witches' plans were now that Mona was protecting The Shade. Annora hadn't told any of us. I didn't care, as long as I never had to go near the island again. I wasn't sure if human abductions were to continue as usual, or whether she would continue harassing The Shade until she managed to penetrate it.

Somehow, I suspected the latter. But it didn't concern me. I'd already made clear to Annora that I wanted to be left out of visits to The Shade from now on.

There was a knock at my door.

I swallowed the last of my drink before opening it. Annora glided in and sat down on the edge of my bed.

"I wasn't expecting you early today," I said.

"I'm in a good mood." She loosened her robe, allowing it to slide down her shoulders and reveal her silk underwear.

She stood up, roughly unbuttoning my shirt and throwing it aside. She manifested a knife and ran it across my chest, leaving a line of blood. I barely flinched. She crawled back onto the bed, kneeling and beckoning me over. I remained still.

"What?" she snapped.

Breathing steadily, I held her gaze, taking in her dark beauty. Her long hair, sharp cheekbones, cool grey eyes, pillowy lips. How I used to yearn for this woman. She'd once been my vision of perfection.

It wasn't often that I reminded myself of the life

Annora and I used to share. The promises we'd exchanged. The plans we'd made. But now I did. Perhaps it was because the vision of Rose was still fresh in my memory, her soft voice still ringing in my ears.

Rose likely considered me a coward. Weak. For running away. For not being willing to fight for what we had. Of course, I couldn't expect her to think anything different. She didn't understand.

I'd already witnessed the wilting of one blossom. I wasn't about to risk the petals of another. Least of all Rose.

The princess still haunted me and it was all I could do to distract myself from the pain.

That night, I touched Annora in a way I hadn't for decades. Instead of extending my claws and cutting her, I gripped her waist and pulled her against me. Running my hands down her back, I caught her lips in mine.

Her eyes widened, and I thought I saw within them a flicker of emotion as I crawled over her, still kneading my lips against hers. But I could have been mistaken, for it lasted but a moment.

I closed my eyes and remembered. *Annora. The girl who'd once owned my every thought and breath, whom I would have done anything for. The girl I'd sworn to marry.*

I knew better than to expect Annora to feel anything other than mild boredom at my advances. But it didn't matter.

She pushed against my chest.

"Caleb?"

I ignored her. I lay beside her, pulling her flush against me as I continued caressing her lips, running my fingers through her sleek hair.

To my shock, she began returning my kisses. I thought for a moment it was out of passion, perhaps even hunger for me. But then her hands slid down my back and spasms erupted at the base of my spine.

She broke away from my kiss, her eyes sharpening.

I shouldn't have allowed myself to hope for anything different. The only thing that aroused her was pain. Violence. So I positioned myself over her, dug my fangs into her neck and pressed down hard, sinking her into the mattress.

She moaned and squirmed beneath me.

She wanted to feel pain. I'd make her feel it.

Chapter 1: Sofia

There wasn't much we could do other than just wait and hope for the best. We didn't know when or if the witches would attempt to attack us again with more force, and whether Mona would be able to keep them out if they did.

Our other witches weren't of any real help to Mona in securing the spell. The security of our island, and all our lives, depended entirely on this witch we barely knew.

Derek and I had done our part in preparing the island for an attack. We'd had all the storage chambers in the Catacombs cleared out and filled with food, water and bedding. But really, if Annora managed to penetrate the island, it would only be a matter of time before we were all brought down.

For now, Kiev and his people had agreed to stay. We just had to hope that they wouldn't change their minds any time soon.

Although we were all on edge, we had to continue with our lives. Ben and Rose resumed classes at school, and the witches went back to teaching.

While I had been making an effort to acquaint myself better with our guests, now living in the northwest of the island, Derek took any opportunity to shut himself in our apartment. Whenever he didn't have a meeting, or some other important matter to attend to, he stayed indoors. I didn't need to possess more than a few brain cells to realize why that was.

So far, I had paid a visit to Matteo, Mona and Kiev, his siblings and a few other vampires. Now I planned to spend some time with Saira and the other werewolves, and then stop by Brett the ogre's cave on the way back.

Before leaving the apartment, I poked my head through the door of Derek's study. He sat at his desk, sifting through a pile of papers. I approached and looked over his shoulder. I recognized Eli's meticulous handwriting. He'd had a meeting with Eli earlier to discuss reconsidering our lookout spots around the island.

I wrapped my arms around Derek's neck, placing a slow, tender kiss beneath his right ear.

"Hey," I whispered.

"Resorting to seduction now, Mrs. Novak?" he muttered, not bothering to look up from his work. "I thought you were more classy than that."

I giggled, tightening my grip around his neck. "What about resorting to force?"

He leant his head back, staring up at me with his blue eyes, calmly raising a brow.

"You can always try, darling. Though I don't suggest it if you place any value on the time you spent combing your hair this morning…"

I squeezed his cheeks and pulled a face at him. I couldn't stop grinning as I knelt next to him. I removed one of his hands from the desk and held it.

"Derek, seriously. You're king of this island. They are now your citizens. You need to get to know them."

"It's not required that both of us get to know them. You're queen. My other half. My representative. You going is the same as my going. It's a waste of time both of us doing the same task. Besides, I already spoke to Matteo. And as for Kiev, I know more about that vampire than I can ever hope to erase from my memory."

"You don't know him. He's different now."

"So it seems. But you've already told me his story. There's nothing more I require."

"But, Derek—"

"Sofia, I don't owe him anything. He owed us. That's why he did what he did. Now we're even."

I sighed and stood up. It seemed that Derek would rather swallow a mouthful of nails than agree to my proposal.

I walked round to the back of his chair as he focused his attention once again on his work. I placed my palms over his forehead, brushing back his thick dark hair, and kissed his temple.

"Okay, baby. I'm not going to keep trying to force you. I just hope that one day you and Kiev will be able to accept each other for what you both are now...

family."

Derek remained silent.

I rolled my eyes and left the room.

Since the last meeting, Derek had resisted all my attempts to rope him into another meeting with Kiev. And vice versa. The truth was, as much as the two men's stubbornness was frustrating, it was also beginning to amuse me. Kiev and Derek could pull off passive-aggression like I'd never seen before. As I walked out of the apartment alone, I determined to somehow bring the two of them together again. And something told me that I would have fun doing it…

I descended the elevator and began walking through the forest toward our guests' residences. My father was approaching Yuri and Claudia's tree.

"Hey, Dad," I called.

"Hi, Sofia," he said. He looked exhausted, his skin grey, eyes dark with fatigue.

I hugged him and kissed his cheek. "Are you all right?"

"Yes," he said, pulling a strained smile.

"I'm just on my way to meet some of the werewolves," I said.

"Oh, great. I won't keep you then, honey. I'm just paying a quick visit to Yuri."

"We need to make some time for each other." I could hardly remember the last occasion we'd sat down and spent quality time together.

"We will."

I hugged him again and we parted ways.

It took me about ten minutes of sprinting to reach the stretch of beach that was lined with the werewolves' townhouses. I headed straight for Saira's door. I knocked three times and waited. No answer. I peered through the window, but the curtains had been drawn. I knocked again. When there was still no answer, I tried knocking on the house next door. Again no answer. I knocked on each door next to hers for about five doors. When not one of them opened, I stepped back onto the beach, frowning.

Strange. Perhaps Matteo knows where she is.

I continued walking along the beach toward the vampires' residences when I saw a large bonfire in the distance. A group was huddled around it, laughing and chattering.

Brett the ogre towered over the fire, skewering fish

and holding them against the flames. He wore a stained waistcoat over his muddy brown chest, and grubby-looking pants that were a little too ripped for comfort.

I looked around at the crowd. All werewolves—still in their human forms since it was daytime, for which I was grateful. It still felt strange to hold a conversation with a giant wolf. I hadn't yet gotten used to the way they replied in their deep gravelly voices.

They stopped laughing and chattering as soon as they saw me approach. An awkward silence descended. It was broken by Brett, who pointed to a spare seat near the fire. "Have a seat, why don't ya."

All eyes were on me as I sat down on the sand. I was glad to see Saira a few feet away from me. Her plump face split into a smile.

"Hello, Sofia."

"Hello."

The rest of the group began chattering again, though still glancing at me curiously.

"So, how are you finding The Shade so far?"

"Very comfortable. Certainly, these accommodations are more luxurious than what we're used to."

"Good."

We needed to go out of our way to keep them all as comfortable and satisfied as possible.

So far, there had been no reports of attacks of their vampires or werewolves on our humans, which a part of me was definitely surprised about. Despite their assurances that they were house-trained, I had still harbored doubts. But they seemed to stick to their area of the island and not encroach on ours.

The ogre roasted several skewers of fish at once. I nodded toward the fire. "I see you're doing all right for food."

"Yes," Saira said. "This fish and the meat here... it tastes very different to what we're used to. But we're getting used to it."

"The fish are easier to catch," said a voice from my left.

I turned to see who had spoken. A handsome young man—he looked no older than twenty—with sandy blond hair that licked the sides of his face. He had a broad forehead and hazel eyes.

"And your name is?"

"Micah."

I reached out to shake his hand and smiled.

"Nice to meet you, Micah."

It truly was a pleasant surprise to see how easy to please our guests were. They seemed to be grateful just to have clean beds, fresh water and food, basic amenities everyone in The Shade took for granted.

Brett started handing out skewers to the werewolves, who began eating hungrily. He looked at me apologetically.

"It's a shame you can't try any. This batch is scrumptious." He licked his thumb as he removed three fish from a skewer and guzzled them down.

"That's kind of you, Brett."

I had to admit that I did miss food. Often. Blood became so boring. Especially animal blood. Mealtimes were just a means of sustenance. There was never any pleasure in them. I'd tried eating regular food a few times, but I'd had a similar reaction to Derek's the time I'd tried to stuff toast down his mouth. It was tasteless and I wasn't able to digest it. I'd tried eating my favorite breakfast, toast with jam, but each attempt had resulted in a severe stomach ache that had lasted for days afterward.

I moved over, squishing closer to Micah as Brett

plodded toward me, attempting to sit on a patch of sand that was clearly far too small for him.

I watched with a mixture of intrigue and disgust as the ogre devoured his meal. It was fascinating how he used his tusks. His teeth seemed to be all around quite blunt. It was his tusks that he pressed the fish against, tearing the flesh into pieces.

No wonder they always look so greasy.

"Micah here caught these fish," he said through a mouthful, pointing a sticky finger in Micah's direction while spraying pieces of meat down the back of a female werewolf sitting directly in front of him.

"Ugh! Brett!" She stood up and began shaking herself down, brushing away the meat which had crept down the back of her collar. "How many times have I told you not to sit behind me when you eat?"

"Sorry," he blurted, wiping his mouth with the edge of his waistcoat.

I had to fight to suppress a grin. *I think I'm going to like Brett.* He certainly seemed to be the gentle giant Matteo and Saira had made him out to be.

"So, Micah, you're a fisherman?" I said.

Micah smiled. "Yeah, you could say that."

"He's the best we have," Saira said fondly. "He always comes back with the juiciest catches…"

I chatted with Saira, Brett and Micah for about an hour before standing up and brushing the sand off my clothes. They seemed to be more than content with their setup. None of them voiced any complaints even when I asked the whole group. My business with the wolves was done for now.

My vow to bring Derek and Kiev together still playing on my mind, instead of going straight back home, I decided to pay an unexpected visit to Kiev.

I approached the vampires' stretch of beach and knocked on Kiev and Mona's front door.

Mona answered the door.

"Hi, Sofia. What brings you here?"

"I wanted to talk to Kiev again. It's about Derek."

"Oh." She gave me a knowing glance and rolled her eyes. "Good luck with that."

She swung open the door, allowing me entrance.

"Kiev!" Mona called up the staircase.

There was a click of a bolt and the sound of a door creaking open. The floorboards groaned overhead and Kiev descended the stairs. His dark hair was wet and he wore nothing but a towel wrapped loosely around his waist.

"You could have put something on," Mona said, wrinkling her nose as she looked Kiev over.

"Mrs. Novak could have warned of her visit in advance," he replied, eyeing me steadily.

She rolled her eyes and looked back at me. "I'm sorry, Sofia. Kiev's manners are still a work in progress... Well, I'll leave you two to it. I'm off to see if there's anything left over of Brett's cooking."

I wished that she wouldn't go. It felt so awkward to be standing here alone with the half-naked vampire.

I averted my eyes from his rippling muscles to the floorboards and walked briskly into the living room. He glided in after me and drew up a chair at the table. He gestured that I take a seat.

I sat down on the sofa at the opposite end of the room, as far as possible from him. He leaned against the edge of the dining table. Crossing his arms over his chest, he gazed down at me.

"Well? What does her highness want with me?"

"It's, uh, about my husband."

His mood darkened instantly. His jaw tightened, his

16

biceps tensed.

My husband's name always had been a trigger word for Kiev. I remembered how it would bring about fits of violence when I'd been under his care in The Blood Keep.

Ignoring his reaction, I continued. "I'm trying to find a way to make things less uncomfortable for the two of you, and the rest of us, and I could use your cooperation."

His gaze remained steely.

"Stop being so passive-aggressive around him. I'm trying to get him to do the same. But it would make my job a hell of a lot easier if you threw me a bone. Look, Kiev, I'm not asking you to be friends with him. I just want the two of you to grow up."

More silence followed. His eyes were still on me, his face unreadable. "Is that all?"

"Yes."

"Then you can leave me to get dressed."

I glared at him. I didn't need to be a Seer to know that he wasn't going to budge one iota from his stance.

I stood up and walked toward the front door. He made no motion to follow me, so I shut the door myself on my way out. I sighed, staring out at the ocean. It was like trying to shift two mountains.

How am I ever going to do this?

I lost myself in thought as I made my way along the beach. I kept drawing a blank, but as I reached the foot of our tree, it dawned on me all at once. It was obvious now that I'd thought of it.

If the two men can't put aside their egos, I'll just have to create new ones for them…

I could barely keep the smirk from my face as I entered our penthouse.

Chapter 2: Caleb

After Annora left, I collapsed on the bed. I ran a thumb over my lips, recalling the few seconds she'd returned my kiss.

I tried to fall asleep. But I kept thinking about her, and the night she'd decided to leave me forever.

She'd lost some of herself after I turned her into a vampire, but she'd still been mine. She was dark, but she still loved me. She still kissed me like I was the only man in her world. But when she'd given herself over to the witches, she'd become unrecognizable.

To this day, I didn't know what they'd done to her.

She'd told me they'd agreed to make her a Channeler—one of the most powerful witches of their kind, receiving direct empowerment from the Ancients themselves. She wouldn't explain to me what the induction involved. She'd said she was forbidden to. But when she came out of it, she was a shell.

My thoughts drifted to the blonde witch, Mona. Her powers were clearly equal to, if not greater than, Annora's. I wondered if she'd been inducted in the same way. She seemed to still have life left in her.

What I wouldn't give to have Annora back even for an hour. Even just a small piece of the girl she used to be…

My thoughts were interrupted by the creak of my door. I looked up to see none other than Annora approaching my bed.

I sat up. "What?"

Tears glistened in her bloodshot eyes. She reeked of alcohol. Staggering forward, she sat down on the edge of my bed.

Truth be told, the only time I welcomed Annora's company was when she was drunk out of her mind. Although I never detected anything other than sorrow in her, I drew comfort from her display of emotion. It was a welcome change from the ice-cold woman she was when sober.

I reached for her hair, brushing it away from her face.

Her lower lip trembled. "Y-you didn't ask why I was in a good mood," she said.

I stared at her. She was right, I hadn't.

"You want to tell me?"

She nodded slowly, letting out a hiccough. She paused, and a small smile spread across her lips.

"The Shade will lose its King and Queen soon."

My breath hitched.

"What?"

Her smile broadened. "I put a spell on them. Neither of them are aware of it."

My throat tightened. "Wh-when did you put the spell on them?"

She reached out and gripped my jaw, frowning. "It doesn't matter when I cast it. Why aren't you excited?"

She leant over me and caught my lips in hers, kissing me hard. Her tears moistened my cheeks. She gave me another half smile, then disappeared from the room leaving me staring after her, winded.

I tried to steady my breathing as I stared out of the

window at the snowy peaks.

No. I can't get involved with that family again.

Chapter 3: Aiden

"Five hundred years," I muttered, my eyes glazing over as I puffed on a cigarette. I was sitting next to Yuri on his porch. "That's how long your brother's been celibate. It's just my luck…"

"I'm sorry, man," Yuri said, placing a hand on my shoulder. "I had no idea you were into Adelle like that. I'd seen you talking to her, but I didn't know you were planning on making a move."

"Yeah," I said grimly, blowing out smoke. Yuri had told me that he'd decided to help put Eli out of his misery and convinced him to ask Adelle out. I couldn't blame Yuri for it. It was what any good brother would have done.

"If I'd known, I wouldn't have said anything to him. Eli's had his eye on Adelle for a while now. I've never seen a woman capture his attention like Adelle. It was becoming agonizing to watch."

"She might have not said yes to me anyway," I said. The vision of Adelle embracing Eli was still fresh in my mind. It sent pain shooting through my chest each time I recalled it. Shaking the thought away, I tossed my cigarette and stood up. I patted Yuri on the shoulder. "Well, I wish your brother all the best. Finders keepers, right?" I forced a smile. "Forget we even had this conversation. I'd rather all this remained between you and me."

"Rather what remained between you and Yuri?"

I groaned as Claudia appeared in the doorway, hands on her waist.

"Oh, it's nothing, Claudia," I said.

I motioned to walk away, but the little spitfire never was one to be brushed away. She moved in front of me, blocking my exit.

"Come on, Aiden. I can keep a secret."

I heaved a sigh, looking back at Yuri for help. He shrugged. Claudia grabbed my hand and pulled me inside their penthouse. She led me into their living room and pushed me down on the couch.

"It's really nothing interesting. It's just…"

"Just what?"

"Adelle. Okay? I like her."

Her lips curved in a small, knowing smile.

"Well, you're not telling me anything new. The way you gawk at her… it's obvious to anyone but a complete moron. Why don't you tell her, then?"

I looked from Claudia to Yuri. Evidently she hadn't been informed yet about Eli.

Yuri cleared his throat. "Babe, Eli's going out with her. I encouraged him to ask her out."

Her face contorted with shock. "What?"

"You heard right," I said heavily.

"Eli? Your brother?"

"There's no other Eli on this island," Yuri said.

"Why didn't you tell me before?" she asked, turning on Yuri.

"I didn't even know he'd taken my advice to heart before Aiden told me."

She sank onto the couch next to me. "Wow, that really sucks."

"Yes," I said through gritted teeth. "It sucks."

I motioned to stand up and leave, but Claudia caught my arm and yanked me back down again.

"Honey, what are you going to do about it?"

"Nothing, Claudia," I said, staring at her in bemusement. "She likes Eli. And neither you nor Yuri are to talk about this with anyone, do you understand?"

Claudia bit her lip and looked at her husband. Concern filled her eyes. The silence that followed was painful. If there was one thing I loathed more than being beaten to a woman, it was being pitied.

"It was all a stupid fantasy anyway. I'm much too old for her."

"Nonsense!" Claudia scolded. "I'd take a bite out of you if Yuri didn't own me."

Yuri rolled his eyes.

I chuckled. "Well, thank you, Claudia. That's good to know."

"Seriously, Aiden. As much as I want my brother-in-law to get laid, I think you're a better match for Adelle. I think she's all wrong for him."

Yuri stared at her in half surprise, half amusement. Neither of us had expected Claudia would have such a strong opinion on the matter.

Mrs. Claudia Lazaroff. Quite the relationship counselor.

"What makes you say that?" Yuri asked.

"Eli's so goddamn serious, he needs someone younger to force some life into him."

"I'm sure Adelle will have no trouble with that," I muttered.

"She's too experienced. She doesn't look old, but God knows how many years she's actually been alive. It could be a thousand years for all we know."

"Yeah, well… as much as you might like to make this choice for them, Eli's already made his choice, and so has Adelle."

"You don't know what either of them feel for each other," Claudia pressed. "For all you know, they could decide they're not right for each other and split up."

Somehow, I doubted that. By the boathouse, their chemistry seemed to be on fire.

"And even though she's dating Eli," Claudia continued, "you should still tell her how you feel. Then she can make a choice. If you'd have gotten to her beforehand she might have chosen you instead of Eli."

I scoffed and stood up. I might have been many things, but, as much as I longed for Adelle, I wasn't the type of man to poach another's woman.

I'd had enough of this conversation. It was utterly nonsensical. Adelle was going out with Eli, at least for the moment. There was nothing more to discuss. I stood up, and although Claudia attempted to seat me again, I brushed her away and headed for the front door.

"She's right for you, Aiden," Claudia called after me as I walked out. "Don't give up on her. God knows, I'm thankful every day that Yuri didn't give up on me."

"Yeah, whatever…"

Chapter 4: Sofia

I sat opposite Corrine in her bedroom. I'd just finished explaining my plan to her. We both stared at each other and burst out laughing.

"I never knew you were so devious, Sofia."

She handed me a pen and a piece of paper. My idea was to start a letter correspondence between the two men. Derek would find himself receiving apologetic letters from Kiev, and vice versa. Of course, I would be writing all the letters. Corrine would put a charm on my handwriting so that it didn't look like my own.

I breathed out, scratching my head with the pen. We

still had to work out exactly what to say. How to pull this off without arousing suspicion from either of them. Eventually, they'd realize what I'd done, but by then—if all went to plan—the ice would have already been broken between the two of them.

I placed the tip of my pen on the paper. I was about to start writing when Corrine gripped my forearm. Mischief sparked in her eyes.

"Wait. I have a better idea."

"What?" I put the pen down and stared at her.

She walked over to her bookshelf and reached for a heavy book bound in burgundy leather. She heaved it off the shelf and plonked it down on the table next to me. She took a seat and began flipping through the pages.

"You know, I think we can get a bit more hi-tech with this…"

I was burning with curiosity as she stopped on a page. Scrawled over it was an ancient language I didn't understand.

She made me wait in silence for ten minutes before she finally looked up, grinning again.

"Yes, I think this will work."

"What?" I urged.

"What if Kiev went to Derek personally to apologize, and vice versa?"

I stared at her. "Well, obviously that would be the best option, but how on earth—"

"How on earth do we get those two stubborn mules to ever do it? Simple. We don't."

"Huh?"

"There is a spell I believe I can pull off." Corrine stood up and began pacing the room. "But we're going to need Mona's help."

"What spell?"

"I can give you Derek's appearance. And also Kiev's appearance."

I gasped. "That's brilliant, Corrine. So I would look exactly like them? My voice would sound like them too?"

Corrine nodded, grinning from ear to ear.

I pushed the pen and paper away from me.

"And why do we need Mona?"

"I need some form of both of the men's DNA. A hair will probably be the easiest and least... unhygienic."

"Okay. We'll ask Mona. I'm sure she'll agree. She's

not happy with the tension between the two of them either."

"We just have to trust that she won't blab to anyone about it," Corrine said.

"I trust Mona," I said immediately. How could we not trust her about something as small as this when we'd already placed our faith in her to protect the entire island?

"I do too."

Corrine and I stared at each other as the weight of our planned deception fell upon us. I just hoped that I'd be able to keep a straight face while doing all of this.

"Okay," I said, standing up. "I'm going to get one of Derek's hairs now. I'll get it from his hairbrush."

"No," Corrine said. "It needs to be freshly plucked. It will be more potent that way, and the effect of the potion will last longer."

"Oh. I hadn't thought about that. How long does the potion last?"

Corrine scratched her head and consulted the book again.

"Hm. I'm not sure exactly."

"Well, it should last at least a couple of hours, right?"

"It should do…"

She didn't appear confident, but this was an idea too delicious for me to pass on.

"All right, let's think," I said, beginning to pace up and down the room myself. "I should turn into Kiev first, and visit Derek. It only makes sense that he would be the one to approach Derek first, since he has a lot more to be sorry for. Then once the spell wears off, I'll visit Kiev as Derek."

"So we need Kiev's hair first," Corrine said. "That means I need to fetch Mona."

"Okay, I'll wait here."

Corrine vanished. I sat down again, drumming my fingers over the table. I paged through her spell book, but not being able to understand a single word, I soon got bored.

She returned about half an hour later. Mona appeared by her side carrying a pair of pants and a shirt over her shoulder, clutching a hair between her fingers.

"How did it go?" I asked, eyeing the hair.

Mona looked at me, bemused. "Are you really sure this isn't all going to backfire?"

"No. I'm not sure. But things can hardly get any

worse than they are now."

"Let's go into my potion room," Corrine said, leading us out of her bedroom. "Oh, and you might want to bring one of those sheets with you," she added, pointing toward the bed.

We walked through the halls of the Sanctuary until we reached Corrine's potion room. Mona laid the hair down on a plate near the sink. I bent over the hair, studying it more closely. I wasn't sure that I dared ask where she'd plucked it from.

"From his leg," Mona said, as though she'd read my mind.

"Great," I mumbled.

"Trust me, there are worse places it could have come from."

Mona and I hovered over Corrine for the next fifteen minutes watching as she stirred ingredients into a cauldron and brought them to a rolling boil. The liquid hissed and turned a bright green color. A foul smell began emanating from it.

"Okay," Corrine said. "This is done."

Mona and Corrine exchanged glances, then both set their eyes on me.

"Ibrahim isn't expected back, is he?" I asked, glancing at the door.

"No," Corrine said, "he's not due back for a few hours. Now, I'm going to leave the room for this. Mona will take things from here. Good luck." She patted me on the shoulder and left the room.

I looked at Mona nervously.

"The first thing you need to do is strip."

I looked down at my dress. *Strip. Of course.*

Mona held the sheet around me while I undressed. Once I was done, I clutched the sheet against me as Mona let go and began pouring the potion into a goblet. She passed it to me.

"Drink up."

Holding the cup to my lips, I took the first sip. It was hot, but surprisingly tasteless. I downed the rest. Mona took the empty goblet from me and walked over to the sink. Picking up the hair, she returned with it.

"Now you need to lay this on your tongue. Don't swallow it."

"Can you at least wash it first?" I grumbled.

"Hygiene should be the last thing on your mind right now."

I opened my mouth, allowing her to lay the hair on my tongue. I almost gagged.

She placed her hands on my head and began muttering some kind of chant. She continued for five minutes before letting go.

I looked at her nervously, waiting to feel something. Anything. Ten minutes passed. I was beginning to think the spell had failed.

"Mona, are you sure—"

And then I felt it. A strong tingling at the tips of my fingers, spreading through my arms toward my chest, then neck, face, stomach. Soon my whole body prickled. It wasn't painful, just an odd itching sensation. I began to rise inches above the floor. Whereas previously Mona was taller than me, now I towered over her. I reached up a hand to touch my face but Mona stopped me.

"Wait," she said. "Don't touch yourself until the transformation is complete. I'll tell you when."

I waited for ten more minutes until finally Mona nodded. "You've changed as much as you're going to change."

I looked down and saw a muscular chest and

powerful arms. Thankfully, I couldn't see further than that. I was still holding the sheet tight against me. I became suddenly aware of all the extra weight I was carrying.

Crap. I really didn't think this through.

I held the sheet tighter against me, looking at Mona in despair.

What have I done?

"I'd better be able to change back," I croaked.

Mona chuckled. "You will."

This was perhaps the most bizarre experience of my life. The only thing I could think of that came close to it was when the Elder had possessed me and taken control of my body.

Mona approached and to my horror, yanked the sheet away from me.

"No!" My eyes shot up to the ceiling. "Give it back!" I reached out my hands desperately.

Mona broke out laughing.

"It's okay," she chuckled. "I've see Kiev before. Just keep looking at the ceiling while I help you change."

She grabbed the clothes she'd brought with her. She pulled my arms through the shirt and buttoned it. My eyes followed her as she reached for Kiev's pants.

"No sneaking a peek at my man, girl."

I glared at her. "I wouldn't dream of it." My gaze shot back up to the ceiling as she helped me step into the pants.

I hope Derek will forgive me for this when he finds out...

CHAPTER 5: SOFIA

I ran my hand along Kiev's rough stubble.

"Okay," I said, taking a deep breath. "I have to go now."

Both of the witches were still eyeing me with amusement.

"Good luck," Corrine said.

I left the room and made my way toward the exit. I stopped short a few feet away from the front door. *I'm making Kiev walk like a girl. How do guys walk?*

I slouched slightly, let Kiev's arms swing more loosely at my sides, and spread out my feet. I tried walking again. Although I felt far from confident, I didn't have time for more practice. I'd just have to stand still in front of Derek.

I walked out the door and scanned the courtyard. I was terrified that I might bump into Kiev on the way. I jolted forward and flew across the clearing, into the woods. I avoided the main pathway as I made my way toward Derek's and my penthouse. Kiev was at least twice as fast as me. Underestimating the speed at which I was traveling, I almost collided head-first into a tree. It took a while to get used to his agility.

I arrived at our tree and took the elevator up to the verandah. I walked to the front door. Clearing my deep throat, I wiped sweat from my brow with the bottom of my shirt.

Then I knocked. Again, not being used to Kiev's strength, it was far louder than I'd intended. It sounded almost aggressive. *Not a good start…*

I held my breath as footsteps approached. The door unlatched and Ben appeared in the doorway.

His eyes darkened.

Great, now I have two Novak men to deal with. Ben was supposed to be in school.

"What do you want?" Ben asked, leaning his arm against the door frame.

It was unsettling having my own son stare at me with such disdain. I supposed that Kiev was used to everyone looking at him like this.

"I'm here to see your father," I said.

I was horrified by how off Kiev's voice sounded from what I was intending. I'd been trying to adopt a more docile tone of voice, but it came out far too soft and husky. It sent chills down my own spine. *Christ. If I keep this up, Derek will think Kiev's come to seduce him.*

Ben raised a brow.

"For what?"

Nosey child. Just bring your father.

"It is a private matter," I said, relieved that Kiev's voice sounded more balanced this time.

Ben stepped back and allowed me entrance. His eyes followed me as I approached the center of the room. I was about to head directly for Derek's study when I remembered that Kiev didn't know his way around our apartment. I looked at Ben. He seemed to be enjoying making me feel uncomfortable.

"Where might I find your father?"

"In his study."

"Which is where?"

He glared at me once more before leading the way to Derek's study. He rapped on the door.

"Dad?"

"What?"

"Someone's here to see you."

"Who?"

"Kiev Novalic."

There was a pause.

"Tell him to go away."

Damn you, Derek.

Ben turned to me, raising a brow and shrugging. "You heard him."

I approached the door myself. "Derek. I need to talk to you."

More silence. Then the scraping of a chair. The door opened and Derek's unshaven face appeared in the crack, his blue eyes burning into mine.

"Well?"

"May I come in?"

Derek looked at me witheringly. But then, to my surprise, he conceded. He opened the door. I stepped into his study and stood at the end of his desk.

Derek too remained standing, still staring at me, his fists clenched.

I felt intimidated by his stare. The hair on Kiev's arms prickled.

Chill out, Derek. Geez...

I took a deep breath before beginning. "I'm not a man of words, Derek. I speak through action. I had hoped that you might read into my actions, and not require me to articulate them. But I suppose sometimes words are more direct." I paused, waiting for Derek's reaction before continuing. His gaze remained steady. "You're a busy man and I don't intend to keep you. So here it is: I'm sorry."

I held my breath, scrutinizing Derek's face for any hint of acceptance. Of reconciliation.

Although he still kept a poker face, his fists loosened. I reached out my hand.

Come on, Derek. Take it.

He stepped forward and gripped my hand. Hard. I wasn't sure whether this was more passive-aggression, or whether Derek always shook hands like this with men. Whatever the case, Kiev's visit had been a success. A handshake was more than I'd been expecting to get.

As we stepped apart, he gave me a nod. I couldn't keep the smile from my face. I hoped it didn't look goofy.

Although I could have prolonged my stay to seal the deal further, since I now sensed a fair amount of leeway with Derek, I didn't want to run the risk of the spell wearing off.

"I'll be on my way now," I said and backed out of the room.

"Ben," Derek called.

Ben appeared in the doorway—too quickly. I suspected that he'd been eavesdropping.

"Show our guest out."

Guest. Another grin split my face.

I followed Ben through the glass-covered walkways to the main entrance hall. He eyed me curiously as I exited through the door. Before he shut it, I turned around and gave him a small smile. Reaching out, I patted him on the shoulder.

"Thank you, Benjamin. And... I'm sorry."

He looked at me, confused, as though unsure of how to react. Then he returned a smile, nodding like his father.

Once the door had clicked shut, I rushed into the elevator.

Now I'd better hurry and find the real Kiev before he shatters my illusion.

Chapter 6: Sofia

I raced back to the Sanctuary. Corrine kept me locked up in her bedroom until the spell wore off a couple of hours later. It was a relief to be out of Kiev's skin and back into my own.

Kiev's clothes baggy around me, I changed back into my own clothes before hurrying back to our penthouse. Now, it was time for Derek to bite into some humble pie.

"Derek?"

Silence. It seemed that Ben and Rose weren't in either.

I headed straight for my husband's study. He wasn't there.

"Derek?" I called again.

I tore through the apartment. All the rooms were empty. My heart sank.

I hope he hasn't gone to visit Kiev.

I hurried out of the penthouse again and headed for Eli's tree. Derek might have gone there to discuss the plans he'd been reviewing. I raced up to his penthouse and knocked on the door.

Footsteps sounded and Adelle appeared, wearing a dressing gown. I stepped back, momentarily speechless.

"Um, hi, Adelle. Is Derek here?"

She looked bashful, her cheeks flushing. "No, he's not. It's just, uh, Eli and me. I can fetch Eli if you want."

"No," I said quickly, "don't worry. I'll look elsewhere."

What business would Adelle have in Eli's apartment, dressed like that? While I was happy to assume that Eli had finally found himself a girlfriend, I was also saddened. I knew my father liked her. I hoped their new relationship wouldn't crush him. But I had no time to fret over this now.

My heartbeat doubled as I descended Eli's apartment back to the forest ground.

Where could he be? Think.

The truth was, as king of the island, he could be anywhere. Our assistance could be required at any time, on any part of the island.

I decided to check Vivienne and Xavier's apartment first. Perhaps his sister would have a better idea where he'd gone.

Thankfully, I didn't need to travel that far. I caught sight of Derek strolling through the woods with Matteo.

I caught up with them.

"Hi, Matteo," I said.

He smiled back. I turned to my husband.

"Derek, I'm in a hurry," I said, "Ashley invited me over to her place and I'm late. I'll catch you later, okay?"

I wrapped my arms around his neck and planted a kiss on his cheek. Reaching my hands into his hair, I plucked a strand as I drew away from him.

He winced.

"Sorry, my bracelet got caught... I've got to go. I'll catch you later. Bye, Matteo."

"Bye, Sofia."

I hurried off, clutching Derek's hair triumphantly in my palm.

***

I returned to the Sanctuary to find Corrine still waiting in her bedroom.

"You said you'd be gone fifteen minutes."

"I'm sorry. Derek wasn't in the apartment," I said. "Anyway, here's the hair."

I placed it down on the wooden table. Corrine picked it up and we headed back to her potion room.

"We've no time to lose now," she said, tipping ingredients hurriedly into a black cauldron and bringing it to a boil.

"Oh, no," I blurted out, realization dawning on me. "I forgot to bring Derek's clothes!"

"We'll just have to borrow some of Ibrahim's. If they don't fit, it won't take long for me to tailor them."

She was right. I didn't want to risk going back to the apartment in case Derek was back by now and wanted to talk. I removed my clothes and once again wrapped a sheet around me.

"Where's Mona?" I asked.

"She's back home," Corrine said, handing me the goblet. I swallowed it more confidently this time, downing it all in one gulp. Then I opened my mouth. Corrine placed the hair on my tongue, reminded me not to swallow—as if I needed to be reminded of that—held my head in her hands and muttered the same chant Mona had. The tingling sensation spread across my skin again. And then my body once again expanded, growing heavier and taller until Corrine's hands could no longer reach my head.

I stared down at Corrine, waiting for her to inform me that the transformation was complete. Finally, she nodded.

Keeping the sheet firmly around my—Derek's—body, I returned with Corrine to her and Ibrahim's bedroom.

Corrine swore beneath her breath as soon as she stepped into the room. My eyes fell on Ibrahim.

His jaw dropped as he saw Derek wearing nothing but a thin white sheet, entering his bedroom with his wife.

"Ibrahim," I blurted out, my voice rumbling through my chest, "It's not what you think. I'm not Derek. I'm Sofia." I walked forward and placed a muscular hand on his shoulder, gripping him perhaps a little too desperately. Ibrahim winced. "You can go and verify it for yourself if you don't believe us—Derek is likely back at our apartment now. You can go and see him."

Corrine reached up and kissed him. "You didn't really think I'd cheat on you, did you, honey?"

Ibrahim's fists loosened. He stared at the two of us, bewildered. "What the hell are you two girls up to?"

Corrine and I eyed each other and burst out laughing.

"Good question," she said. "One that has no simple answer. I'll tell you as soon as Sofia's out of here. We don't have time to waste. Oh, she needs to borrow some of your clothes, by the way."

Ibrahim watched in bemusement as Corrine whipped around the room, rummaging in drawers and cupboards, finding suitable clothes for me to wear. In the meantime, I walked over to the full-length mirror in the corner of the room.

I couldn't help but grin as I caught sight of Derek's reflection in the mirror, that cute boyish grin I loved so much. I flexed Derek's biceps. I stroked his jawline. I ran both hands through his thick hair. I frowned, glared and bared his fangs.

Hm. So this is what it's like to be Derek Novak.

"Finished?"

I turned to face Corrine, who was looking at me in amusement.

I chuckled. "Yes."

Ibrahim was shorter and less bulky than Derek, but it was nothing Corrine couldn't handle quickly. She took Derek's measurements, then lengthened the trousers and widened the shirt until the clothes fit Derek's physique perfectly.

Corrine handed me the clothes. Still holding the sheet around Derek's body, I took them with one hand.

"I don't need help getting dressed this time. I can handle my husband..."

Chapter 7: Caleb

I'd been desperately trying to forget the princess. But Annora's revelation had planted her right back in my mind again. And no matter what I did, I couldn't get rid of her.

I have information that could save Rose from the pain of losing her parents, yet I'm choosing to sit here and do nothing.

I couldn't stop thinking about what she'd think of me if she ever found out. Even though the thought was nonsensical—Rose would have no way of finding out—I couldn't stop the guilt clawing at my chest. It scared me. It wasn't even Rose's life at risk here. It was her parents'. *Can I really have fallen that hard for her?*

I tried to shake myself to my senses. There was no way I could risk meeting her to warn her. I'd gone out of my way to be as cold with her as possible the last time I saw her. She might have even moved on from me by now. Saving her parents would only strengthen her attachment for me again. Something that would ultimately be fatal.

Unless there's a way I could send a warning without her ever knowing that it was me…

I stalked onto the balcony, staring out at the ocean as I racked my brain.

Then it hit me.

Mona. A witch I desperately want to speak to anyway. What if there's a way to contact her, make her swear confidentiality, get the information I want from her concerning Annora, while also warning her about Rose's parents?

I began pacing my room furiously as a plan formulated in my mind. I had no idea how many days had passed since Annora had cast the spell on them. If I was going to go through with this, I had not a second to lose.

Even though my plan was reckless and downright insane, something told me that if I wanted to ever find a semblance of peace within myself again, I had no choice but to at least attempt it.

Since Annora had failed to gain entrance to The Shade and we were almost out of humans, we were due to leave late the next evening to collect more humans.

I just had to hope I wouldn't be too late by then. I didn't have a choice. I couldn't propose we left earlier without arousing suspicion from Annora once she discovered Derek and Sofia had survived the curse.

I spent the rest of the day trying to distract myself with books in my study, but all I was really doing was thinking about Mona, and how I would go about this without her blasting me out of the water the moment she saw me—that was, if I even managed to catch her attention.

I knew it wasn't as impossible as it sounded though. Even though I had no idea where she was staying on the island, I'd spent enough time around witches and this island to know that there were ways of calling attention to the caster of a protective spell. If Mona was the same breed of witch as Annora, which I was confident she was, the spell she'd put around the island would be similar.

I recalled a time, soon after we'd first arrived on this island, when we hadn't had the systems in place that we did now. Annora had still been getting used to the spell as a newly turned witch, and she hadn't yet set up a system whereby we could enter and leave the island without her assistance. I remembered we'd had to attract Annora's attention first to be able to gain entrance. I was willing to bet that the same method could be used to call Mona's attention.

An hour before we were due to leave, I climbed the stairs to Annora's apartment. I eased the door open. She wasn't due to be around at this time. I had to hope that her plans hadn't changed. Hurrying from room to room, I stopped in her study. In the far end of the room was a chest of drawers. I bent down and opened the bottom drawer. I breathed out in relief on seeing its contents. Apparently untouched even after all these years, the drawer was filled with small conch shells. But no ordinary conch shells—a charm had been cast on these. Once blown, they emitted a sound audible to any witch within a hundred miles.

I pocketed one and hurried out of the study. Annora wouldn't notice it was missing. I'd just have to find a way to discreetly replace it once she'd returned.

I returned to my apartment and, after making final preparations for the excursion, I descended the stairs to the entrance hall. A dozen vampires already waited for me there.

"Let's go," I said.

I pushed open the main doors and we all hurried down the steep mountain slope, through the forest until we reached the harbor. I slipped through the hatch of the largest submarine and headed straight to the control room. Frieda entered and sat in the seat next to me.

I prepared the submarine for departure.

"Is everyone ready?" I asked.

"Yes."

I backed the vessel out of the port and began speeding ahead.

I'd picked the beach nearest to us, even though we'd hit it many times before. Beach parties were harder to come by, but I was sure that we'd find enough tourists taking strolls to collect enough humans to keep Annora satiated at least for the next few days. I needed to get this job out of the way as soon as possible and didn't have time to go further afield.

"Hopefully soon, there will be no more need for these trips," Frieda muttered. "I know the first thing that I'm going to do once I get on that island. Wring that little wench's neck."

"I'm not sure that Annora would want you doing that," I said, careful to keep my voice free of emotion. "They may have other plans for the twins."

Frieda scowled. "Well, if I can't wring her neck, I'm going to at least take a bite out of her."

We passed the rest of the journey in silence. I breathed out in relief when we arrived at our destination.

I stopped the submarine near a remote part of the beach.

"Let's go." I jumped to my feet and Frieda followed me out of the cabin. Vampires rushed along the passageway toward the hatch. We climbed out and slipped into the ocean. I scanned the length of the beach as I swam toward it. There were no large groups of people in sight, as I'd expected, but there were couples and individuals walking along the beach.

We climbed out of the water and rushed toward a patch of shrubbery bordering the sand. We couldn't afford to be seen in plain view anymore on this beach. We'd simply hit it too many times before.

I was the first to creep out from the bushes. I ordered Demarcus, a tall wiry vampire, to follow me. We ran up behind a couple and, withdrawing our syringes, injected them both at once. Two more vampires ran out of the bushes, grabbed the humans we'd tranquilized and began swimming back to the submarine. In this way, over the next hour, we poached humans who passed by our stretch of the beach until we'd caught about a dozen. Enough for now.

I turned to the vampires crouching in the bushes beside me.

"Back to the sub."

"Are you sure we have enough?" Demarcus asked.

"Yes, enough for now. I don't want to take too many from this beach."

"We could go to another beach," Sabine, a vampire to my left, said. "I'd rather just get a whole bunch at once rather than making so many separate trips. We're already halfway to Hawaii. It makes no sense turning back now when—"

"Who's in charge here?" I glared at them.

Sabine and Demarcus bowed their heads.

"Just keep silent and obey."

I checked the beach again. It seemed to be all clear.

"Okay," I whispered. "We make a run back in three, two, one…"

We all sprang from the bushes and raced toward the water.

What happened next was a blur. A blast of light overhead blinded me. Something heavy slammed down against my shoulder, making me stumble and lose my footing. Lying on the sand, I looked up to see a giant cage fall around me and several other vampires who hadn't yet made it to the waves. I scrambled to my feet and gripped the bars, pulling at them with all my strength. They wouldn't budge. I tried to dig my fingers into the sand and slide them beneath the bars, but as soon as I did, a sharp metal surface shot out from the edges of the cage and closed beneath us above the sand. Had I not leapt up in time, my feet would have been severed.

One vampire wasn't as fast. A scream erupted behind

me. I whirled around to see Frieda lying on the floor, writhing and nursing two oozing stumps where her feet should have been.

The cage jolted and began lifting us into the air.

"No!" I yelled.

I strained my neck upward. A black helicopter hovered above us.

What is this?

I looked back down at the ocean. Our submarine had already disappeared beneath the waves along with the vampires who'd escaped, and all chances of reaching Mona in time.

Chapter 8: Sofia

Once I'd pulled on Ibrahim's clothes, I left the room. I found Corrine and Ibrahim in the corridor.

"Wish me luck."

"Good luck."

I walked to the exit. Again, before darting through the courtyard, I poked my head out and scanned the area. A couple of vampires crossed the clearing and headed back into the woods on the opposite side. Once they had gone, I launched forward and ducked into the bushes. I headed northwest of the island, again careful to travel off the beaten path. Having experienced Kiev's powerful form, it wasn't as much of a shock getting used to Derek's prowess, and I was more graceful as I rushed through the trees.

I reached the beach and ran to the line of townhouses. I singled out Kiev and Mona's house and, holding my breath, rapped on the door.

I tried to steady my breathing as the door creaked open. Mona stood in the doorway. She gave me a knowing smile and opened the door wider. "Come in… *Derek*."

I followed after her cautiously, looking about the hallway as I entered.

"Take a seat in the living room. I'll get Kiev."

"Thank you."

I couldn't have been more grateful that she was here. If I pushed the wrong buttons and Kiev snapped, she was powerful enough to intervene.

Kiev entered the room, but froze at the doorway as soon as he laid eyes on me.

I stood up and cautiously closed the distance between us.

"Kiev," I said, holding his gaze even though he intimidated me. "I've come to apologize."

Kiev's face remained steely, impossible to read. Just as Derek's had been. *It should have been obvious all along that they're related.*

"I've allowed memories of the past and my prejudices to blind me from seeing what's in front of me. I've spoken with Matteo and he tells me that you have changed. You saved us from Annora, brought Anna back, and now you and Mona have agreed to stay to protect our island. I'm not sure I can ever forget the pain you caused us, but I want to apologize and at least try to put the past behind us."

I hoped that I hadn't made Derek sound too cheesy. But when I reached out a hand, Kiev gripped it.

"Okay, Novak."

I stepped back and cleared my throat. "Well, I ought to be going now. But I would like to invite you round for late lunch tomorrow, if you'll accept."

He nodded slowly. Mona appeared at his side. "We'll be there, Derek," she said, grinning and looping an arm though Kiev's.

"Good. Let's say, four o'clock?"

"That's fine," Mona replied.

The two of them stepped aside as I made my way

out. I opened the front door and walked out into the front yard leading up to the sandy beach. I turned back once more to smile at Mona as she closed the door.

Four o'clock tomorrow. I supposed that I could have invited them round much earlier, for dinner this evening. I should have had more than enough time to turn back into myself. But something made me want to play it safe. I scanned the length of the beach for people and, on seeing the coast was clear, hurtled back toward the woods. I hurried as fast as I could off the path and arrived back in the Sanctuary, slamming the oak door shut behind me.

I hurried from chamber to chamber, looking for Corrine. I found her sitting in the kitchen area, at the dining table, deep in conversation with Ibrahim. They both looked up as I entered.

"So?" Corrine said. "How did it go?"

"It went well," I replied. "Kiev accepted Derek's apology." I slumped down in a chair and looked from Corrine to Ibrahim.

"And now what?" Ibrahim asked.

"I invited Kiev and Mona to come to lunch tomorrow, at four o'clock." I looked anxiously at

Corrine. "So I guess now I just have to wait here until I turn back. I hope that Derek and Kiev won't bump into each other in the meantime. I should be myself again by dinner tonight, right?"

She peeled back her sleeve and looked at her wristwatch.

"Yes, you should be."

And so I waited there at the table with Corrine and Ibrahim, passing the time in conversation as we waited for me to turn back. We waited one hour. Then two. Then three. Then four.

As time pushed on, even Corrine was no longer able to keep the worried expression from her face. My stomach was in knots.

I stood up and walked over to a mirror, getting up close and staring at Derek's face, rubbing his skin, willing myself to see even the slightest bit of transformation.

Come on, Derek.

It was now almost ten o'clock. I'd missed preparing the twins' dinner. They would be wondering where on earth I was. Derek might even be out searching for me now.

"Why am I not changing back?" I asked, wringing my sweaty hands.

Even Ibrahim looked worried now.

"Where did you get that hair of Derek's?" Ibrahim asked.

"From his head."

His brows furrowed. "And where did you get Kiev's?"

"Mona plucked one of his leg hairs."

"Hm."

"What?"

"See, I suspect that hair from the head is more potent than leg hair."

My throat went dry. "How much longer will it take?" I croaked. "Will I be myself again in time for lunch tomorrow?"

"I don't know."

"But isn't there some antidote? Can't you just force me back?"

"We can," Corrine said, walking over to me and placing an arm around my shoulder. "But this type of spell is best left to wear off naturally. Sometimes, forcing reversion of a spell of this type can have...

negative side effects."

"What side effects?"

"Well… let's just say that Queen Sofia could end up with some rather unsightly stubble."

I cursed beneath my breath. I looked up at the clock again. *Thank God I didn't invite them over for dinner.*

"Can't Mona do something? Surely she must—"

"I'm sure she can. But again, it's not without the risk of side effects, same as if I tried to force you back."

"But I will turn back, right?" I asked, my voice trembling.

"Yes," Ibrahim said. "Don't worry. The spell will wear off. It's just a matter of time."

Time. That's just what I don't have.

Chapter 9: Caleb

As we were hauled up into the belly of the helicopter, I looked around the dim aircraft. Three men stood dressed in black. Masks covered their faces. The door closed beneath us and they began circling the cage.

"Who are you?" I snarled.

The man nearest me approached the bars, his light blue eyes boring into mine.

"It was foolish of you to come to this beach again."

"Answer me."

He chuckled and exchanged glances with the other men. "Let's go!" he shouted.

The aircraft lurched, and we began ascending. Blood pounded in my ears, my mouth parched, heart racing.

"You can tell them who we are," a brown-eyed man said, looking me over.

Blue Eyes approached the cage again. Withdrawing a dagger from his belt, he ran it across my fingers where they gripped the bars, slitting a line through my skin. It stung, but I refused to flinch.

"You've hit this beach one too many times, vampire. You should have expected that someone would have clued in by now. You think you can just rip apart families with no consequences?"

"Who are you?" I repeated.

He paused, looking back at the other men before answering. "As you are snakes, we are hawks."

Hawks. I caught a glimpse of a black tattoo on his wrist. The brand of a hawk.

So these are hunters. In all our years of kidnapping, we'd never once met a hunter. Their order had been shut down almost two decades ago. I supposed it was only a matter of time before we provoked them enough to reform.

"What are you going to do with us?" Demarcus

grunted, sweat dripping down his forehead.

Ignoring him, the hunters exited the chamber through a door to our left. I stared at the eight vampires who shared the cage with me. Frieda whimpered in one corner. She looked close to unconsciousness.

I'd known it was a mistake going to that beach again. I'd felt it in my bones. And yet I'd risked it anyway—my life, and those of my fellow vampires.

None of us exchanged a word until the aircraft started to descend. My stomach lurched as we took a dive, and several minutes later, the aircraft shuddered as we hit land.

Footsteps sounded overhead and two men entered the chamber. They circled the cage, attaching metal chains to the bars. A side door opened. Several more men came down the steps and entered the room. They all gripped the chains now attached to the bars of our cage and slid us roughly down a ramp. We hit the ground. We had to grip onto the bars to prevent ourselves from falling on top of each other. Frieda was too weak. She slid across the floor and her head smashed against the bars.

As they dragged us away from the aircraft, I stalked

around the edges of the cage. We'd landed on a cliff. The sea glistened beneath the waning moon in the distance, and there was a steep drop a few hundred meters away. I looked around at our captors. Now ten of them had debarked from the helicopter and were staring at each of us through the bars.

The blue-eyed man pulled off his mask. His jaw was square and covered with a bristling black beard. His skin was tan, his nose long and pointed. The other men followed his lead, revealing their own faces for the first time. All of them were men except for one. The female hunter looked as tough as the men. Hardened features, marred with scars. They were built like military veterans.

They gathered together in a huddle and started talking in hushed tones. Though of course I could hear every word they spoke.

"Anthony, what first?" the woman asked, looking at the blue-eyed man.

Anthony cast another look at us.

"Bring our families."

"Already?"

"Yes. They'll want to be here to watch every moment

of this."

The woman nodded, her face stony and resolute, and hurried back toward a small helicopter parked fifty feet away from the black helicopter we'd arrived in. She climbed aboard with three other men and launched into the sky.

I turned my attention back to Anthony.

"You asked what we're going to do with you. You won't have to wait long now to find out. Don't worry."

If these hunters were as powerful as the hunters who used to roam the human realm decades ago, our chances of survival were practically non-existent. As I looked around at my comrades' ashen faces, I was sure that they knew this too.

Man to man, they stood no chance against us. But the technology they possessed was enough to overpower us. One shot of one of their bullets into our flesh and we'd burn alive from the inside.

"Declan, Crispian," Anthony called. "We may as well start preparing for the show."

Two men ran up the ramp into the helicopter and returned minutes later, each carrying metal chests.

"Since the police are useless, I'm sure you can

understand why we had to take this matter into our own hands. I'm so sorry," Anthony said, looking at me with mock sympathy. "You're the leader of this lot?"

I didn't respond, though he didn't seem to require my answer. He'd already seen me leading the way to the submarines when we were still on the sand.

I glanced at the horizon. The sun was close to rising. I looked up at the ceiling of the cage we were trapped in. It was solid, no holes. But the sun would shine right through the bars that lined the sides of the cage. There would be no escaping it. Perhaps this was their plan.

The men unlocked the chests and started withdrawing an array of weapons, many of which I'd never seen before in my life and couldn't put a name to. But all were clearly torture devices. Sharp hooks, butchers' knives, chains and handcuffs. Wooden stakes. And guns. Lots of guns. Their intentions were clear from one brief glance at the display they were laying out on the grass before us. *Torture equipment and then guns to finish off the job.*

"You see," Anthony said as they unpacked the chests, "we couldn't risk turning you into the police. They'd likely lose you. We had to take matters into our own hands. I'm sure you can understand."

Anthony stooped down and picked up a stake in one hand, a dagger in the other. He crouched down on the floor, the wood leaning against his knee as he began to sharpen it.

Still I refused to discourse with him. I kept my face expressionless. If this was going to be my last hour, I wasn't going to give them any more satisfaction than they already derived from seeing us caged here like animals.

I turned my back on the sight of him sharpening the stake and faced my companions. I looked at each of their dejected faces. Despite the many years I'd known them, I'd never gotten close to any of them. Our relationship was merely functional. I doubted that they had relationships amongst each other either. Everyone on our island just did what they had to do to get by and avoid trouble. I might as well be dying in the company of strangers.

I walked over to the other side of the cage and stared out again at the brightening sky. A cold breeze caught my hair, bringing along with it the scent of freshly blooming flowers.

I tried to calm my mind, stop thinking about what these hunters were about to put us through.

Soon enough, the sound of the small chopper returning roared over the mountaintop. A crowd of humans bundled out of the helicopter. More than a dozen of them. Men and women, young and old. They approached the men sharpening their tools and stared into the cage at us. Hatred burned in their eyes.

Anthony stepped forward with a young woman and an elderly man. "Meet Stacy, my wife, and Raymond, my father-in-law. Do you remember kidnapping Tobias? My brother-in-law? No, I didn't think so."

Another hunter stepped forward, his lip trembling as he held the hand of a teenage boy. "What about Justin, my son? Why don't you explain to Sean where his brother is?"

More hunters stepped forward, one by one, introducing themselves. I looked down at the floor of the cage, no longer willing to look into their eyes.

"You see, vampires." Anthony broke through the crowd again. "There are many more like us. What you see here is just a small sample of lives you've affected."

Now that the Hawks were no longer on earth to

manipulate the hunters' cause, the agenda of these humans was simple. Vengeance. And none of us vampires could blame them. Hell, I'd join their cause if I weren't a bloodsucker myself.

"Our organization is small now. But we are rebuilding fast. Gathering funds. Investing in weapons, surveillance systems, aircraft, training new recruits. Many are still afraid. That's why occasions like this are important. Occasions where we demonstrate that, behind bars, you're nothing more than animals. Animals that can be tamed... perhaps. We shall see how much desperation can tame you."

He paused, his cold eyes surveying the cage. They stopped on Frieda, who lay curled up in a corner, still nursing her bloody stumps.

"We'll start with the weakest first, shall we? Put her out of her misery."

There were murmurs of approval from the crowds behind them.

Frieda squealed, backing further into her corner against the bars of the cage. Two hunters circled the cage with stakes, poking them into her back to force her to the center of the floor. Five men aimed guns at us as

Anthony approached the entrance of the cage.

"One movement from any of you, and my men will take you down." His eyes were fixed on Frieda. "Come here, girl. Come on." He beckoned her over as one would a dog.

Her eyes sparked with fury at his humiliation. But she was helpless. We were all helpless. One movement, and the bullets would be lodged in our bodies, burning us from the inside out. Anthony entered the cage, gripping Frieda by her arm and holding a gun against her temple. He dragged her out even as she screamed. A woman fastened the door behind him as he stepped out into the clearing. He dropped her to the grass, in clear view of all of us.

"Make sure you all watch this," Anthony said, addressing the crowd of hunters. "Spread out if you have to."

He gripped a machete and brought it slamming down against her right arm. Steel sliced flesh. Blood spurted everywhere, soaking the grass. Frieda's screams could have brought hearing to the deaf.

She writhed around on the grass so violently, four men had to bend over her to keep her still. As she tried to lash out at them with her remaining claws and bite them with her fangs, one man lodged a metal ball into her mouth, choking her, tying it around her head like a muzzle. The other men raised stakes to the air and brought them down, digging straight through her shoulders and pinning her down against the soil.

The crowd's eyes flickered with anticipation. Hungry for blood. Hungry for death.

Anthony hovered over, cutting away her clothes with his blade. Then, using its tip, he etched the mark of a hawk into her skin. Blood seeped from the brand.

They didn't prolong her pain much longer. Anthony grabbed a stake from one of the men and stabbed it through her throat. He pulled it out again, and finally pierced her heart.

The first weak rays of the sun were now beginning to peek out from behind the horizon. I dropped down to the floor along with the other vampires to avoid being hit by them. A few more minutes, even half an hour, and the sun's angle would make it impossible to avoid its rays any longer. We'd burn alive, unless they decided to kill us first.

"Don't worry," Anthony said, his eyes gleaming as he

severed Frieda's head. He dug a stake into the ground like a mast and mounted her head on top of it. "We won't keep you here long enough for the sun to have all the fun."

Chapter 10: Sofia

I ended up staying the night in the Sanctuary. I'd had to ask Corrine to pay a late-night visit to Derek. She explained to him that I'd decided to have dinner with her and we'd ended up having a little too much to drink. She said I'd already fallen asleep on her sofa and would return tomorrow. It wasn't the most plausible of stories, since Derek knew it wasn't in my character to get drunk, but it was the best I could come up with in my panicked state.

To my dismay, as the clock struck half past three the next day, I still hadn't turned back.

"Corrine," I said, my voice shaking, "you and Ibrahim need to step in for me."

"Hey, I didn't sign up for this."

"I know. I know. But all of this will be for nothing if they don't at least have one meeting together where they behave civilly, as themselves—"

"That's all very well said, but what do I tell Derek? He's going to wonder where the hell his wife is."

"Just..." My voice trailed off as I desperately racked my brains. "Just tell him I'm at Anna's place. I left the Sanctuary and decided to visit her and Kyle."

Corrine stared at me, her eyebrows raised. "That's ludicrous. Derek's never going to buy this. He was doubtful enough about the story I told him last night. Besides, he's going to wonder why Kiev turned up on his doorstep."

"Just tell Derek that I invited Kiev round for lunch without telling him, hoping they could both make amends. In preparation and without my knowledge, Kiev came to apologize yesterday, to make sure things weren't awkward over lunch. Tell Derek I invited you too. He'll have to assume that I've gotten held up with Anna and you can suggest that I'll probably be back home soon."

"But—"

I crossed the room and gripped Corrine by the shoulders... a little too hard.

"Ouch," she said irritably, wriggling away from my grasp.

"Sorry. But look, please Corrine, I'm begging you. You have to step in for me. I know it's a stupid story. But we just need to get them together, okay? Ibrahim can go with you."

She paused, biting her lip. "Ibrahim!" she called.

I breathed out in relief.

He appeared in the room.

"What?"

"As you can see, Sofia still hasn't turned back, so she's going to have to stay here while we go and help Derek with his lunch guests."

Ibrahim looked less than enthusiastic at being roped into this.

He opened his mouth but I bulldozed over him. "Just try to keep the conversation away from the visits they made to each other yesterday—by any means necessary. They won't be very talkative, so you two must take the bull by the horns and lead the conversation places where the subject won't crop up. Remember, Mona will be there too. She's smart enough to realize what might have happened and she'll help in keeping the conversation on other topics."

Corrine looked less tense at mention of Mona. "All right. I'll do my best." She looked again at Ibrahim. "So, will you come with me?"

He sighed. "All right."

"Good job vampires are easy to feed," she muttered. "I suppose I'll have to cook something for us witches though, and the twins."

"You'd better hurry," I said glancing back up at the clock to see ten more minutes had passed. I prayed that Kiev and Mona wouldn't arrive early.

Corrine grabbed Ibrahim's hand and they vanished.

I sighed heavily and sat back down in a chair. I drummed my fingers on the table, watching my hands closely, hoping to detect any sign of change.

But another hour passed, and Derek's large hands showed no signs of shrinking even in the slightest. I stood up and started walking around the chambers of the Sanctuary, trying to distract my mind. But it was impossible to stop thinking about the time.

A second hour passed. And then a third.

I was surprised that Corrine and Ibrahim hadn't returned by now. I had expected the lunch to last one to one and a half hours at most. This could mean only two things: either the lunch party was going exceptionally well, or most horribly wrong.

Sweat formed on my brow as I made my way back into Corrine's dining room and resumed my seat at the table.

Leg hair. I should have pulled a damn leg hair.

Finally, Corrine and Ibrahim reappeared in the kitchen. My stomach dropped on seeing the expressions on their faces.

"What happened?" I said, leaping to my feet.

Corrine walked up to me and held my hand.

"Vivienne's had another vision. I tried to delay this as long as possible, but you need to return to Derek now."

"But—"

Corrine ignored my protests. She gripped me and we both vanished.

Chapter 11: Caleb

"We'll take the leader down last," Anthony said. "It's only right that his pain be prolonged."

The five men resumed aiming their guns as Anthony once again entered the cage. He dragged out Demarcus. I couldn't bear to watch this time, but Demarcus' cries were enough to tell me that they were no less merciful to him than they had been to Frieda. I winced at the sound of gargling, and the final tearing of flesh.

The sun was now treacherously high. Its rays singed my right shoulder. I tried to huddle closer into the shade, but all of us vampires remaining had the same idea.

One by one, Anthony came in and pulled out the rest of them. Someone from the crowd kept insisting that Anthony was ending them too soon, and since Anthony obliged, my wait was prolonged.

By the time my last companion's head had been mounted on a stake, my skin was on fire. I'd torn off my shirt, trying to cover myself with it. But the fabric was torn and thin.

The gate creaked open for a final time as Anthony stepped inside, his heavy boots thudding against the cage's metal floor.

He reached down and gripped my hair, placing the barrel of his gun against the base of my neck. He dug the metal in hard, forcing me into standing position. As I stepped out of the cage, the morning sun blinded me. I had to squint, and even then it was all a blur. Anthony tore away the shirt from my hands, and now the sun hit my bare chest. My body erupted in agony, as though a thousand daggers were piercing me all at once.

He pushed me down on my knees. A chain tightened around my neck like a collar. They were going to humiliate me before killing me, watching the life drain out of me as I lay helpless as an animal.

No.

I may die this morning, but not like this.

I forced my eyes open and scanned the edge of the cliff. I couldn't imagine I'd survive the fall. But I preferred to take my own life rather than have these hunters take it from me. Of course, I might end up with a bullet lodged in my back before I ever made it off the cliff. But it was worth trying. It wasn't like I had anything to lose.

I didn't have any semblance of a plan. My adrenaline took over.

I took a deep breath, my heart hammering in my chest. Just as Anthony had finished sharpening the stake and the men had begun to approach me to pin me down, I sprang up, slamming my elbow backward and catching Anthony square in the jaw. My sudden motion knocked him off his feet. I had a few split seconds before they started firing bullets. I reached Anthony just in time. Gripping his neck, I held him before me as a shield as I backed away, closer to the edge of the cliff.

Men tried to run up behind me but I was too fast. I'd reached the edge of the cliff too quickly. There was no way they could fire a bullet without hitting Anthony. Anthony tried to struggle against my grip, but without his weapons, he was no match for my strength—even with the sun's torture. I extended my claws and dug them against his neck.

"Stop struggling, or I'll slit your throat," I growled into his ear.

He chuckled dryly.

"So what's your game plan, vampire? Pray tell. Once you kill me, there will be nothing stopping these men shooting at you. And even if you don't kill me, there's only so long you can stand here with me before the sun cooks you alive."

He was right, of course. I doubted I'd last more than an hour, at most, standing here with the sun beating down on me. Ten men now stood armed and ready to shoot the moment I gave them a chance.

Attempting to calm my racing heart, I pushed Anthony to the ground in front of me. A symphony of bullets erupted. Facing the sun and the edge of the cliff, I kicked with all the strength my legs could muster and dove. Bullets grazed my skin just as I fell.

My limbs knocked against overhanging rocks, bone

splintering, as I spiraled down in a free fall. I was sure I'd broken my leg. The wind rushing past my ears deafened me. I didn't know where I would land, whether I would hit water deep enough to survive. I hadn't had time to calculate before I jumped.

The hunters had taken us to such a height because they'd thought not even a vampire would be so insane to jump from it.

They had grossly underestimated the insanity of Caleb Achilles.

Chapter 12: Sofia

We reappeared in the penthouse. I was afraid to open my eyes as I felt the soft living room carpet beneath my feet. Gasps erupted around the room.

Derek sat on the couch, an arm around Vivienne, who was trembling uncontrollably in his arms. His jaw dropped to the floor as his eyes fell on me. Xavier sat next to them, equally stunned. Ben and Rose, also hovering over the couch, stared in my direction with a mixture of horror and bewilderment. Their eyes travelled from their father to… their father.

I expected to see Kiev and Mona. But neither were in

the room. I supposed that I should have been grateful that at least Kiev wasn't here to witness this second Derek.

"What the—?" Derek swore. He looked like he'd just seen a ghost. I imagined how bizarre it would be to see myself across the living room floor.

"You asked for Sofia," Corrine said, nudging me forward.

I stepped forward, wincing as I looked at my husband. "It's me," I said in Derek's baritone voice.

"Wha—How?"

"It's a long story," I said. I was about to cross the room and place a hand on Derek's shoulder, but I held myself back. Touching my husband would hardly make him feel more comfortable. "I'll explain it all to you, I promise. But..." I walked closer to the sofa, looking down at Vivienne. "What happened?"

Since everyone still appeared to be recovering from the shock of seeing me, Corrine answered. "Vivienne came a few minutes after Kiev and Mona left. She's had a vision. It seems she's still having one now."

I approached my sister-in-law.

"What's wrong, Vivienne? What did you see?"

She moaned and continued shaking in Derek's arms. Vivienne was so in a world of her own, she didn't seem to have noticed that Derek's double had just appeared in the room. I reached down and brushed her cheek gently with a hand.

Her eyes flickered open, though they were glassy and distant. Her lips trembled as she parted them.

"Time is slipping," she said in a voice barely louder than a breath.

"What do you mean?" I urged.

"It's drawing close. Too close."

"What is?"

I looked at Derek, who was still staring at me in bewilderment.

"What do you see, Viv?" Xavier urged, forcing his eyes away from me to look back at his wife.

"Derek and Sofia," she murmured. Her eyes rolled and she closed them again. Her lips moved, but no more words came out.

Xavier stood up, carrying Vivienne in his arms. "I think she needs to rest." His voice faltered as he looked at us.

"Stay the night with us," Derek said, "I want to be

able to check on her." He stood up and led them to the spare bedroom.

Now I was alone with my twins. They stared at me, their mouths agape.

"Mom?"

"Yeah," I sighed, running a hand through Derek's hair.

"How? Why?"

I was about to answer when Derek reentered the room. Glancing at Corrine, he gripped me by the arm and pulled me out of the living room into our own bedroom.

He closed the door behind us and glared at me.

"Explain."

I sighed and sat down on the edge of the bed.

"I wanted to break the ice between you and Kiev," I said. "So, I initiated apologies from both of you. I took a potion, two potions, one to turn into Kiev—"

"You turned into Kiev?"

"Yes," I said, steeling myself. "I came to visit you in your room and apologized. Likewise, I visited Kiev as you and invited him round to dinner…"

Derek gaped at me. "I can't believe you would do

that."

"Really?" I said, my blood pressure rising. "If you hadn't been so stubborn, I wouldn't have been driven to such desperate measures. You think I enjoy being a hairy man? Huh? And now the spell's not even wearing off—" My voice broke. It was disturbing, hearing Derek's voice get all sentimental like a girl's.

"What? What do you mean it's not wearing off?"

"It was supposed to wear off yesterday," I said, trying to keep my voice steady and swallow back my tears.

"What does Corrine say?"

"She says it will wear off... Look, I'm probably just overreacting, okay? It's been a long day. It will wear off."

He bent down and motioned to touch me, I guessed in comfort, but then stepped back.

"Agh, I can't do it."

"Don't. It's weird." I breathed out and looked up at him, wanting to change the subject. "How did dinner go?"

"It went all right," he muttered, averting his eyes to the floor. "Kiev and I talked."

"Good." *At least it wasn't all in vain.*

My thoughts drifted back to Vivienne. It had been a long time since Vivienne had experienced such an intense vision. The last had been when this island was riddled with darkness and the Elders' influence. We'd lived without her ominous visions for almost two decades now. Her having them now again was perhaps the most discomforting thing that had happened since the twins were first kidnapped from Hawaii. Because Vivienne's visions, although not always accurate, were rarely far off the truth.

Derek too seemed lost in thought. I was sure that he was also feeling disturbed about Vivienne.

The stress of the day was taking its toll on me. I yawned, rubbing my face with Derek's big hands.

"Maybe things will be clearer in the morning."

"Maybe," he said.

"Let's get some rest," I said, removing Ibrahim's shirt from Derek's chest and lying back in bed.

Derek remained frozen to his spot in the corner of the room.

"What?"

"As much as you might think me a narcissist, Sofia, sleeping with myself is something I have never felt the urge for. I'll rest in the spare bedroom next to Xavier and Vivienne."

He turned to leave the room. Despite the heaviness surrounding us, I couldn't help but chuckle at the horror on his face at the notion.

Grabbing his pillow and laying it on top of my own, I nestled Derek's heavy head down against it. "Suit yourself," I mumbled as he closed the door. "Just be grateful Mona stole a leg hair. Or it could have been Kiev dribbling on your pillow tonight…"

CHAPTER 13: CALEB

Hundreds of bullets rained down on me. If even one of them found its way into my flesh, I'd burn up inside.

I'd been right about one of my legs breaking during the fall. My right arm was also dislocated. But I had no choice but to force my wrecked body to start moving as soon as I hit the water. The salt stung my singed skin as I swam deeper, away from the edge of the cliff. I looked back up toward the top of the cliff, my breath hitching just looking at the crazy jump I'd just taken. Then I caught sight of a black helicopter descending toward me.

Ducking my head beneath the water, I strained my aching muscles to kick down further, deeper. If they lowered their cage again, it wouldn't be difficult to catch me.

More bullets fired into the water. I swam deeper and deeper, and although my lungs felt the strain and my head began to feel light, I couldn't let up. I would hold my lungs until they burst if it meant avoiding death in their hands.

As I touched the bottom of the ocean, it was also darker, and although the salt still stung, at least the sun's rays reached me less down here. Parting seaweed, I swam with my stomach grazing the floor. I looked upward and spotted the shadow of the black wasp above the water, although now about two hundred meters away, not directly over me. I kept swimming, every few minutes glancing back up at the shadow which seemed to be slowly losing track of me.

I waited until I was about half a kilometer away before giving relief to my screaming lungs. I allowed myself to surface for no more than ten seconds, keeping a close eye on the helicopter skimming the waves, before submerging myself again.

The helicopter remained nearby for what felt like an hour. Although it drew dangerously close again, I managed to stay deep enough beneath the water for them to not notice me. Perhaps they presumed me dead. Whatever the case, I was just grateful they didn't send divers down to look for me.

I continued swimming for hours, far past the point where I thought my limbs would collapse. Only once the helicopter had completely disappeared did I resurface.

Now that I resurfaced and felt the full force of the midday sun beating down against my skin, escaping the hunters felt like child's play. My body was too weak to continue swimming so deep under water, and yet I couldn't resurface and float without being roasted alive.

I reached for my belt. It still had the small conch shell fastened to it. I removed the belt from my pants and fixed it securely around my neck. Then I ripped off my pants and, tearing the fabric, wrapped it around the top half of my body as best I could. Although the sun still dug into my flesh, the dark pant fabric at least helped to bear the brunt of it.

I dove down to the sea bed again and plucked

handfuls of seaweed. Resurfacing, I added this as an extra layer against the fury of the sun—however pathetic it was.

My throat was parched, my whole body trembling.

I lost track of time. I faded in and out of unconsciousness, my body being carried further and further out to sea. The water became colder and colder, indicating how much deeper I was being sucked. The ocean that had been my savior from the hunters was now my enemy. I didn't know what nasty surprises it might hold within its depths. I just had to hope there were no sharks in these parts.

***

I woke up to the feeling of cords tightening around my body, restricting my breathing. I opened my eyes. I was surrounded by slimy brown rope, closing in around me and lifting me upward. I was too weak to struggle. My torn pants and seaweed slipped off me as I was pulled over a ledge and landed on a hard floor.

"Hey. It's okay. I've got you."

I looked up to see a young man towering over me. A cigarette hanging from his mouth, he was dressed in faded dungarees stained with blood.

I was on a small boat. Nets of fish writhed on the front deck, an assortment of hooks and fishing equipment scattered about. Spotting the dark entrance of a cabin, I dove for shelter from the sun.

The young man followed me, leaning against the doorway. He grimaced as he looked at me.

"Sweet Jesus, you're a mess. You're lucky I found you. You wouldn't have lasted much—"

My hunger took over. I launched for him, gripping his throat and pinning him to the ground. I tore through his jugular. My body heaved as I drained every last drop of blood from him. I gasped for breath, knocking him away from me and leaning back against the wall. I closed my eyes. His fresh hot blood felt like ecstasy flowing through my veins. The sensation drowned out my feeling of guilt.

I stood up and searched the boat. I found a small bathroom beneath deck. I looked in the mirror. I barely recognized myself. Every inch of my skin was covered in swollen sores and blisters. I trusted that the blood would speed up my recovery.

I sat back down, allowing myself a few more minutes'

rest as my body worked on healing itself. But then I got up. I had no idea how much time had passed since we'd been kidnapped by the hunters on the beach, but now that I was alone, I had to try to complete my mission no matter how doubtful I was about it being too late.

I hurried to the control room. My eyes rested on the electronic navigation device. I studied the map. I wasn't as far away from The Shade as I'd feared I might be.

I examined the boat's controls. It was a small vessel. I didn't know how much fuel was left in it, but I had no choice but to attempt this now.

Chapter 14: Caleb

The vessel did end up running out of fuel, but thankfully I'd found a spare jerrycan below deck.

It was close to the early hours of the morning by the time I arrived outside the boundary of The Shade. The boat shuddered as I brushed against the boundary, sending papers and equipment flying everywhere.

I reached for the conch in my belt. Taking a deep breath, I blew into it. I wasn't able to make out the sound, but if Mona was still on the island, she would hear it.

I waited. And waited. I blew the conch again.

After an hour of waiting, I thought she wasn't going to turn up. Perhaps the spell had worn off the shell after all these years. Or she had come to the edge of the boundary, seen it was me, and returned, not being willing to give me the time of day. The possibilities were endless.

But then she appeared out of thin air on the deck a few feet away from me, a dressing gown wrapped around her body, her long blonde hair tied up in a bun. I realized how strange I looked wearing nothing but my underwear. At least my wounds had mostly healed by now.

"You?" Her eyes narrowed on me. "What are you doing here?"

"I'm here to make a trade with you. I have a piece of information that you need to know. In return you must answer a question."

Her lips parted, her brows furrowing.

"You realize that I could blast you and this boat out of the water with a flick of my finger?"

I nodded, trying to keep my expression calm, even as urgency coursed through me.

"I don't think you'll want to do that until you've

heard what I have to say."

"What?"

"Once I've told you, you won't be able to keep yourself from running off. I need you to answer my question first."

She crossed her arms over her chest, her eyes darkening.

"Look, vampire. You've just woken me up, drawn me away from my bed—"

"As you did when you came to fetch me for Rose."

"You're in no position to be calling the shots. Tell me your information first, then we'll see what question you have."

I stood my ground.

"No. You answer first, or I'll not tell you the information I came here with."

She closed the distance between us, gripping my jaw.

"I could torture the information out of you," she hissed. "You do realize that?"

I chuckled dryly. "I'm quite beyond responding to torture, believe me."

She glared into my eyes for several more minutes. I returned her gaze steadily. Then, breathing out in frustration, she said, "Well, spit it out."

"I believe you were inducted to become a Channeler. Correct?"

"Yes."

"How did you… become one, without losing yourself in the process?"

"That's what you came all this way to ask me? Why, are you thinking to become a Channeler?"

"Just answer the question."

Her brows furrowed, and she paused. "What makes you think I didn't lose myself?"

I stared at her, examining her heart-shaped face.

"You just strike me as… different from any Channeler I've come across before."

She sighed and leaned against the wall of my boat.

"You're right. I am different. Though I did lose myself. I was just lucky enough to have someone to remind me of who I was. To save me."

"What do you mean?"

"I had someone who was able to help remind me of who I was before I lost myself."

"Who?"

"Someone I was—am—in love with."

"How?"

She frowned. "I thought you said one question."

"Just answer me, will you?" I said irritably.

"I... I honestly don't know how he did it. I just somehow... saw myself in him. And then all the memories came flooding back in waves."

"Perhaps if I tell you the purpose of my question, you will better be able to help me," I said after a pause. Although I hated the thought of baring myself before this stranger, I had to if I wanted a useful answer from Mona. "It's about Annora. She's lost herself completely. We were lovers and I'd do anything to get her back to how she was."

Mona looked intrigued.

"You were in love with Annora, huh? Hm. Were you there with her during her induction?"

I shook my head. "What goes on in the induction? What is it?"

Mona's eyes darkened. She shuddered, wrapping her night gown more tightly around her.

"I don't want to talk about it. I'm still recovering from it myself. I don't want to bring those dark memories back. What I can tell you is... it's carried out in the supernatural realm by someone called Lilith. If you're interested to know more, I suggest you ask someone else about her."

I brought my fist down against the side of the boat. It rocked from the force of my blow.

"There is nobody else I can ask."

Mona showed signs of irritation again.

"Look, vampire. I've answered your questions. I've given you a lead. Now tell me what you came for."

I heaved a sigh. She was right, I supposed. At least I had a name. I made a mental note to raid Annora's library when I returned. If this Lilith was such an influential person, perhaps she would be mentioned in one of Annora's books.

"Are Derek and Sofia still alive?" I asked.

Mona's eyes widened. "Of course. Why wouldn't they be? You know they escaped—"

"Listen carefully," I said, stepping forward and gripping her shoulder. "What I'm about to tell you— nobody can ever know that you heard it from me. Nobody can know that I came here tonight to talk to you. Not any of the Novaks, nobody in The Shade, and certainly none of the witches. You must promise to not breathe a word to anyone."

"All right, but—"

"Just promise me."

She hesitated, confusion lining her face, then reached out her hand for me to shake.

"All right. You have my word. Just spit it out."

I took a step back. "Annora cast a spell on Derek and Sofia Novak while they were with us. A binding curse. They have seven days from when she cast the curse… and I have no idea when that was."

Shock turned to urgency. Mona swore and vanished in an instant. She would now do what she had to do.

I returned to the control cabin, the stench of the fisherman's corpse lingering in the warm night air.

And now it's time for me to return to my icy prison before my own seven days are up.

Chapter 15: Derek

I didn't think it possible for that night to bring more surprises.

But not long after I'd drifted off to sleep, the door to my room burst open. I jolted upright. The spitting image of myself stared down at me. The mist of sleep still partially upon me, it took a few seconds to remember it was Sofia. Mona hurried into the room after her.

Sofia put my strong arms around me and shook me. "Get up," she shouted in my deep voice.

"What?"

She hauled me out of bed and pushed me down to kneel on the floor.

"Sofia, what is—"

Mona gripped both of our heads and pushed us further down against the floor until our heads were touching it. Her fingers digging deeper against my scalp, agony erupted in my chest, as if my heart had just ruptured. A white mist fell over my eyes. I began coughing up blood. I heard Sofia choking by my side.

What is she doing to us?

I tried to look up at the witch, but as I forced my head upward, a burning heat seared through my spine. I collapsed again on the carpet.

"What are you doing?" I managed.

"Shh," the witch hissed.

A blinding headache came on. It felt like my brain was splitting in two. I didn't think that it was possible to experience worse pain than what Annora had put us through in her study. But now it paled in comparison to Mona's torture. I wasn't sure how much longer I could maintain consciousness.

My body was on the verge of giving in, when Mona finally released her grip on us and stepped back.

Slowly gathering myself, I managed to find the strength to sit up. Panting, I stared from her to Sofia.

"What was that?" I tried to shout, unable to contain my anger, but my voice cracked.

Sweat shining on Mona's forehead, she looked down at the two of us.

"Annora cast a binding spell on you."

I stared at her, my mouth dropping open.

"What?" Sofia croaked.

"When you were her prisoners, she bound you to her island. You had seven days to live since the day you escaped."

My lips opened, but no words came out. I stared at Sofia, whose shocked expression mirrored my own. *That's what the bitch must have done to us in her study.*

"H-how did you know?" Sofia stammered.

"I… I just felt something was wrong. I suppose as the time grew nearer, the spell was gathering potency. I just felt it."

"I-is it completely off us now?" Sofia asked.

"Yes. I think so."

I leaned back against the bedpost, trying to steady my breathing as the pain ebbed away from my body. I gazed blankly at the wall.

"That's what Vivienne was disturbed about," I said quietly, more to myself than anyone else. "She had sensed something wrong too…"

Silence filled the room.

"Now if you two don't mind," Mona said, "I'm going to return to bed."

With a snap of her fingers she vanished from the spot. I should have thanked the witch before she left, but I was still too stunned to think straight.

I looked at Sofia. "Do you remember how many days have passed since we were in Annora's study?"

Sofia squinted, biting her lip as she racked her brains. "It must have been about a week, or very nearly a week."

"That was close. Too close."

I should have suspected that Annora wouldn't have let us get away so lightly. If it weren't for Mona, we would be dead—yet another way we were now indebted to her.

***

The next morning, I woke early and went to our

bedroom. Sofia still showed no signs of changing back. I shook her awake. She stumbled out of bed and looked in the mirror, breathing out heavily.

"What if you're stuck like this forever?"

"I won't be," she said. "I told you, Corrine said I just have to wait." She climbed back into bed and leaned against the headboard. "Tell me exactly what happened with Kiev."

I frowned, running a hand through my hair.

The truth was, as much as I hated to admit it, Sofia's plan had worked. The dinner with Kiev and Mona had gone far better than I could have expected. Kiev had behaved civilly with me, and I'd tried to respond in kind—even if I was still a bit stiff in some of my remarks. Having the witches there to guide the conversation had definitely helped.

I wasn't sure how long this truce would last. I was certain that we would still clash—that just seemed to be in our natures. But something told me we'd come to an understanding. Perhaps even a sense of respect for one another. At least this seemed to be enough to satisfy Sofia. I supposed, now that I'd recovered from the shock, I was grateful she had done what she had.

"There's not much I can tell you," I said. "Kiev and I didn't do a lot of talking, but we were civil to each other. The witches led most of the conversation."

She smiled. "I'm glad."

She reached for my face instinctively, her—my—hand brushing against my cheek before I could stop her.

I flinched and stepped away. "I want my wife back."

Chapter 16: Sofia

It took longer than any of us could have expected but, finally, I turned back into myself.

I managed to convince Derek to keep my trick a secret from Kiev. There was no need for Kiev to know. It would only be detrimental to their newly formed relationship. I still regretted Derek finding out. If Vivienne's vision hadn't been such bad timing, neither of them would have ever discovered my trick. Still, the two men were now on speaking terms. And that was all that mattered.

I'd never been so happy to look in the mirror. I

stared at myself for several minutes once the transformation was complete, touching my face and running my hands along my skin. Derek was overjoyed. He scooped me up in his arms and kissed me hard.

Now that I was back, and Derek and Kiev were on civil terms, we needed to call a meeting to discuss the map they'd found. Derek arranged for a meeting in the Great Dome that evening. Kiev, his siblings, Mona, Matteo and Saira were already seated in the dome when we arrived. Mona slid the map toward Derek and me.

Black crosses covered the parchment, scattered across every continent. North and South America, Europe, Asia…

I exhaled sharply. The shock in Derek's face mirrored what I felt. Vivienne, Xavier and other members of our council gathered behind us, peering over our shoulders at the map.

"I suspect that some of those gates are no longer functioning properly—like the one we entered through," Mona said. "But more skilled witches than myself will be able to break through them regardless."

"Do you think there's any chance other creatures know about these gates?" Derek asked.

Derek's question sent my head reeling. I didn't think I could handle another intrusion of Elders and Hawks. We'd been there, done that. Gotten the postcard.

"I very much doubt it," Mona said. "I believe only the witches know about these portals. They keep them secret. They wouldn't want other supernatural creatures meddling with their plans here."

"Thank God," I said.

"Are you capable of closing gates?" Derek asked.

Mona bit her lip, frowning. "I haven't tried, but I think so. Gate opening is a much more skilled process, but closing I believe I can manage."

"The Ageless was able to close gates," I said. "You're as powerful as the Ageless, aren't you?"

Mona's face twitched. "Yes." She looked down at the table uncomfortably. "But I don't think it's going to help. There is one warlock who is especially powerful. Rhys. I thought I might have killed him, but I can't be sure. If he is still alive, I believe that he might have developed the skill by now to open gates. He's one of the most advanced warlocks of our kind. He is—or was—a Channeler, like me. Only more experienced and disciplined in black magic." She paused and glanced up at Kiev before continuing. "Close one gate, and another could just be opened the next day. I don't think closing gates is the answer."

I looked at Derek. Neither of us seemed willing to accept her statement.

"Well, closing these gates would be a start."

"You forget that I can't leave this island," Mona said. "The Shade could withstand the attack of one witch without my presence, but more than one—hell, I'm not even sure that I could hold up the spell even if I was present."

Derek turned to Ibrahim. "Can't you close gates?"

He nodded. "I can."

"Then you can go. Take another witch with you. Close as many gates as you can."

Even Ibrahim looked dubious. "Derek, if what Mona says is true, this isn't going to solve anything."

Corrine gripped Ibrahim's shoulder. "And how do we know these gates aren't being guarded by black witches capable of overpowering Ibrahim? I don't want to risk losing him again for a mission that probably won't even be effective."

It was Kiev who spoke next. His eyes traveled from

me to Derek. "Perhaps we all need to accept that supernatural creatures will always be drawn to this realm. So long as they are, they will find ways to break through. Perhaps there never will be a safe Earth, and rather than putting effort into preventing their entrance, we need to adapt to survive alongside them."

Ah, Kiev. Always the ray of sunshine.

The trouble was, it seemed that living alongside us was the last thing these witches had in mind.

Chapter 17: Caleb

Lilith.

The name played over and over in my mind as I navigated back to my island. I racked my brains for any mention of her throughout the time I'd spent with these witches, but drew a blank.

I just knew one thing: she was the person I had to seek out if I ever wanted to understand how Annora had lost herself, and whether there was any chance of recovery.

The boat was considerably slower than the submarine and it wasn't until the following evening that I finally arrived back on the island. I'd dropped the dead body in the ocean hours ago, but its stench still lingered in the cabin.

I left the boat moored in the harbor and made my way back up to the castle. I was glad to find the entrance hall empty. I was in no mood for answering questions now.

I had almost made it back to my room when I came across Annora on the staircase.

"Caleb!"

I groaned internally, lifting my eyes from the stairs to look at her.

"Frederik and the rest told me you were lifted up into an aircraft."

"We came across a group of hunters," I grunted.

"Hunters," she said, wetting her lower lip, eyes glazing over as she considered my words. "Where are the others?"

"Dead. The hunters murdered them."

There was no sadness in her eyes at the news, just irritation. "How did you survive?"

"By turning into a madman. I leapt from a cliff. Almost died in the process. I managed to come by a fisherman at sea and... here I am." I looked at her impatiently. "And now, if you'll excuse me..."

Her eyes scanned the length of my dirty, almost naked body, and she stepped aside for me to continue on my way.

I locked myself in my apartment and the first thing I did was take a shower, soaping myself from top to bottom, trying to get rid of the sand and salt water. When I looked in the mirror, my skin had mostly healed itself of the burns and blisters, but areas of my back which had been particularly exposed to the sun were still sensitive.

I dried myself and climbed into bed, stretching out my aching limbs and closing my eyes.

Memories of the hunters came drifting back. The sick torture, the loss of several companions I'd spent decades with... I just felt numb to it all. I'd become desensitized. I realized that was partly Annora's influence on me, and in that way, I'd become like her.

Now that I had time to think in the silence of my own room, and pushing aside thoughts of my encounter with Mona for the time being, the true implications of what had transpired dawned on me.

Annora wouldn't want to risk losing more of her vampires. If this type of ambushing was going to become a more regular occurrence, we needed The Shade's humans more than ever.

CHAPTER 18: ROSE

The whole island was shaken by what had almost happened to my parents. It just reinforced how dependent on Mona we were now. In the face of Annora's cunning, it seemed that only Mona could protect us. Goosebumps ran along my skin to think what would have happened if Mona hadn't figured it out in time.

I remembered asking Caleb what happened to vampires bound by Annora's curse who stayed away longer than seven days. He had refused to tell me.

Caleb. The memory of him disappearing with Mona,

not even looking up to say goodbye, still haunted me.

I supposed I should have been thankful to him. He'd made the break quick, clinical. I understood why he'd done it. There was no way that we could be together now.

I put thoughts of Caleb aside as I approached the foot of Zinnia and Gavin's tree. I went up in the elevator and walked onto their balcony, knocking on the front door.

Griffin opened the door and smiled.

"Hey, Rose. How are you?"

"I'm fine."

"Do you want to come in?"

"No," I said, "I wanted to talk to you, Griff. Could we go for a walk along the beach?"

I couldn't miss the excitement in his eyes as he grabbed a sweater from the back of the door and pulled it on.

"I'm going out," he called into the apartment before stepping out onto the balcony with me and shutting the door. We descended in the elevator and it wasn't until we had hit the forest floor that I felt comfortable enough to begin.

I caught Griff's hand and squeezed it, looking up at him in the eye.

"I owe you an answer," I said. Griff stared at me intently, barely breathing, even though I could tell he was trying to be cool. "I'm just going to be honest with you, okay?"

"I wouldn't expect you to be anything but," he said.

I held Griff's hand tighter. "I love you, Griff. And I hate to say *but*, but there is a *but*. I think my love for you is strongest as my friend."

I looked up at him. His eyes were on the forest ground. He was quite expressionless. He nodded slowly. But didn't answer.

We walked the rest of the way in awkward silence as we reached the beach.

"Are you all right?"

This time he looked directly at me. "Of course I am," he said, smiling. "Having you love me as a friend is enough."

I squeezed his hand tighter. "But things won't be awkward? Now I know what you really feel about me…"

He sighed. "I can't pretend that I haven't wished we

had more than friendship, but things don't have to be awkward."

"But I feel awkward about it," I said. In a way I wished he'd never told me.

"Well, don't," he said, stopping in his tracks.

We continued walking, but I wasn't convinced.

"I guess you just have to see the situation for what it is," Griff said, "I won't feel awkward around you, I promise. And neither should you."

I draped my arms over his shoulders, lifting myself up and planting a gentle kiss on his cheek. His face flushed red, almost matching his hair color.

"But if you go doing that too often, it might get awkward," he said, grinning.

I reached for his arm again, looping mine through it, as we continued our walk along the beach.

"Okay. Thanks, Griff."

We began chatting about other things, like Mona, Kiev and my parents almost dying. After about a mile, we caught sight of Ben and Abby walking toward us from the opposite direction.

I raised my eyebrows on seeing the two of them together. Even when Abby was round our house, she barely talked to Ben. It was a shock to see them both strolling alone together like this, Abby bunching up the hem of her dress in the waves, holding Ben's arm.

"Hey," I called, as we neared within ten feet of each other. "What's up?"

"We were just taking a walk with—" Before Ben could finish his sentence, there was a heavy pounding against wet sand and Shadow came into view, hurtling toward us. He carried in his mouth a thick tree branch. He halted at the last minute and dropped the branch in front of Abby.

I leaned over and stroked Shadow's head. Then regretted it instantly. He tried to leap up on me. He would have flattened me—albeit affectionately—had Abby not grabbed his collar and hauled him away. He continued to thrash about, straining to lavish his slimy affections on me.

"Whoa, boy," Abby said. As a vampire, she was the only one powerful enough to control him. Shadow's strength still scared me, even though I knew I owed my life to him for carrying my mother out of The Blood Keep.

Griff and I decided to keep walking along with Ben

and Abby, who were now headed back toward the direction of the Port. As we were approaching, Abby stopped short. Shadow's ears pricked up. They both turned their eyes toward the ocean.

"What?" Ben asked.

"Listen," Abby said, placing a finger to her lips. "Someone is calling for help."

We all strained our ears once more, and finally I heard it. Abby was right. Far in the distance, someone was yelling for help.

Abby squinted, scanning the shoreline with her supernatural vision. Finally she pointed.

"Someone is out there, beyond the boundary."

Ben looked in the direction of the harbor and pointed toward one of the submarines. "Let's go see."

We hurried over to the port and bundled into a submarine. We followed Ben into the control room. He navigated us away from the jetty, toward the boundary of the island. I hoped nobody had seen us. Our parents didn't like us going near the boundary.

As we looked through the glass screen, human legs came into view.

"Go up," I said.

Ben surfaced and we hurried back to the hatch. Ben climbed up first and stuck his head out.

"It's Micah!" he called down, before climbing out.

"Who's Micah?"

"One of the werewolves."

"Careful, Ben," Abby called up as he balanced on the slippery roof.

I lifted myself up through the hatch. My eyes fell on the spot where a young man with shoulder-length blond hair was floating in the water, one of The Shade's small wooden boats beside him, capsized.

"Micah," Ben shouted.

Micah looked around wildly, unable to see the source of the voice since he was outside the boundary.

"Are you all right?" Ben asked.

"Yes," he replied. "I just strayed too far by accident. I didn't mean to go outside the boundary."

"Hold on," Ben said. "I'm coming for you."

Ripping off his shirt, Ben dove into the water and reappeared on the other side of the boundary. He reached Micah, gripped hold of his arm and pulled him toward the submarine.

"Thanks," Micah panted. Griffin reached down and

helped haul Ben onto the submarine, and then Micah. Micah towered over me, a small net of fish hung over one shoulder. I stepped aside.

"How is it you weren't able to come back in?" Griffin asked. "I thought Mona gave you all permission to come and go as you please."

"Yeah. Knowing my luck, I think I was out fishing during the meeting she called to put that charm on us. It seems I'm able to exit but not re-enter."

We all dropped back down through the hatch and made our way to the control room. Ben began navigating us back to the shore.

I recognized Micah now that I eyed him more closely. I'd seen him among the crowd before, but had never spoken to him. He sat in the passenger seat directly opposite mine and was making no attempt to hide the way he was staring at me. I found it off-putting and turned my attention to Griff.

"Why don't you come back to my place after this and I'll cook us both something?"

"I'd love that." Griff smiled down at me.

I looked up again at Micah. His hazel-brown eyes were still fixed on me. I got up and pulled Griff with me out of the control room and into the passenger area to avoid Micah's gaze. He was a beautiful specimen of a man, but I didn't understand why he was looking at me so unashamedly. It occurred to me that maybe—since he was a werewolf, and also from the supernatural realm—I shouldn't be so quick to judge him. Maybe their manners were just different. The fact was that until Kiev's arrival on the island, I'd never encountered a werewolf in my life. They intrigued me, but I had no idea how they behaved. They seemed to be less reserved than vampires.

Whatever his reason for staring at me, I didn't feel comfortable and was happy to retreat to the passenger room toward the back of the submarine while we travelled back to the island.

Griff and I let the others exit first. Micah was the last we were waiting for. He picked up his fish net and dragged it up through the hatch, some fish still alive and flapping. We followed after, Griff pushing me up first. Ben and Abby were already making their way toward Shadow, who was waiting on the sand. Micah stopped midway along the jetty and turned back to face us.

"I was going to roast some of these." He gestured to the fish. "Just thought I'd invite you both to join me."

I'd been looking forward to spending some quality time with my best friend, but I wasn't sure how to turn Micah down without sounding rude. He already knew we were hungry and I intended to cook for Griff and myself.

I looked after Ben and Abby. They'd already disappeared into the woods with Shadow.

I looked at Griff. He shrugged.

"Thanks. That would be lovely," I said. I reached out a hand and Micah shook it, his grip wet and intense. "I'm Rose, by the way."

"Oh," he said, smiling, "I doubt there's anyone on this island who doesn't know who you are, princess."

I brushed my hand against Griff's shoulder. "This is Griffin."

Micah and Griffin shook hands.

"Where do you plan to cook?" I asked.

"On the beach. Nothing like cooking in the fresh sea air."

We walked along in silence for a few minutes before Micah stopped on a particularly rocky part of the beach.

He laid the fish down on the sand and ran over to the boulders a few meters away. He grabbed two large rocks—one beneath each arm—and walked back over.

"Thanks," I said as he set the two stones down for me and Griff to sit on. He returned to the spot and came back with one more for himself. Then he fetched a fourth longer slab and placed it between us. He collected some wood from the forest nearby and, with two pieces of flint, started coaxing a fire to life. Griff and I stood in the direction the wind was blowing, helping to block its force as the fire gathered strength.

I wondered what kind of life Micah had lived back in the supernatural realm. Clearly they'd learned to be resourceful. They didn't seem to take anything for granted and my mother had commented how happy and grateful they seemed just to have roofs over their heads.

Griff and I watched as Micah went about cleaning the fish in the sea and, after removing a dagger from his belt, began preparing them.

I cleared my throat. "I take it you're used to eating fish."

He looked up at me and nodded with a smile.

It wasn't long before Micah was handing both Griff and I platters of roasted fish. No salt. No seasoning. Micah sat down with a platter of his own opposite us and began to dig in.

Since Griff wasn't making much conversation, I asked another question.

"So, uh, how do you become a werewolf? How does it work? Is it like with vampires where you get infected? Are there Elder werewolves?"

Micah swallowed a mouthful before replying.

"We have no Elders, unlike vampires. We are a species in our own right. And despite the folklore, it's not true that humans can turn into werewolves. We're not like vampires where we can infect others with our nature. You're either born a werewolf, or you're not. We have humanoid features, but even in our daytime forms, we are not truly humans."

"Do you have your own realm in the world of supernaturals? Like The Sanctuary? Or Cruor?"

He nodded again, biting into another large fish.

"What's it like?"

"Mountains, forests, open fields... And plenty of wild animals."

"Do you eat just animals?"

He wiped his mouth with the back of his hand.

"We don't have a chance normally to eat much else. I've never tried human flesh before. Can't say I'm not curious to try it. Though I've heard that it ruins the taste of animal meat forever. Humans are rare in our realm. The witches tend to hog them all. Either the witches, or the ogres who have a way of getting large supplies of them… More?" he said, eyeing Griff's and my empty hands.

"No, thanks." I looked at Griff.

"No, thanks," he said.

"I hope it was to your liking," Micah said, more to me than to Griff as he glanced at me sideways. He went about preparing seven more large fish for himself before continuing. "So anyway, you don't have to worry about that with us. As much as it's tempting, we're well practiced at surviving on animals. I believe there's only one werewolf in the whole pack who's tasted human flesh before."

"And who's that?" I asked.

"His name is Ianto. Big, burly fellow. Probably the largest of all of us. Hard to miss."

"I'll be staying clear of him then."

"But like I said, even he is used to animal flesh. I wouldn't be afraid of us. What you need to worry about is what will happen once more witches join forces with Annora. We don't know if Mona will be strong enough to hold up this protection…"

Thanks for reminding me. I'd been trying to push this thought from my mind since there was nothing we could do about it.

Griff stood up and walked over to the waves to wash his hands and mouth.

"Griff?"

"I'd better get going," he said quietly. "I told my mom I'd be back by now. There's something around the house she wanted me to help with."

He was avoiding my eyes as he spoke. Something wasn't right. I hoped it didn't have anything to do with the attention Micah was paying me.

"Okay, well, stop by tomorrow, will you?" I closed the distance between us and held his hands, forcing him to look at me.

"Sure," he said, giving me a forced smile before turning on his heel and striding away.

"Bye, Griffin," Micah called.

"Bye," Griff muttered.

I watched him leave, then turned back to face Micah, an uncomfortable silence now falling between us.

He walked to the water and washed his hands in the waves.

Although I was disturbed by Griff's behavior, I couldn't deny that I was glad to have more time with Micah. I was curious to know more about werewolves and discover what other myths about them were untrue.

"What's it like to turn every time the sun goes down? Does it hurt?"

He took a seat back down on the sand, removing his wet shirt and spreading it out on Griff's empty slab before replying. "No. I'm so used to it, I don't even think about it."

"I see," I said, drawing my eyes away from his tan chest. "I've never seen a werewolf turn before."

"You should watch me tonight," he said.

"I'd like that."

He stood up and reached his hand down to help me up. I took it and he pulled me to my feet. He flashed me a smile, revealing a set of perfect teeth—a little too sharp for a human's. "I'll come to fetch you just before sundown, if you like. But be ready, because once it happens I have no control over it."

"Okay," I said, returning his smile. "It's a date."

Chapter 19: Abby

I wasn't sure what we had, Ben and I.

For the past few days, he'd shown up at my doorstep each afternoon to accompany me in taking Shadow for a walk. We strolled around the island, mostly sticking to the beaches because that was where Shadow liked it most.

It was a strange feeling. We'd grown up together, spent most of our lives together on the same island, yet it felt like we'd only just been acquainted. The conversations we had were those of strangers getting to know each other.

But I didn't know if it was anything more than that. In the submarine I'd told Ben he didn't need to be timid around me. And he wasn't. He was true to his word in treating me like he would any other person. But I wasn't sure if it was just an obligation he felt, or some kind of morbid curiosity, rather than spending time with me because he genuinely enjoyed my company.

There wasn't really a way for me to know. But since he kept calling on my door and insisting on accompanying me for several days in a row, I guessed he got something out of hanging with me.

I felt embarrassed about my feelings toward him, especially while we were out together. It was hard to relax. I felt on edge, self-conscious, not sure where I stood with him. Or how I should relate to him. I was afraid to hope. After all, that was how my own brother had gotten his heart broken.

Expectations. Assumptions. I was careful to harbor none.

The most I held was a light optimism that Ben might want to keep joining Shadow and me on walks.

Because whatever it was we had, or were beginning to have, I was glad for his company.

Chapter 20: Aiden

I'd been avoiding Adelle like the plague and she was beginning to notice it. The fact that my daughter and son-in-law had almost died gave me some excuse for my reclusiveness, but even that was beginning to wear thin for the witch. She'd visited my penthouse twice in the past twelve hours. I'd ignored her. But when she knocked a third time, I decided to answer the door.

She stood on my porch, clutching a pile of papers in one arm. Her long fiery hair was tied up in a bun and she wore her signature summer dress, showing just enough of her long smooth legs to make my breath hitch.

"Aiden!" she gasped, reaching an arm around me and drawing me in for a hug.

I hugged her back awkwardly and stepped away as soon as she released me.

"I haven't seen you around. How are you?"

"Fine."

I stepped aside to allow her entrance into my apartment. She set her papers down on the dining table and drew up a chair.

"I'll put some tea on," I said, turning my back on her and busying myself brewing the chamomile tea I knew she was fond of. It was all I could do to avoid looking at her.

"So you've recovered?"

"Just about."

"I knocked twice already. I guess you were sleeping."

"Yeah…"

An awkward silence fell between us as we both listened to the electric kettle heat up. I reached into a cupboard and started rubbing a kitchen towel against an already bone-dry cup and saucer.

"I just, um, finished work at school. I stayed late

today."

More silence.

Eventually I could find no more excuses to keep my back to her. Once the water had boiled, I poured it into a teapot and placed it down on the wooden table along with the teacup and saucer.

Then I drew up a seat opposite her. I looked up. She was frowning.

"Are you sure you're all right, Aiden?"

"Of course. Why do you ask?"

"You just seem a bit… uptight."

"Ah, well, I've been through a lot recently. I guess it's still taking its toll."

I drummed my fingers on the table, desperately racking my brain for something to change the subject, help me forget the pain that consumed me at having her sit so close to me, our knees almost touching beneath the table. *So close, yet so far…*

She sipped her tea.

"Mmm," she said, smiling. "You know how I like it."

But not as well as Eli… As much as I mocked myself for it, I couldn't stop the childish thought from flitting through my head. I was sure now that any innocent statement she made would cause my mind to start comparing myself with Eli.

"How's, uh, everything at school? Is everything back to normal now?"

"Pretty much…"

"Good."

More silence followed. I hated how stilted things had become between us. Even though it hurt, I realized that the only way to dissipate the awkwardness was to tackle it outright.

"Yuri tells me that you and Eli are going out. Congratulations."

Blood rose to her cheeks, giving them a rosy glow.

"Uh, yes, actually." She frowned. "I just wonder, how did Yuri know? Neither Eli or myself have told anyone yet."

I cursed myself. In my hurry to make things right, I'd forgotten that I was the one who told Yuri about them.

"I'm not sure," I said. "Perhaps he or Claudia caught sight of you somewhere."

I made a mental note to talk to Yuri and Claudia to make sure we kept this story straight.

"Ah, okay…" Adelle's voice trailed off and she busied

herself sipping tea again.

I cleared my throat, picking up a pen and fiddling with it. I felt like snapping it.

"So, uh, how did it happen? He asked you out?" I asked, throwing her a casual glance.

"He did. Soon after we both returned from Caleb's island." She paused, smiling fondly. "There's a side to Eli that you wouldn't expect. He's got a great sense of humor once he comes out of his shell."

I recalled the way she'd been laughing that fateful day I'd discovered the two of them in each other's arms in the boathouse by the lake.

"I'm sure," I said, my jaw tensing. "Unfortunately, I've never had the privilege of seeing that side of him before."

"Maybe you need to get to know him better."

"Clearly."

She swallowed the last of her tea.

"Do you want some more?" I asked.

"No, thank you. It was lovely though. I really have to get going. I just stopped by to check you were all right."

We both got up from the table and she picked up her papers, replacing them beneath her arm. I led her back to the front door.

She gave me another hug, her perfume tantalizing my senses.

"I'll see you around, okay?" she said, squeezing my arm.

"Yeah. Bye."

She threw me another smile and vanished from the spot.

Late for a date with Eli, no doubt…

CHAPTER 21: ROSE

There was a sharp rapping at our door just before sundown. I hurried to answer it, but my father got to the door before me.

Micah stood in the doorway, dressed in a shirt and jeans. My mother had arranged for clothing for our guests, since they'd arrived with nothing but the clothes on their backs.

"Yes?"

"I'm here for—" Micah began.

I reached the door and placed a hand on my father's shoulder.

"He's here for me."

My father raised his eyebrows, looking from me to the werewolf, before stepping aside and allowing me to exit.

"Watch your step with my daughter, wolf," he said.

"Of course," Micah said.

"And Rose." My father's eyes bored into mine. "Don't stay out later than nine-thirty."

"Okay," I said, hurrying toward the elevator with Micah before he could impose more restrictions on me.

"Don't mind my dad," I muttered as we descended to the forest ground.

"I think it's hard for anyone to not mind your father considering he's the king of this place."

I let out a dry chuckle.

As we hit the forest path, I looked around. "So where do you plan to turn?"

"Wherever it starts to happen. It won't be long now. We may as well keep walking."

We continued walking in silence. I kept shooting glances at him, expecting to see fur start sprouting through his skin. It wasn't until we reached the beach that he grunted and stopped short.

"It's time," he said, his voice constricted.

I took a few steps back and stared as he sank to the floor, on his knees and hands. His body began to shake. His clothes burst beneath his expanding form and lay strewn on the ground. His head expanded. Thick fur grew over his skin. His teeth lengthened and became razor-sharp. His hands and feet balled up as his legs took shape. His whole body rippled with muscle as the transformation completed and he lifted himself up onto all fours.

"Normally, I'd try to be undressed during this time to avoid this." His voice gravelly, he jerked his head toward the shreds of clothes on the ground. "But present company precluded that…"

I gave him a weak smile.

He shook his thick brown coat and stretched out his limbs.

"Well, you've seen it. What did you think?"

"Um, it was faster than I thought it would be."

"Want a ride?"

"A-a ride?"

"Yes."

I bit my lip, eyeing his broad back. Of course I

wanted a ride. How many girls could say they'd ridden a werewolf before? But I felt shy to admit it. I'd only just met Micah.

"No?" he said.

"Okay. Just a short ride."

He knelt down so I could mount him. I gripped the fur nearest his head and hauled myself up, one leg over either side of his back.

"Holding tight?"

"Uh, not yet," I said, burying my hands into the fur at the back of his neck and gripping tight. "Does this hurt?"

His back shook as he laughed. "No."

I gripped harder—just in time. He lurched forward, knocking the breath right out of me. We hurtled along the beach, spray and sand flying everywhere. I dug my heels into his sides, holding on for dear life. Werewolves seemed to be as fast as vampires. We raced around the island and soon enough my nerves cooled and I started to enjoy myself.

He ran once around the island, and then he left the beach and started whipping through the woods. I ducked down and closed my eyes on his order to avoid the low-hanging branches. We reached the door of the Black Heights and he began scrambling up the mountain. This was a level of daring I hadn't been prepared for. We were almost at a sixty-degree angle as he scampered up.

"Micah," I gasped, the blood draining from my knuckles. "I'm slipping."

Either he didn't hear me or he deliberately ignored me as he continued racing up the mountain. I fought to hold on, and in the end ended up locking my arms around his neck in an attempt to secure myself.

After a particularly bumpy patch in which I was sure I would finally lose my grip, we arrived at the top of the mountain. I let go of him and collapsed on the ground.

Christ. This wolf is insane.

Micah cocked his head to one side. "You didn't slip."

I sat up and glared at him. "I almost did." I dared peek over the edge of the cliff and gasped at how high up we were. Strong gusts of cold wind swirled around us. I was afraid to stand up lest I lose balance. He'd brought us to a particularly narrow peak, and with Micah already hogging most of the space with his giant frame, I stayed where I was, flat against the ground.

"I wouldn't have let you fall," he replied.

My eyes narrowed on him.

"Life is more fun with risks," he said.

"That wasn't fun. That was just stupid. And now we have to make our way all the way down again…"

"I'll go gentler with you on the way down," he said. "I promise."

He fell silent as we both set our eyes on the magnificent view. I should have been terrified to be all the way up here, away from everyone with a giant wolf. But somehow I trusted Micah. Even though I barely knew him. But perhaps that was just my naiveté again.

I'd lost all track of time. It was only now that I was no longer preoccupied holding on to the werewolf's back for dear life that I glanced at my watch. Ten o'clock.

"Crap. I need to get home now. It's past nine-thirty."

He looked disappointed, but said, "If that's what you want…"

I climbed on to his back and held my breath as Micah jumped from the cliff and began making his way down. *So much for going easy on the way down.*

I could have sworn his fur was thinner behind his

neck by the time we arrived back at my penthouse. I slid off him, holding on to his head for support as I steadied my weak knees. As I approached the elevator, Micah motioned to follow me. I turned to him and shook my head.

"It's best you stay here," I said. Although I was still annoyed with him, I wasn't keen on him getting an earful from my father. I'd rather take the brunt of it myself.

"Good night then," Micah said.

"Good night," I said.

It was hard to be angry with Micah. There was something refreshing about him. Something wild and raw. I liked the fact that he wasn't inhibited by social norms.

He was about to turn, as was I, but before we parted, I walked over to him and stroked his fur.

"Thanks. Tonight was fun. I'd like to do this again some time."

"You know where to find me?"

"Which house number?"

"Sixteen."

"Okay. I'll see you around."

He went running off into the dark woods while I ascended the elevator back to the apartment. I held my breath as I stood outside the front door. I knocked.

Ben answered the door.

"You're in trouble," he muttered, stepping back and allowing me entrance.

"What's new?" I said.

My father emerged from his study, glowering at me.

"Do you know what time it is?"

I looked down at my feet. "Sorry, Dad," I mumbled. "I lost track of time."

I moved to walk past him and lock myself in my bedroom but he was having none of it. He stood in front of my bedroom door, blocking my way.

"You're grounded."

"What?"

"For the whole weekend."

I huffed and puffed, but there was no budging my father. I pushed past him and entered my room, slamming the door shut behind me.

I couldn't have expected my father to act any differently. I'd gotten myself into enough trouble recently. It was only to be expected that my parents' discipline would tighten now.

As I collapsed in bed, I found myself worrying about Micah. When I didn't reappear, he might think that it was something he'd done or said. And despite him almost dropping me from the Black Heights, I wanted him to know that it really wasn't.

Chapter 22: Caleb

Annora gave me space after I returned. I supposed that she'd seen the state I was in and thought it was best I recovered my strength before she visited me again.

But I wasn't able to give my body the sleep it was crying out for. My mind was too alive. I tossed and turned in bed, trying to fall into slumber, but eventually gave up.

Rose had left a flavor in my mouth, familiar, yet distant. A flavor I hadn't tasted since Annora's better days. And now I hankered for more of it.

I sat up in bed, looking out the window, watching as

the sun began to rise beyond the boundary. My conversation with Mona still plagued me. *Lilith.* She was the only straw I had to cling to.

***

The next day I waited for Annora to leave her apartment before sneaking inside. I headed straight for the library and began pulling books off the shelves, searching for any mention of Lilith—any clue as to what she was and where I might find her. Most of Annora's books were written in the ancient witch tongue. I'd picked up a little of it over the years, and I could understand enough to look out for Lilith's name.

After twenty minutes, I was already realizing that this was an impossible task. For one thing, Annora had many dozens of books in this room. Even if I had the time to search through every page, there was no guarantee that I would find mention of Lilith.

Careful to replace everything in the room exactly as I'd found it, I slipped back out of the apartment and headed downstairs to my own quarters. But my apartment suddenly felt claustrophobic. Instead, I went down to the ground floor and began to pace from chamber to chamber, seeking to avoid bumping into anyone. Thankfully, solitude wasn't hard to come by in this castle.

Annora was the only witch we had contact with. If I didn't know who Lilith was after all these years of serving the witches' cause, there was no way any of the vampires would know about her.

It seemed that the only way to Lilith was through Annora. I guessed I'd known this all along. But I'd been hoping to avoid mentioning Lilith to her because it would bring about awkward questions. How would I know about Lilith to begin with? I began to wonder what possible explanation I could give her.

As I walked from hall to hall, the solution finally hit me.

If I can't mention Lilith to Annora, I just need to get Annora to mention Lilith to me.

I shuddered as a plan started to formulate in my mind. There was only one way to do this. I had to convince Annora that I wanted to become like her.

Chapter 23: Vivienne

I turned my back on Xavier as he sat at the dining table. I busied myself at the kitchen counter, trying to hide the way my hands were trembling. I poured two glasses of deer blood and passed one to him before taking a seat myself.

I tried to keep a calm demeanor, but inside I was burning up. I'd begun to feel the disturbance when we were held hostage by Annora. It had taken root in the pit of my stomach and I'd had to bear it every day since. Then, once I'd had the vision, it had intensified tenfold.

"What's wrong, Viv?" Xavier asked, his gorgeous eyes

settling on me. "You haven't been yourself lately."

His eyes always made me feel like he could see right through me.

I cleared my throat and reached out to touch his hand resting on the table. Squeezing it, I forced a smile.

"I'm fine. There's just something I need to talk to you about."

"What is it?"

I held my breath, anticipating his reaction. "Xavier… I want to have a child."

His jaw dropped. It took a few moments for him to find his voice again.

"Are you serious?" he choked.

I nodded.

A smile broke out on his face. He stood up and walked round the table to me, pulling me up and drawing me into an embrace.

He looked down at my face, studying me closely. "Why now? After all this time… What's changed?"

I nestled my head against his chest, breathing deeply.

"The time we spent trapped in that dungeon at Annora's mercy… it just made me realize that I need to stop taking this life for granted. Even as vampires, it can end at any moment. I need to stop delaying what I know we both want."

The joy on Xavier's face made me feel like my heart might burst. Xavier had wanted children for a long time. Since the day we got married, he'd made no secret of it. I was the one who'd been delaying it. Because I was a coward. I knew the risks that came with having a child. I'd already suffered the loss of most of my family—my mother, father and brother. And I had come so close to losing Derek on more than one occasion. I didn't want to risk losing Xavier, or myself, by taking the cure. Derek had told me how agonizing it was. And then, even if we managed to become humans, I was afraid of being a mother. I didn't know if I was capable of being a good one. My head was so in the clouds sometimes, I was worried that I wasn't present enough to properly care for a child.

Yes, having a baby scared me. But now the prospect of not ever being able to have one scared me more. As with most things in life, you only realized what you wanted when it was taken away from you.

I realized how much I wanted to have a child with Xavier.

"But are you sure, Viv? I'm afraid you're just doing this for me."

I shook my head. "No. I'm not."

"But now of all times? When the safety of the island is still in the balance? Is now the best time for us to turn back into humans and for you to bear a child?"

I'd considered this already. How could I not have?

Holding my husband's head in my hands, I kissed his cheek. "There never will be a perfect time. I've come to realize that. It could be that in the future it will seem even more impossible. We're safe for now with Mona. I… I don't want to delay any longer. Who knows what could happen in even ten years?"

"But—"

"Something tells me we're as safe now as we'll ever be. There will always be some danger lurking round the corner. We just have to do the best we can to protect our child, like Derek and Sofia."

His thumbs brushed the sides of my face, his eyes still drilling into mine. "But darling, this is a time when we need to be strong. Stronger than ever. There was a seventeen-year gap when nothing happened… when we could have…"

"I know," I said, swallowing back the lump in my throat. "I know. It was a mistake not having one before. But I don't want to look back at this period and realize we made the same mistake again."

"Neither do I," he said. "But I also don't want us to regret having one now. I think we should wait—a few weeks—to see how things play out with Annora. For all we know, we could be driven out of this island by then."

I sighed. "All right. A few weeks. But after that, no more waiting."

Chapter 24: Rose

The weekend passed slowly. Griffin came to visit me on Saturday, for which I was grateful. He seemed to have cheered up a bit from the last time I saw him. I guessed that it was the absence of Micah. For whatever reason, Griff seemed to be tense around him, so I was careful not to bring him up. However, when Griffin asked if I wanted to go for a swim after lunch, I had no choice but to mention the werewolf.

"I'm grounded," I said, scowling.

"What did you do?"

"I got home too late."

"How come?"

I looked down at my empty plate and fiddled with my fork. "I wanted to watch Micah turn. And then, well, things just got a bit out of hand. He gave me a ride on his back and… Anyway, my dad grounded me this weekend."

"That's a shame," Griff said. "It's a beautiful day on Sun Beach."

I groaned. "Yeah, I bet. Well, don't let me stop you. I've got homework to catch up on anyway."

I stood up and began washing the dishes. Griff took the hint and got up too.

"Okay," he said, patting me on the shoulder, "I'll see you around then."

"See you, Griff."

As soon as he'd left the apartment, I sought out Ben in his room. He was lying on his stomach in bed, listening to music and doing algebra, still in his pajamas.

I placed a hand on his shoulder and pulled away one of his earbuds.

"I need you to do me a favor," I said, bending down to his level.

"Hm?"

"Micah. I just need you to tell him that I've been grounded for the weekend, or he'll think I'm rude for not showing up today. We'd agreed to meet on the beach this evening."

"All right," Ben grunted, replacing the earbud in his ear. "I'm going out later. I'll let him know then."

"Thanks," I said, ruffling his hair and leaving the room.

I finished tidying up the kitchen, then headed to my own bedroom where I proceeded to finish the homework that was due in on Monday. It was late afternoon by the time I'd finished a particularly grueling set of calculus exercises.

I flopped back on my bed, only to sit up a moment later on hearing a knock at my door.

"Come in," I said.

My mother appeared in the doorway.

"Hi, Rose," she said, sitting on the bed next to me and brushing a hand over my arm. "Dad told me you've made friends with Micah."

"Yeah," I mumbled, wanting nothing more than to just take a nap.

"He seems a friendly, talkative type."

"It's not like I've known him for more than an afternoon," I said, frowning at her.

I found it odd that she'd come to talk to me about Micah when he was barely more than an acquaintance. I sensed that my mom had detected I had felt something for Caleb, though I was thankful she'd never expressed her thoughts to me, saving me from embarrassment. Perhaps now she was happy I'd made friends with another guy.

I was relieved when she changed the subject.

"We're going out. Your father and I have a meeting with the Novalics. We'll probably be back late. I just wanted to warn you not to try to go out while we're away. Grandpa's agreed to stay here on Dad's request— so don't bother."

Although it hurt that my father didn't trust me, I could hardly blame him. I'd given him little reason to trust me of late.

"I don't plan to," I said curtly. "I still have more homework to finish anyway."

"Okay, honey," she said, brushing her fingers through my hair and kissing my forehead.

I watched her leave the room, then reverted my attention back to calculus. I was finding it hard to concentrate. My thoughts drifted to Sun Beach, and how much I wanted to join the others in bathing. I managed to eventually finish up my math homework, even though it took twice as long as it should have.

It was early evening by the time I tucked all my homework back into my bag and made my way to the music room. I was bursting for some creative output after all the left-brain work I'd been subjected to. On the way, I checked Ben's room. He'd left already, perhaps hours ago, and had likely been enjoying the sun all this time.

I walked over to the bookshelf in the corner and began sifting through music sheets. I settled on one and sat down at the piano. Smoothing the paper out on the music stand, I began to play.

I'd barely gotten halfway through the piece when a thump came from the opposite end of the room. I stood up in time to see Micah crawling through the semi-open window, his broad shoulders squeezing through the gap.

"Micah!" I hissed. "How on earth…?" I hurried over

to him and stared out of the window. Just looking downward made my stomach flip. "Don't tell me you climbed all the way up here."

Twigs were caught in his hair. He breathed heavily as he looked down at me, a smirk forming on his lips. "Your brother told me that you've been… grounded? I think that's the word he used."

Before he could utter another word, I rushed to the music room's entrance and pulled the door shut.

"You need to be quiet. My grandfather is here. He might have heard you already."

Micah's amused expression didn't leave his face as he walked around the room, surveying our instruments. He stopped at the grand piano, running his fingers along the keys.

"I've never touched one of these before," he said. "You play?"

"Yes," I replied with a sigh. "Look, Micah, you shouldn't be here. I'll be allowed out again after the weekend. I can see you then."

He wet his lower lip, a spark of mischief in his eyes. "I just think it's an awfully nice day to be grounded."

"Yeah, well, there will be plenty more nice days to

come."

He fell silent, and began pacing around the room again, this time moving back toward the window, to my relief. But then he stopped again.

"I could unground you, for a while…"

He held out his hand, cocking his head to one side.

I bit my lower lip, staring at him. My conscience was ordering me to tell him to beat it. But another side of me, a wilder side, the side that was fed up of being inside on this beautiful warm day, was telling me to take his hand.

Eventually, the latter won over.

I blew out, hoping that I wouldn't regret this decision. Holding a finger to my lips and glaring at him, I grabbed his hand and pulled him out of the music room. I led him into my own room.

"Wait here," I said, and closed the door.

I found my grandfather in the living room with a book on his lap. He looked up as I entered.

"How's the homework going, darling?"

"I've finished," I said, letting out an exaggerated yawn. "I'm exhausted now. I'm going to have a nap, so please don't let anyone come in my room. I'll probably be sleeping for the next few hours…"

"I'll make sure nobody disturbs you," he said.

I returned to my room and placed my Do Not Disturb doorknob sign outside my door just as an extra precaution. Micah already had my window pulled open, expectation alive in his eyes.

"Well?" he said.

"Unground me."

Chapter 25: Rose

Micah bent down to allow me to climb on to his back. I felt more secure around him in his human form. He was easier to cling to, at least. I locked my arms over his broad shoulders, my legs around his muscular waist. I closed my eyes as he swung himself out of the window. I gripped so hard I thought I might be strangling him as he leapt several feet over a sheer drop into the branches of a nearby tree.

"Where are we going?" I asked, gasping as he began leaping from branch to branch. His hands gripped my legs and held them in place.

He didn't respond as he continued to leap down with furious speed.

"We can't afford to bump into my parents," I pressed.

"Don't worry, Princess. I'll make sure that we won't."

I was breathless by the time we reached the forest ground. I was expecting him to set me down on my feet. But he began racing through the trees.

"My parents are probably having their meeting in the Great Dome. So don't go anywhere near there."

I realized soon enough where he was taking me. We were headed for Sun Beach. He set me down on the sand as soon as we arrived. I cast my eyes around. Ben swam in the waters with some of his friends. I also saw some of my own girlfriends. Micah unbuttoned his shirt and, heading straight for the waters, dove in and began swimming about.

I dawdled over to the edge of the waters, wishing I'd brought my bikini. I would have to make do with just dipping my feet in the enticing ocean water.

Micah swam up to me. "Are you not coming in?"

Before I could answer, a familiar voice called out my

name.

I turned to see Griffin walking over to me, wearing his swim shorts.

"Hey, I thought you were grounded?"

I looked at him sheepishly.

"I am… Micah helped me escape through the window."

"Oh," he said, his eyes falling on Micah who'd now stepped out of the water. "Well, are you going for a swim?"

"I would, but I left my bikini at home."

"Bi-kini?" Micah wrinkled his nose as he looked down at me.

"Uh, it's what girls go swimming in." I pointed to a group of girls further along the beach. "Like what they're wearing."

"Tell me where it is, and I'll get it for you," Griff offered.

"Nah, don't bother. I'll just hike up my skirt—"

"Where is it?" Micah said, towering over me, his tone of voice more of a command than a question.

"Um, it's in the bottom drawer of my big wardrobe. And if you're going to bother getting it, you may as well bring a towel too. I have one hanging on the back of my chair, near my bed. Just don't get caught by Aiden."

He dashed off, leaving me standing alone with Griff. Griff turned his eyes toward the ocean.

"Griff, I…" I'd opened my mouth before considering the rest of my sentence. The look on his face was killing me. Disappointment. It was subtle, but I knew him well enough for it to be pronounced for me.

Unable to bear the silence, I caught his hand and pulled him into the water after me. I began wading into the waters, lifting my skirt up above my knees.

But we weren't alone for long. Micah returned about ten minutes later, my towel over his bare shoulder, my bikini scrunched up in his large fist. I left Griff and took both from him.

"Aiden didn't catch you, I hope?"

He shook his head.

I left the beach and found a quiet part of the forest to change. Returning to the waves, I laid my towel down on a dry patch of sand before wading back into the water. Griff had moved toward Ben and his group of friends, leaving Micah swimming alone in the waves.

My brother stood up, finally having noticed me.

"What are you doing here?" he called.

I grinned and shrugged my shoulders. He looked at me disapprovingly.

I waded back into the water, toward my brother and Griff rather than Micah, who seemed to be busy swimming. But the werewolf caught up with me in the water as soon as he noticed me. He stopped in front of me, blocking my way.

"Come with me," he said.

"Huh?"

Before I could object, he pulled me toward him and fastened my arms around his neck. He began swimming in the opposite direction of my brother, deeper into the ocean.

Great.

I was beginning to feel nervous at how deep we were swimming. The waters were becoming rougher and rougher and we were nearing the edge of the island's boundary.

"What are you doing?"

"I want to show you how I fish," Micah said, tightening my hold on him.

"Micah!" a sharp female voice called. Micah stopped

and turned around. Saira was swimming toward us, her bushy brown hair tied up in a bun over her head. She swam faster than I could have expected for such a short-limbed woman.

"Don't go past the boundary again," she said, swimming in front of us and blocking Micah. "Especially not with the princess."

Micah looked disappointed but shrugged it off. He turned around and we approached the shore again. I let go of him once we were in shallower waters and swam over to join my brother and Griff. Micah followed me. I introduced the werewolf to those who hadn't already met him, and we spent the next few hours until sundown swimming around in the cool waves, escaping the heat and humidity of the day, soaking in the warm sunshine.

Once the sun had set, we built a bonfire on the beach and Micah fetched some fish. Brett also joined us and helped him with the roasting. I made sure to sit next to Griff during the meal, talking to him about anything other than the werewolf.

I had to leave early, just in case my parents or Aiden checked in on my room. I hoped that they hadn't already. Micah noticed me stand up and took the opportunity to walk over to me.

"I'll take you back now?"

"Yes, please."

I said good night to Griff and the others, annoyed that I couldn't stay for marshmallows. Micah helped me climb on to his back once again and we headed back to my penthouse. I held on tight, my breath coming harsh and uneven as he leapt up the branches. I closed my eyes and buried my head against his back, scared one of the branches might gouge my eyes. When he stopped, I looked up. We were now parallel with my window. He took a giant leap that made my stomach flip and gripped hold of the window sill, pulling us both inside.

I was relieved to see that my door was still closed. Hopefully I had arrived just early enough to not be caught.

"Thank you," I said.

"When will I see you again?"

I found his question odd. As though he was now expecting our meetings would be a regular occurrence.

"Tomorrow, after school, I guess," I said.

I heard voices in the corridor outside.

"Go. Now!" I hissed.

He climbed back out of the window and hurled himself back onto the tree a few meters away. I closed the window and dove into bed, pulling the covers over me up to my forehead.

My door creaked open.

I'd made sure to bathe in the showers on the beach before leaving, but hoped the scent of ocean wasn't still on my skin.

A weight pressed my mattress down. Too heavy for my mother. It was either Aiden or my father, but I dared not look up. I continued pretending that I was sleeping.

I felt a hand on my forehead, brushing hair away from my skin, and then a gentle kiss.

My father stood up, walked across the room and then clicked the door shut.

I breathed out slowly. If I'd arrived back even a minute later, he would have caught me out of bed. I didn't think I could have borne the disappointment in his eyes that I'd betrayed his trust yet again.

CHAPTER 26: ROSE

Micah was keen to see me most days after school. It seemed that he didn't have much of an agenda of his own. While I gave Griff first priority on my time, since he had more homework than me to complete that week, I ended up seeing more of Micah than I'd expected.

I agreed to meet Micah at the bottom of our tree. I'd recommended this rather than the penthouse since he hadn't exactly made a great first impression on my father, although my mother didn't seem to have any objection to him.

One evening, we ended up walking by the lake—

somewhere I hadn't been with him before.

I still didn't feel I knew much about this werewolf, and I wasn't sure why he was interested in me so much. I also wasn't sure why I'd agreed to spend so much time with him. Caleb still being very much on my mind, I began to wonder if I was just using Micah as a distraction. As some kind of rebound. Still, he was a good distraction. When I was in his company, it was easy to get lost in conversation. There were still so many things about him and the supernatural world I wanted to know.

As we approached the boathouse, I stopped in my tracks. I gripped Micah's arm, pulling him back. He looked at me questioningly.

"Wait," I breathed.

I crouched down in the bushes, pulling Micah down with me. I stared through the leaves, barely able to believe my eyes.

Our headmistress, Adelle. She was making out with... Eli?

All the other girls in my class were convinced that Eli would never get himself a girl—after all, he'd been a bachelor for several hundred years already. Now, watching him locking lips my teacher, it was shocking. It took me a few moments to pick up my jaw from the ground.

I dared not whisper in case they heard. I pointed and we began retreating. There was a snap. Micah had just trodden on a branch. My eyes shot toward the boathouse. It was too late. They'd spotted us.

Adelle looked mortified as she disentangled herself from Eli. I wasn't sure why Adelle would look so guilty. It was embarrassing, yes, but it wasn't like she was doing anything wrong.

"Hello, Rose." Her cheeks were almost as bright as her hair.

"Hi, Ms. Ardene," I said.

She smiled awkwardly, then, wiping her lips with the back of her hand—smudging her lipstick even more— she gripped Eli's hand and they walked away into the woods.

"We may as well go sit there now," I said, once they were out of sight.

I leaned against the windowsill, staring down at the blue water lilies beneath us. We both stood in silence. I glanced up at Micah. For a change, he wasn't looking at me. He too was staring into the water.

"Do you have family?" I asked.

He shook his head. "Not anymore."

"What happened?"

He took a deep breath and paused, running his tongue over his lower lip.

"I left them in my realm when I was banished. I haven't seen them since."

"You were banished?"

"Yes. Most of us in Matteo's crew are outcasts."

"I see. Do werewolves live forever?"

"No. We live a long time, often as long as witches. But not forever."

"Why exactly did they ask you to leave?"

He swallowed hard and shifted his feet on the floorboards. "I was in love with a girl I had no business being in love with."

Huh. I remained silent, not daring to urge him to continue even though I was burning with curiosity. As it turned out I didn't need to.

"And she was in love with me. Or so she said. But she was the daughter of our chieftain. She already had a betrothed…"

"I'm sorry," I said.

"I had to either leave, or be executed. I still remember the night they caught us. The fear in my family's eyes. I didn't have time to pack anything. I just had to sail away in a boat. Leave and never return. I had no idea how I'd survive. I'd never been outside my own realm before. By some mercy, I came across Matteo and his crew. They gave me a cabin in their ship. The rest is history. They're my family... and now, the people here in The Shade." His eyes roamed me again.

"Do you think you'll ever see your family again?"

"No."

"But you came to Earth via the werewolf realm, right?"

"Yes. But if anyone had caught me there, I wouldn't have gotten out alive. Mona put an invisibility covering over all of us as we made our way to the hidden gate." He shook his head again, as if clearing his thoughts. "Anyway, she... they... are all gone now. I won't ever be going back there. It's my past."

Silence fell between us again.

"I know what it's like to love someone you can't be with," I said. I didn't understand why I would tell

Micah this, when I hadn't even told my own brother.

He turned to look at me, an eyebrow raised. Coaxing me to continue.

I didn't feel comfortable speaking Caleb's name out loud somehow. It just didn't feel right. So I just said, "We fell out over a… misunderstanding. To be honest, I'd rather not talk about him either."

"That's okay," Micah said, holding my hand. "I understand."

I gave him a faint smile.

We left the boathouse and walked around the lake a bit more before heading home. It was getting late now, and to avoid another grounding, Micah carried me on his back the rest of the way home.

He stopped at the foot of my tree at my request. I checked my watch. I had ten minutes to get my butt upstairs. I looked up at Micah. We hadn't spoken much since our conversation in the boathouse. I found the look in his eyes unsettling. He looked… restless somehow. As though there was something he was hiding, something he was bottling up.

"Well, good night," I said and turned to leave.

Strong hands gripped my shoulders and turned me

around.

Before I could make sense of what was happening, Micah gripped my jaw and drew me closer. His lips pressed against my cheek, the tip of his hot, rough tongue brushing against my skin.

I staggered back, reaching up to where his mouth had been. His hazel-brown eyes looked fierce.

"Good night," he growled.

He spun around and sprinted away. I stared after him. His limbs began transforming and he hit the ground on all fours as he pounded away into the distance.

That boy is wild.

Chapter 27: Rose

I wasn't sure what to make of Micah's kiss. A part of me felt deeply uncomfortable about it, whilst another had lit up with a passion I was finding hard to ignore. I was glad that we were having tests that week. I could bury myself in study and avoid thinking about both Caleb and the werewolf.

In my free time, I found myself going on longer walks by myself, deliberately avoiding the parts of the beaches where the werewolves tended to gather. As I walked along the beach one evening, on my way back home, I heard a gruff voice behind me.

"Hello."

I whirled around to see the ogre.

"Oh, hello, Brett."

This was the first time I'd really spoken to him since I'd met him the day they arrived on the island.

He stood at the entrance of a large cave. I'd forgotten that he lived on this side of the island.

"You wanna come in?" His meaty hand beckoned me over.

As much as I'd been assured by everyone that he wasn't dangerous, my heartbeat doubled as I walked toward him over the boulders, slowly and cautiously. His appearance was so imposing, I couldn't help but feel nervous.

He was grinning from ear to ear as I stepped into the cave, looking down at me with sheer delight.

He lumbered further into his home, leading me forward. I glanced around. There was a mound of straw in one corner with a heap of dirty clothes at the end of it. And in the center of the cave was an axe, a saw, small carving tools, a log of wood and half of a chair.

Brett looked at me sheepishly. "Sorry there's nothin' for a princess to sit on yet," he mumbled. "I need to work faster. I don't get many folks visiting me, you see."

I took a seat on his straw while he sat on the floor opposite me.

I still couldn't wrap my head around the fact I was sitting next to an ogre. I hadn't even known such things existed until recently. I remembered my father reading stories involving ogres to Ben and me when we were younger, but I'd thought they were nothing more than that—stories. Then again, it wouldn't take much getting used to, having grown up with vampires as parents.

I looked at his work in progress on the floor, admiring his handiwork.

"That's looking pretty," I said. "How long will it take you to complete it?"

He shrugged. "Going slower than I'm used to. I don't have as good tools as I did back home. I had to leave them all," he said, wiping his runny nose with the back of his hand.

"I'm sure we have extra chairs if you need any. The witches are good with that sort of thing. And what about getting you a more comfortable bed? This straw seems spiky to sleep on."

"I like creating my own stuff. And I like straw too. It's good for itches. You should try it sometime."

"Hm, maybe I will."

I stood up and crouched down closer over his half finished chair. I was impressed by how delicately designed it was—there were beautiful etchings in the wood around the seat. I wondered how long he had been laboring over it.

"So this is what you do with your time?" I asked. "You create beautiful things."

He cast another wistful glance at his half-finished chair and sighed. "Yeah, well, it was my job before. When we were back on our own island. Captain Matteo gave me the job of creating things. 'Cos I don't like to fight."

"Fight?"

He eyed me. "Yeah. Like when nasty people tried to enter our island. I don't like it."

"Oh, okay. I understand." I reached out and patted his leathery forearm. "I don't like fighting either."

A pang of sadness hit me as I looked once more around his damp empty cave. It occurred to me how lonely this creature must get, being the only one of his kind on the island.

"Have you always lived alone?"

He looked taken aback by my question, as though the answer should be obvious. "Yes." Then he chortled and shook his head. "There isn't anyone who'd want to share my cave with me."

I paused, looking into his face. It was innocent, good-natured. Much like a child.

"We need to find you a pretty girl ogre to keep you company, Brett."

He blushed. He actually looked sweet—a word I'd never thought I'd use to describe an ogre.

"Agh," he said, waving a hand dismissively. "Girls are trouble…"

I giggled. "But have you ever had a girlfriend?"

"G-girl…" He paused, frowning. "Saira is a girl friend."

"No. By girlfriend, I mean like a lover. A girl you're in love with."

He furrowed his brows as though deep in thought. "No. I have never had that."

"Then how do you know girls are trouble?"

He looked away from me, as though hoping that

avoiding my eye contact would also avoid the subject. His expression was not unlike a four-year-old trying to hide from an uncomfortable question.

"Well?"

"Fights always start when they're around."

"That doesn't have to happen. There are lots of couples who don't fight."

"Yeah, well, you don't know about girl ogres. They're mean."

There wasn't much I could say to counter that argument. Brett was the only ogre I'd come across, and from what I'd learned about ogres so far, Brett was an anomaly. Most ogres were cruel-hearted beasts, and that was why Brett was an outcast. He didn't like violence.

"Sometimes," he continued, "it's better to be alone. There's no fighting. It's peaceful. No troubles."

I bit my lip, looking out at Brett's view of the sea. We were both quiet for a few minutes, listening to the waves crashing against the shore.

"You have a boy-lover, don't ya?" Brett blurted.

I frowned and shook my head.

A grin spilt his face and his eyes narrowed on me. "Yeah, you do. Don't think I haven't seen you with that

Micah boy."

"Oh," I said. Now it was my turn to blush. "Micah is just a friend. I barely even know him."

"Yeah, well, I've seen the way he looks at you. He thinks you're his girl-lover."

I wasn't sure whether to laugh at Brett's turn of phrase or be mortified that even an ogre had picked up on this. My expression was likely somewhere in between.

"Well, what do you think of Micah?" I said, eyeing him with amusement. "Do you think he would make a good 'boy-lover'?"

Brett paused and furrowed his brows, clearly taking my question as no light matter.

"Yeah, I think he's a good fella."

"Anything else you can tell me about him?"

Brett thought for a moment longer. "He's a good fish-catcher… though he doesn't roast them as well."

"Uh-huh." It was clear that this was all the insight Brett was planning to offer. "Well, thanks for that, Brett. I'll bear it in mind. Because roasting is important."

"Yes."

"I should probably be getting home now."

"Oh, princess. You could stay for dinner if you wanted."

"I would love to, Brett. I truly would. But my parents want me home early."

He looked mildly disappointed, but was probably expecting that answer. I doubted there were many on this island who spent dinner alone with Brett, unless they couldn't be bothered to cook.

"Well, thanks for visiting, Princess Rose."

"I promise I'll visit you again soon," I said as I left the cave, and I meant it.

"I'd like that. I will try to have the chair finished in time for you. Can't have the princess sitting on my straw again," he mumbled.

"I'll bring my brother Ben with me too, if you don't mind. And we don't mind sitting on the straw."

He positively beamed at the thought of two visitors.

We said goodbye and I climbed down from the cave across the boulders and back onto the sandy beach. I didn't know how it would ever happen, but I was determined to make it my personal mission to one day find a companion for Brett.

Chapter 28: Caleb

I sat in my bedroom the following evening, waiting for Annora to knock. It turned out I was right in assuming that her nightly visits would resume now that I'd had some respite.

She arrived at the stroke of midnight, in her usual black silk coverall and lingerie.

I stood up and as she approached me, I gripped her arms and sat her on the bed while I towered over her, looking deep into her steely gray eyes.

"What?"

"I've put it off long enough."

She frowned at me. "Put what off?"

"I want to become a warlock."

She blinked, her lower lip twitching.

"Warlock?" she breathed.

"Not just any warlock. I want to become a Channeler of the Ancients' power."

"Y-you're serious?"

I nodded slowly, studying every flicker of emotion that crossed her face. What I saw confused me. She looked shocked at first. That I could understand. But now she looked disturbed. Worried. Desperate even.

Her hands began to tremble and she stood up, gripping my forearms.

"Why? Why don't you want to remain as you are?"

"For the same reason as you. Power. Influence. Surrender to our cause."

She began shaking her head.

"No." Her voice cracked. "No, Caleb. I-I…" She clasped a palm over her mouth. She sank back down on the bed, her chest heaving. "Caleb, no."

I didn't know what game Annora was playing by refusing something she herself had coaxed me to do for so long. I bent down to her level, gripping her jaw and forcing her to look directly into my eyes.

"Why?" I repeated, my mouth inches from hers.

She flinched and closed her eyes, shaking her head.

Ignoring her discomfort, I continued to press.

"Who do I need to see about this? Who turned you into a Channeler?"

"But Caleb—"

"Just answer my question."

"H-her name is Lilith."

"Lilith. Who is this Lilith? Where do I find her?"

"I-I can't tell you."

I tightened my grip on her jaw. "What do you mean you can't tell me?"

Tears spilled from her eyes. She fought free from my grip and hurried out of the room, slamming the door behind her.

I stared after her, stunned, listening to the sounds of her footsteps disappearing down the corridor outside.

I'd never seen Annora crumble like that. And the way she'd just left... as though she'd completely forgotten what she'd come for.

I left the apartment and considered following her, but decided against it. At least for this evening. Instead,

I went downstairs to the kitchen, intending to pour myself a glass of blood. I exhaled in frustration on finding all the jugs empty in the cellar. Topping up the jugs had been Frieda's job. I guessed it was my fault I hadn't yet appointed another vampire to do the job. I'd have to do it myself tonight.

I left the jug on the kitchen counter and entered the dungeon in the corner of the room. Gasps and cries echoed around me as I descended into the dark prison.

I looked around the cells, trying to decide which human looked most likely to quench my thirst that evening. I settled on the plumpest, a young boy. Opening his cell, I pulled him out and handcuffed him. I was about to exit the dungeon with him when I noticed a strange scent. Not human. Not vampire. Not witch. It was quite unlike anything I'd smelt before. Chaining the boy to the wall so he wouldn't cause trouble, I walked toward the scent.

I stopped outside a cell containing a wolf. A giant wolf. Slumped in the corner, it raised its head as I approached the bars.

"Werewolf?"

It looked up at me with brown eyes.

"What does it look like?" it said hoarsely.

Since when are we keeping werewolves in our dungeons? New blood rituals, perhaps.

"Who brought you here?"

Leaning against the wall, the wolf struggled to stand up. I could see now that he was male. His two hind legs were severely disjointed and soaked with blood.

"And what's it to you?" he growled. "You going to help me escape?"

"Just answer my question."

He scowled, his eyes darkening. "Some black-eyed warlock caught me while I was out fishing. He didn't tell me his name."

"What's your name?"

"Micah Kaelin."

Chapter 29: Rose

I'd been expecting Micah to keep his distance from me after that kiss. But he showed up the very next day as I swam with Griff and my girl friends on Sun Beach. He walked up to the edge of the water, fully dressed, and beckoned me over. I glanced apologetically at Griff before walking over to him. Micah's blond hair was tied in a bun. The sides of his face were rough and unshaven.

"I was hoping you might take a walk with me," he said softly.

"Um, okay."

I pulled my clothes on over my bikini and followed him into the woods. *Back into the woods with the big bad wolf.*

"I'm sorry for what I did," he said, as we lost sight of the beach. "I hope it didn't offend you."

I felt my cheeks growing red. "It didn't offend me."

"I'm glad. Because I was worried. I wasn't sure if I'd overstepped my mark. I know we haven't known each other long."

"It was just a peck on the cheek," I said. *Understatement of the year.* "It's no big deal."

"Good... I fixed the fishing boat, by the way. It's strong enough for two now. Can I show you?"

"Show me the fishing—?"

He caught my waist and threw me over his shoulder. He began racing through the forest.

"Micah? What are you doing?"

"Just hold on," he said.

He stopped running once we reached the Port. He ran up to the jetty and put me down. He pointed to a small fishing boat bobbing next to the submarines. He stepped in and held out his hand.

"Allow me?"

I eyed the small boat, the slimy nets bunched in one corner.

"Where to?"

"We'll stay within the boundaries," he said. "I promise. I just want to show you how I fish."

"Because my parents don't like me straying beyond them."

"I promise we'll stay within them."

Hesitating a few moments longer, I took his hand and stepped into the boat.

He clutched the oars and began moving us away.

I wasn't sure why he was so bent on showing me how to fish. I'd never shown much interest in it. But since he kept going on about it, I decided to just humor him. I dipped my hand into the water, feeling its warmth gradually fade as we got deeper and deeper.

"You can start unraveling those nets if you want."

Grateful for the distraction, I untangled the slimy nets and, under Micah's direction, spread the largest one out so that it hung over the end of the boat.

I bent over the side of the boat and washed my hands in the water. Only once I'd finished the task and looked up did I realize how close we were drawing to the boundary. Micah was showing no signs of slowing down.

"Micah? What are you doing?'

His eyes were focused forward, his arm muscles tensing as he rowed faster.

"Just trust me," he said.

"But the boundary—"

And then it was too late. We were out in the blinding sunshine. Outside the protection of the island.

I glared at Micah.

"You promised we wouldn't leave the boundary." My shock turned to confusion, then annoyance. "Why did you lie?"

I reached for one of the oars. Micah's right leg shot out, kicking me beneath my knee. Something cracked and pain seared through my leg. I fell to the floor, groaning and clutching my knee to my chest.

What is happening? Why would Micah do this?

I had no time to try to recuperate from my injury. Despite still being in shock, I had to scream for help before it was too late.

"No! Help!" I screamed at the top of my lungs.

Micah stood up and roughly stuffed a piece of old

rag into my mouth. I choked, the smell of rotten fish pervading my nostrils. It was all I could do to stop myself vomiting. He fastened my wrists and ankles with ropes.

I looked daggers at him, trying to read his face as he hovered over me. His eyes were expressionless. Hollow.

And then it happened. His hair began to shorten and curl at the roots. Its blond color faded and darkened. Warm hazel eyes turned pitch black. He grew taller, his shoulders broadened. Even his clothes changed—into a long black cloak and heavy leather boots.

There was no trace left of Micah in the man standing over me.

I struggled and tried to scream more desperately than ever, but it was no use. The stranger placed a long finger against his lips and gripped my forehead.

"Hush, Princess," he said in a voice much deeper than Micah's. "Sleep."

CHAPTER 30: CALEB

We sat on the edge of my father's finest ship, dipping our feet into the shallow waters, watching the sun duck beneath the horizon. Annora rested her head on my shoulder, while I had an arm around her waist. The warm summer breeze caught her black hair, making it dance in the air. I looked down at her delicate fingers. The gemstone in her engagement ring glinted in the evening light.

I held my breath, anticipating the excitement that would shine in her beautiful eyes as soon as I told her.

"My father agreed to let us take this ship."

She lifted her head and looked up at me, gasping.

"He really did?"

I nodded, smiling as I brushed my lips over her forehead.

"For how long?" she asked.

"Two weeks. Now you just need to decide where you'd like me to take you."

She bit her lip, facing the sunset once again.

"Mmm. How about somewhere far away... like Asia?"

I laughed. "We could. But that really would be a long time at sea. I'm not sure my father would be willing to part with me for that long."

She sighed, once again falling into thought. "Where do you want to take me?"

"We could stay within Europe and do a tour. Maybe start with France, work our way down to Italy, perhaps head for the Ionian Sea..."

"Just the two of us?"

"Just the two of us."

"All right, my love. Let's do that," she purred. "And then after?"

"What do you mean?"

"What will we do after?" She rested her head on my lap, reaching her hand up and playfully twirling my hair in her fingers.

"I don't know," I said, stroking her forehead.

"Come on, Caleb," she said, "Tell me a story."

"A story, huh? Well, after is when our life together will really start. We'll find a house near the shore, away from the bustle of the town, and move in together. I'll take over managing the dock while my father retires. We'll keep our own boat, and whenever I can afford it, we'll take trips. I'll build the business and train workers well enough to be able to manage without me. We'll make time to travel the world together. We'll go to Asia. And the Americas. And explore the North Pole. South Pole. Any Pole you want..."

I paused, watching as her face grew impatient for the next part.

"And?"

"And once we're tired of touring the world, we'll return to our quiet house on the shore, and we'll start a family."

"How many children will we have?"

"Eight. Four boys and four girls."

"What will we name them?"

I paused again to think. As always, Annora wanted details. I'd give her details. "Our first child will be a boy. His name will be Hector. Next will be Jennifer. Then Jason. William. Laina. Laurence. April. And lastly, sweet Isobel."

"And will we travel the world again with them when they're old enough?"

"If that's what they want… The end."

"But what happens next? You can't just stop a story like that," she said. "Not before you get to the happily ever after."

"All right," I said, chuckling and rolling my eyes. "And we'll live happily for the rest of our lives. We'll die old and wrinkly holding hands in our bed. We'll be buried in the same grave. And the worms will digest our bodies, leaving only our bones forever entwined in the soil… Is that far enough?"

She giggled. "What if there's an afterlife?"

"Then that would make this a very long story indeed…"

She sat up and knelt, her face level with mine. I could lose myself forever in those sparkling grey-blue eyes. Draping her arms over my shoulders, she leaned in closer. And then her sweet lips were on mine in a chaste caress. She allowed me to taste their nectar for but a moment before drawing away. Sitting back down next to me and clearing her throat, she looked around as if scared someone had seen her.

That kiss sparked a bonfire within me that only she could extinguish. I didn't care any more whether someone *saw us. Everyone in the town knew we were to be married soon. I reached for her waist and pulled her closer again. I held her head in my hands. My thumbs touched the sides of her mouth.*

She shut her eyes.

"Don't be afraid," I whispered.

Closing my lips around her mouth, I tasted her fully for the first time. A gentle blush warmed her cheeks as I pulled away.

I felt like the luckiest man in the world, and whatever lay ahead of us, I knew we'd find bliss. We'd find our story. Our happily ever after.

"Maybe that's what ours is," she breathed as our lips touched again. "A never-ending story."

I woke up in a sweat. I looked around my room, reality returning to me.

Once I'd drained the human and downed a glass of blood, I'd returned to my room and slept. Now I hoped it wouldn't take long to drift off again. But then I heard it. A sound I'd heard countless nights before, but somehow this night it resonated louder in my ears.

Crying. In some dark hall of the castle. The dining room, I suspected. That was Annora's usual haunt.

I lay back in bed, closing my eyes and trying to block it out as I usually did. But I couldn't. Every draw of breath, every wretched sob, every moan of sorrow echoed around in my head.

Groaning, I got out of bed and paced the room.

I couldn't remember the last time I'd gone to her during her fits of sadness. It had been so long I was sure that she couldn't remember either.

Wrapping a robe around me, I left my apartment and descended the staircase to the ground floor. My suspicion had been correct. Annora was a creature of habit and this night was no different.

I stood silently by the doorway of the dining hall as she howled into the wind, her whole body wracked with sobs.

I couldn't help but ache at the sight of her.

Oh, Annora. What made you give up my love for pain?

It was on nights like this when she showed her humanity that I longed to ask her this question. Even though I knew the answer, I longed to ask again, hope welling within my chest that perhaps, this time, the answer would be different.

I crept into the room. She didn't notice I'd entered

until I reached out and touched her shoulder.

She jumped back, pausing to breathe, her sobs subsiding.

"Annora," I whispered. That name. Once honey to my lips. Now poison to my heart.

She flinched as I held her hands.

"Why are you crying?"

She slipped her hands out of mine and looked out of the window again. I held her arm and forced her to face me.

"Leave me," she said, her voice rasping.

I knew she could easily vanish if she didn't want me in her presence. The fact that she didn't meant that she didn't really want me to leave.

I stood next to her by the window, sliding an arm around her waist. Tears fell afresh from her eyes.

"Why wouldn't you answer my questions last night?" I asked. "If you help me become a Channeler, it will bring us closer. I'll better be able to understand your needs."

She closed her eyes, her lips trembling.

"Because I don't want you to become like me."

"And what is like you?"

She smiled bitterly. "You know what I am."

"But I've never heard it from you. What do you think you are?"

"In pain."

She backed away until she hit the wall at the opposite side of the chamber. She leaned her head against the stone as she bit her lip until she drew blood.

Even if Annora was back to her usual numb self tomorrow, it didn't matter. Because I'd just seen all I needed to see. A glimmer of hope that just perhaps, somewhere deep in that black soul, the old Annora was still in there. Trapped. Needing to be rescued. But still alive.

"Caleb," she said, her voice cracking. "Just leave me. Please... Go back to sleep."

I finally gave in to her request. I left her alone in the chamber and returned to my apartment. But I didn't sleep that night. Only one thought kept me awake:

I'm going to find you again, Annora. And, somehow, we're going to pick up our story where we left off.

Chapter 31: Caleb

I woke with renewed strength. I wasn't going to let Annora keep avoiding me any more. I was going to get the information I needed from her.

I went up to her apartment first thing. She refused to speak to me, so I followed her around the castle for the rest of the day. I determined to make myself as awkward as possible. Finally she snapped.

I interrupted Annora in the middle of a meeting with Stellan, who'd come to visit our island for the day to speak with her.

Ignoring Stellan, I barged in and made a beeline for

Annora. I marched up to her in the center of the room and sat down on the tabletop, blocking her view of Stellan. She looked up at me irritably and tugged on my shoulder, trying to move me. I didn't budge. Of course she could have used her magic to get rid of me, but she didn't.

"I'll leave you alone as soon as you give me what I want."

"What? I already gave you a name. Stop pestering me, for God's sake."

I turned around and eyed Stellan, who glared back at me. Annora took the cue and scowled. "Get out, Stellan. I'll talk to you after I'm done with Caleb."

Stellan got up slowly, threw me another dark look, and stalked out of the room.

"Take me to Lilith."

"I told you, Caleb—"

"I may decide not to turn," I said.

She looked at me dubiously. "Lilith is not the type of person whose time is available to waste. If you go, she's going to expect something in return."

Again I burned to ask what Lilith actually was, but right now it was hard enough getting Annora to agree to take me, let alone entertain more of my questions.

"I'll deal with Lilith," I said. "You don't even need to come in. I'll speak to her alone." I squeezed Annora's arm. "Do this and I won't bother you again, I swear."

Annora let out a sigh and slumped back in her chair, rubbing her temples with the tips of her fingers. She cast me a long lingering glance, and I swore I saw worry behind her eyes. "All right. I'll take you to see her."

"I want to leave now."

She rolled her eyes, folding her arms over her chest. "I need to finish speaking to Stellan. Then we'll decide when to do this."

I slammed my hand down on the table, making her jump. "We leave the moment you are finished with him. All right?"

She glowered at me but didn't protest.

I stalked out of the room to see Stellan waiting impatiently outside, shuffling from one foot to the other. He had obviously been eavesdropping. He walked in the room after me. I returned to my quarters upstairs to grab anything I might need. I had no idea what might be on the other side, so I grabbed a wooden stake and a knife and fastened them to my belt.

Then I returned downstairs, and since I couldn't hear talking, I assumed Stellan had left already. I pushed the door open.

Annora waited at the table for me and stood up when I entered. She grimaced as I fastened a cloak around me.

All traces of worry I'd seen in her eyes were gone now, replaced with resignation—something that was both relieving and off-putting.

"Follow me," she said.

We left the chamber and crossed the entrance hall until we reached another hall on the opposite side.

She headed straight for the Chinese carpet in the corner and tugged it across the floor to reveal an old trapdoor. It creaked open as she pulled and we descended into the depths of a dungeon. This was not a room that I had frequented many times throughout my time here on the island, for I rarely travelled back to the supernatural realm—I didn't have permission, for one thing. None of us vampires did. We had to obtain special authority from Annora if we wanted to return for some reason. But now that I was down here again, it looked the same as it always had. I inched over to the edge of the starry crater as Annora bolted the door above us.

I looked at her and she nodded. I dove into the hole, and felt her jump through seconds after me.

We both landed on a stone floor. Another dungeon. We both got to our feet and walked toward the exit that led to a flight of stairs. We climbed them and appeared in a kitchen filled with sharp utensils and black cauldrons.

I spotted an old witch in the corner, stirring deep red liquid that I was sure was blood—human blood from the smell of it. She began chopping up what looked suspiciously like a human torso.

"Annora?" She turned and looked at both of us in surprise, her eyebrows raised. She put the blood down and tucked her gray-streaked black hair behind her ears.

"Isolde, I'm sorry for arriving like this unexpectedly. But I need to pay a visit to Lilith."

Isolde's eyes widened even further as they travelled from me to Annora. "Whatever for?"

Annora glared at me. "Caleb would like to become one of us."

Isolde looked incredulous enough to laugh. "He wants to become a Channeler?"

"Yes," I said, butting in.

"No," Annora said quickly, "There's no way he'd be ready for that yet. He just wants to become a warlock, at least at first."

They were talking about me as though I wasn't present. Still, I didn't mind as long as Annora convinced Isolde to allow us to proceed toward wherever Lilith resided in this supernatural realm.

"Don't waste Lilith's time," Isolde said sternly, looking at me. "Her energy is limited, especially these days."

Annora gripped my arm before Isolde could say another word and led me out of the dark kitchen. We walked through to an entrance hall, very much similar to that of my own castle, and exited the building through a large oak door. We descended a set of steps overlooking an endless ocean. The waves lapped precariously close to the base of the castle.

"So Lilith doesn't live on this island?" I asked.

"No. She lives a few hundred miles away. There's a gate linking her island to the human realm I suppose we could have traveled through. But I wanted to warn Isolde what we were doing first. Now, no more questions. Just follow me."

I followed Annora forward and as we reached the edge of a rock, she said, "Close your eyes."

I did as I was told and we both vanished from the spot. We hurtled through air at the speed of light. Our feet hit solid ground a few moments later.

I opened my eyes to find myself standing on a large black boulder. Above us was the entrance to a cave. I looked up and down the pebbly beach we'd appeared on. There wasn't any sign of life other than a group of vultures that circled overhead. I looked down at Annora who was now looking directly at the cave.

"So this is it? This is where Lilith lives?"

"Just follow," Annora said through gritted teeth. I noted how much heavier her breathing had suddenly become as we neared the entrance.

I'd expected a more salubrious abode for such a renowned witch. At least a castle of some sorts. I found it hard to believe that she could be living in this damp cave.

Annora led me forward, deeper and deeper, until we reached a door. As soon as she placed her fingers on the handle, it clicked and swung open. The next chamber was dimly lit by lanterns that hung from the walls, unlike the pitch-black chamber we'd just left.

We walked for several minutes hearing nothing but our echoing footsteps. After this winding tunnel we reached another oak door. Annora reached out once again, her hand now shaking. I gripped her shoulders and turned her to face me. Her face was pale and sweaty, her lips tightly pursed.

"Just let me in, you can stay here," I said.

She shook her head. "I'll come with you," she said, her voice hoarse.

Although I didn't want her in the same room as Lilith and me while we had our conversation, clearly now wasn't the time to argue. Once I'd come face to face with Lilith, I'd be in more of a position to ask Annora to leave.

She unlocked the door and, as I stepped forward through the door and into an odd circular chamber, I was immediately overwhelmed by the stench. Something dead and rotten, like decaying flesh. The smell was intensified tenfold thanks to the lack of air in this dim room.

The dusty floor sloped downward, leading toward a strange dark pool in the center of the chamber. I scanned the area, but to my disappointment, there was nobody here.

"Where is she?" I asked.

"Shh," Annora hissed.

She gripped my hand and led me down the slope to the pool of liquid. The closer I got to it, the more unbearable the smell became.

Annora seemed quite unfazed by it. She hurried forward until she was standing right at the edge of the pond.

"It is me," she said, her voice shaking. "Annora."

I took a step back as ripples began to form in the dark liquid. Soon enough, it parted to reveal a motionless corpse floating in the water. The corpse of a woman. Until she sat bolt upright. Black eyes shot open, gleaming as they reflected the dim lighting in the chamber. Her skin was thin and rotten. Where it had disintegrated around her forehead, bone was visible. A tuft of hair hung limply from her scalp, which was otherwise shriveled and bald.

"What is this?" I breathed.

"Lilith," Annora whispered. "The last Ancient among us."

Chapter 32: Caleb

Chills ran down my spine as I stared at the ghostly form.

Her shriveled lips parted, and ancient witch tongue spilled out.

"Why are you here?" she croaked, her voice rasping against my ears.

I had been around Annora long enough to be able to detect witch tongue, though when I spoke I wasn't able to express myself well. I wasn't sure that she would understand me but I had no hope but to try.

I was still in shock. I had believed that all the

Ancients had passed from this world centuries ago. I couldn't understand how one could have survived for so long.

Most of all, looking at her, I felt a crushing feeling in my stomach. I'd come in hopes of finding a solution to Annora's misery, in hopes of finding a cure for her, a recourse. Looking at this creature of nightmares, I couldn't imagine she'd do anything but add more darkness to my already pitch-black life.

Annora stepped in front of me and curtsied.

"Your Grace, I have come here with this vampire because he wishes to turn into one of us." She looked conflicted even as she spoke the words, but she knew she had no choice in the matter if she ever wanted to regain a semblance of peace in her life again. Annora knew how stubborn I could be.

Lilith's black eyes settled on me as she clucked her tongue, looking me over from head to foot. She retched suddenly. Black fluid dripped from her mouth into her cesspool. She looked back up at me, wiping her mouth with the back of her sharp bony hand.

"He's not ready," she said, looking back at Annora.

Annora and I exchanged glances. I saw relief in her

eyes more than anything.

It was now time to take matters into my own hands.

"Leave, Annora," I said, "I want to speak alone with Lilith."

Annora glared at me. "Only if Lilith wants. She may not want to waste any more of her precious time with you."

I scowled and turned back to look down at the disgusting creature. In the best witch tongue I could manage, I looked her directly in the eye and said, "I wish to speak with you alone, if you'll let me. There is more to me than you perhaps realize."

Lilith gargled. I wasn't sure whether that was supposed to be a snort or a chuckle. Whatever it was, she was shaking her head. Not a good sign.

"Please," I said.

Annora gripped my arm. "She doesn't want to speak with you, Caleb." She began to tug on me and pull me back toward the door.

I broke free from Annora and glowered down at Lilith. I didn't know what possessed me—I could only assume desperation—but with one leap I dropped into the pool with the odious creature.

I thought the pool was shallow, but I found myself falling, the weight of my body sucking me down into the grime. It took all my strength to not be sucked under completely. I managed to keep my head above water. It was so heavy the substance felt almost like quicksand and it was a constant struggle to remain above the surface. Luckily I had the strength of a vampire. Any mere human would have been sucked right under, probably never to be seen again.

I could have sworn a glint of red flickered in Lilith's eyes and now her face was contorted enough for me to read an unmistakable expression of fury.

Annora gasped and rushed to the side of the pool.

"Caleb!" she screamed. "Get out."

Ignoring Annora's pleas, I waded closer to the witch. And stopped about three feet away from her. I glared into her eyes.

I'd gone to all this trouble getting here. I wasn't about to be brushed away so easily by this old hag. But mostly my desperation was brought about because I knew if I didn't get answers from Lilith, my trail would be completely cold.

Damn it, I wasn't going to leave without putting up

a fight.

"Annora and I have been your loyal servants for years," I said softly. I winced at my broken witch tongue, but lumbered forward all the same. "I have come here requesting to simply talk with you for a few minutes. Is that so much to ask now?"

The Ancient inhaled sharply and stared at me. Without warning, she jolted forward and gripped my forehead, her freakishly long fingers closing around my skull. I remained still, expecting to feel pain. But I didn't. I didn't know what she was doing, what she was feeling for, but after several moments, she let go, leaving a handprint of grime on my head and likely on my face. But grime was the least of my worries right now.

"What do you want?" Her voice creaked like a rusting door joint.

"Firstly," I said, "I want to speak with you in private. I want you to order Annora to leave this chamber while we talk and to not enter until you give permission again."

"Why do you want to talk in private?" Annora blurted out from behind me.

I ignored her, keeping my eyes level with the

Ancient's.

The grime was beginning to give me a headache. I had to fight to fend off the nausea.

She knew what I wanted now and she was either going to bend to my will or banish us both from the room again.

I breathed out as she slowly broke eye contact with me and looked at Annora.

"Leave," she muttered.

I didn't bother to turn round to look at Annora's reaction. I knew she'd be seething. I kept my eyes on Lilith all the while as Annora's footsteps disappeared and the door to the chamber locked.

I waded further away from the witch, placing more distance between us, and gripped hold of the edge of the pond. I hauled myself out and leaned against a wall. The Ancient too made her way to the edge of the pond and, placing her hands against the edge of the wall, she hauled herself up. I did a double-take as her decrepit body emerged from the liquid. She folded like a tray, then straightened up. She was almost twice my height as she stood up, her knees thin as rods, and so shaky I found it a wonder that she could even support her own weight.

I stood up, uncomfortable about her standing while I remained seated. She walked around the pond and headed toward a flight of stairs in a far corner of the chamber. She beckoned to me with a flick of her hand. I followed, keeping a few feet between us.

What is she? Is she even living? Or is she a ghost inhabiting a corpse?

To my surprise, we arrived on a landing with four chairs and a table.

She grunted, pointing to one of the chairs. Her lanky legs folded as she perched on one of the chairs opposite me.

I cleared my parched throat. "Do you remember what you did to Annora?"

I doubted that I could express all that I needed to, especially since Lilith seemed to speak in some kind of antiquated dialect, but I had no choice but to stumble forward regardless.

"Annora," Lilith murmured.

"She came to you. She gave up her form as a vampire and became a witch. She wanted to become a Channeler."

Her lip twitched and she shook her head. "She was not strong enough to become a Channeler."

I stared at the witch. "You're saying Annora isn't a Channeler? How is it she has so much strength?"

"I made her a witch, but not a Channeler. Her mind was too weak. She gave in before she reached the other side."

"Why wasn't she strong enough? Mona was."

Lilith's eyes squinted into slits at the mention of Mona.

"Mona," she croaked. "Traitorous bitch."

"Yet Mona was strong enough to become a Channeler without losing herself in the process. Why did Mona survive it, but not Annora?"

Lilith stood up, her bones cracking as she began to pace the floor in front of me. "Annora was alone. There was nobody here. She had no partner. Mona had somebody."

"What do you mean, partner?"

"I mean what I say, vampire. A partner. Somebody close. A relative. Or a lover, as Mona had."

I shot to my feet, anger boiling within me. "Then why wasn't Annora granted a partner for her transformation? She could have been—"

"She didn't want anybody," Lilith snarled. "She knew she ought to have someone, but she refused. She said she had nobody."

That cut me deep. How could Annora have said that she had nobody? I'd told her a thousand times she owned my heart, every part of me through and through, and I would be there for her no matter what.

I swallowed back the hurt and regained composure, trying to realign my train of thought.

"So if Annora had called someone in with her, she wouldn't have lost her mind the way she has."

The witch pursed her rotting lips into a hard line.

"What is wrong with Annora anyway? I see nothing wrong."

I wasn't sure how to start explaining what was off about my fiancée to someone who slept in a pool of their own festering body juice. I just glared at Lilith. "Annora can no longer feel anything but pain. She was my fiancée. She used to be in love with me. She lost some of herself when she became a vampire, but when she came to you, she returned to me unrecognizable. You ruined her."

"It was her choice," Lilith snapped. "Nobody forced her to become a witch. She knew the risks. She took them."

Again her words sent a dagger though my heart. I clenched my fists and stood up, walking over to where the towering nightmare was pacing.

"Whatever did happen in the past… that's not why I'm here now. I came to ask you if what happened to her is reversible. I want you to undo the spell. Make her into a vampire again, if you have to."

"And why would I do that? Annora is most valuable to us in her current form."

"Then keep her a witch, but give her back her heart. What if you redid the spell—try to make her a Channeler again—this time with me present?"

Lilith stopped pacing and shot a glare at me. "Much like my skin, my patience is wearing thin. I have granted you this meeting only because of Annora's and your loyalty to us so far. But remember, I don't owe you anything. Annora got what she wanted, as did you. Don't forget what we saved you from. You would still be rotting in Cruor were it not for us."

There wasn't much I could say to argue with her,

although it felt like we'd jumped from the frying pan into the fire. What the witches had done could hardly be called saving. They'd taken us as prisoners, preying on our vulnerable state and complete absence of other options.

"You're right that I can't make you do anything, and neither do you owe me," I said. "But in light of our years of service to you, grant this one request. I'll never ask anything of you again. And think of how much more useful Annora will be to you once she's a Channeler. And I too will be more motivated if we can somehow—"

Lilith clucked her tongue and clicked the bones in her knuckles impatiently. "And what makes you think redoing the curse will save your woman?"

"I don't know that it will help. But I want to try."

"There is no guarantee," Lilith said. "It all depends on how strong her mind is, and how deep her attachment is to you. Her trust in you is vital to regaining mental stability, that you are next to her to remind her who she is… You may be willing to try, but what about Annora? Is she willing to try it? Because I'm not willing to waste any more of my time while you try to convince her."

Time that you'd otherwise be spending doing what exactly? I couldn't help but think.

The Ancient was sharp despite her rotten skull. The tension between Annora and me evidently hadn't escaped her notice and now she was trying to use it to brush off my request.

"Grant me five minutes," I said.

When the Ancient hesitated, I reached out and gripped her bony arm. "Just five minutes of your time, in exchange for years of service."

She withdrew her slimy hand from mine and shook me away.

"Very well, vampire," she grumbled. "But no more than five."

I raced down the steps and out of the chamber. Annora waited outside the door. I thought she might have been eavesdropping, but I didn't care now. I just had to get her to agree to what I was proposing.

"Annora, I know you tried to become a Channeler. And you failed," I said, gripping her shoulders. Her face contorted. "The Ancient is willing to give it another shot with hopes that it will be successful this time and this time I will be there with you.'

Annora narrowed her eyes on me. "What does this have to do with our trip? You said you wanted to become a dark witch yourself..."

"And I will," I bluffed. "But Lilith said that before she agrees to it, since you're here with me, she wants to try turning you into a Channeler again."

"No," Annora said, stepping back from me. "I don't want to go through all that again."

"Lilith wants you to," I lied. "But think about it, this is a good thing. You'll be more powerful than ever. You need to take this chance while the Ancient is willing. Her mood might change at any moment. It's now or never. Come on." I tugged at her.

"I'm fine how I am."

I paused, staring at her.

"Do you not remember the pain you feel each night?" My face now a few inches away from hers, I continued to squeeze her. "Do you want to feel that for the rest of your life? Do you remember nothing of the life we used to share?"

She stared at the floor, refusing to make eye contact with me.

"Look," I said. "I don't care any more if you do this for me or for yourself. I'm tired of having to deal with you. Become a Channeler and finish the job. Do it for Lilith, for Christ's sake, but just do it."

"You didn't want to come here for yourself at all, did you?" Annora said, biting her lip.

"It doesn't matter any more." I grabbed her hand and pulled her into the room. She didn't resist this time, although she could have easily. I pulled her down the sloping floor toward the pond.

"Lilith," I called.

The hulking skeleton descended slowly down the steps toward us.

"We're ready," I said, even though Annora looked anything but.

"Are you ready, Annora?" the Ancient asked, her eyes boring into her.

Annora breathed out and looked up at the ceiling. "What difference will being a Channeler make? I'm strong as it is."

"You will be of more use to Lilith and the rest of our kind."

Lilith began clicking her tongue, inching back

toward her liquid tomb.

"No, wait," I said. I pushed Annora toward the Ancient.

Come on, Annora. Don't sabotage this. Please...

Annora glared at me one more time, but finally nodded. Turning to the Ancient, she said, "All right, I'll do it. I'll give it another try. But only if Caleb leaves."

I stared at her in shock. "What are you saying? You need somebody present who's familiar to you. Even Lilith advised this." I turned to Lilith and looked at her desperately. "Didn't you?" Lilith scowled, but nodded. "Otherwise it will just be a repeat of last time and you might even end up worse off."

Lilith coughed up another mouthful of black phlegm and spat it over her shoulder into the pond. "Hurry up!" she rasped.

Annora swallowed hard and then nodded. "Okay, with Caleb present."

Annora folded her legs and sat cross-legged on the dusty floor, while I took a seat next to her.

I looked up at Lilith, who had approached and was hovering over us.

"Let's begin."

Chapter 33: Caleb

Watching Annora writhe and scream, semi-conscious throughout, was perhaps the strangest experience of my life. Her eyes rolled in their sockets. It was as though she was present at times, rested enough to scream, but other times I had no idea where she'd drifted off to.

I didn't know what Lilith was doing to her, or why it caused so much pain. I would have liked to ask, but there simply was no time. Lilith had been on the verge of disappearing back into her black pond and I couldn't afford to agitate her further.

We sat on the dusty floor for what felt like hours.

The whole time Lilith instructed that I keep my hands firmly placed in Annora's, which was becoming harder and harder as she sweated. They were becoming slippery and I had to grip tight as she writhed on the ground and tried to break free.

Annora was so far gone, I wasn't even sure she was aware I was even here for her, or what good simply holding her hands would do. Still, I had no choice but to trust Lilith.

I wanted to ask how much longer, but since Lilith too had her eyes closed tight I was sure she wouldn't welcome the interruption. I dared not say anything lest it interfere with the process and the spell went wrong yet again, leaving Annora in an even worse condition.

Truth be told, I was surprised that Annora had agreed at all. I had thought she'd refuse and just vanish from the spot. A small part of me hoped that perhaps she was doing this for me after all. That there was still a part of her that missed what she was before, when she'd still loved me.

It was impossible to know, and a waste of time speculating about, but I had nothing else to distract myself with. Otherwise, I would just find myself worrying about things out of my control, such as whether Annora would resurface at all after Lilith was done with her.

I knew I shouldn't get my hopes up too high. If she did resurface, she would still be a witch. Still affected by the darkness that had first consumed her when I'd turned her into a vampire. It wasn't like we could erase all that history and bring back the sweet beacon of light Annora had once been. Still, I hoped that she would at least revert to the way she was before she'd attempted to become a Channeler—when I could still recognize pieces of her, rather than seeing nothing but an empty shell.

More time passed, and Lilith still showed no signs of letting go of Annora. At least by now it was easier to keep hold of Annora's hands. She seemed to have passed out completely. Her face was still contorted, as though pain was still coursing through her, but now she was stiller, her breathing more steady.

I was beginning to suspect that we were nearing the end when a click echoed around the chamber. Though I was careful not to let the shock loosen my grip on Annora, my eyes shot toward the entrance.

The door was wide open. And standing in the doorway was a man with pitch-black eyes and pale skin. A dark traveler's cloak was wrapped around his shoulders.

Outraged, I glared daggers at him. I wanted to shout at him, but I was scared to break Lilith's concentration. She hadn't yet looked up at the intruder. Her eyes still closed, she seemed so absorbed in what she was doing, I wondered if she'd even heard him enter.

The man began walking down the stone steps toward us, his heavy black boots echoing around the chamber.

No. Not now. Leave, you bastard. We were so close to completion. We couldn't afford for this to get messed up now. *I need Annora back.*

To my horror, he approached just a few feet away and broke though the silence.

"Lilith. Your Grace. I'm sorry to interrupt."

Lilith shook her head, her thin eyelids fluttering open. She glared up at the man. Then, once she took in this intruder, her face softened.

To my horror, she let go of Annora and stood up. She hurried over to the man's side as though Annora and I didn't exist.

"What are you doing?" I hissed, jumping up. "Did you even finish?"

She ignored me and began speaking in hushed tones with the man.

"Well?" she asked him.

"I've—"

I barged into the man, gripping him by the collar and pushing him back. I took his place in standing next to Lilith and staring down at her. "What is happening with Annora? She's still unconscious! Have you finished—"

Fury sparked in the Ancient's eyes and with one sharp incantation from her I flew backward and crashed against the wall at the far end of the room.

"Tell me, Rhys," she said, scowling at me and then fixing her black eyes once again on Rhys.

He threw me a dirty look too and continued, "I was successful."

"Ah, good, good. Where is the catch?"

"Outside. First I need to speak with you. Alone." Rhys glared at me once more.

Lilith lost no time in issuing me orders. "Take your girl and get out of here," she hissed.

Although my blood was boiling, I didn't see another option but to obey. Infuriating her further might lead her to take her irritation out on Annora. I just had to hope that the spell had worked and now all I had to do was wait for Annora to wake up.

Glowering at both of them and cursing beneath my breath, I brushed past them, scooped the limp Annora up in my arms and stalked out of the room. I took special care to slam the door behind me.

I marched back through the dim tunnel. Although we hadn't arrived through it, Annora had told me that there was a gate on this island. The problem was, I had no idea where it was. I'd have to try to wake Annora up or just wait until she woke by herself.

Still shaking with anger and frustration, I stopped in my tracks just as I neared the exit of the tunnel. My nose caught a scent. A familiar scent, both sweet and terrifying.

I laid Annora down on the ground and followed the smell. It led me to the end of the corridor. I stopped in front of a narrow gap in the wall, just large enough to hold a thin human. A girl. A black-haired, green-eyed girl. Gagged and bound in ropes at her hands and feet.

Blood seeped from her kneecap.

Rose Novak.

CHAPTER 34: CALEB

I almost choked on my tongue.

As soon as Rose saw me approach, her eyes widened and she struggled to sit upright. I stood frozen. My instinct was to reach out and help her, but my hands remained at my sides. It was as if time itself stood still as I stared at the girl.

A wave of longing crashed over me. Longing I'd tried to bury deep. Longing I'd tried to forget. Longing that would only lead to pain and trouble.

Rose began to choke as she tried to talk to me through the gag.

My eyes travelled from Rose in her desperate state, to Annora still unconscious on the ground, then back to Rose.

I didn't know why Rhys had brought Rose here, but I knew one thing—once she stepped into that chamber with Lilith, she wouldn't come out the same. Whatever those two monsters had in store for her, they would take something from her, perhaps her very life.

Rose, the delicate flower I'd tried so hard to shelter from my dark world, had been thrust right into it.

All logic shut down and adrenaline took over.

Despite the pang of guilt I felt about leaving Annora in her helpless state on the ground—a state I wasn't even sure she would wake up from—I approached Rose and scooped her up in my arms.

I didn't know what I was doing, or where I would go with her. I didn't consider what would happen if we were caught. All rational thought escaped me as I raced out of that cave and hurtled down over the boulders toward the beach. All of it blurred into the background as I was left with the one overwhelming urge to carry Rose out of the dark. To not let her witness the nightmares within it.

I didn't want to think about what Rhys might have done to her already. My stomach clenched as I eyed the blood on her leg, which hung limp.

She moaned as I continued ahead full speed, her leg swinging roughly over my arm. Once we'd lost sight of the cave, I dared pause for a breath.

I placed Rose down on the ground and pulled the gag out of her mouth.

She gasped and choked, coughing up dirt and blood. Her lips were parched, her face smeared with blood and sweat, eyes wide and fearful.

She opened her mouth to speak, but we had no time for it.

I shook her silent. "Listen to me, Rose. How did you get here? How did Rhys bring you here?"

"I... Th-there was a... crater. Further up. On the beach. Near the statue."

"What statue?" I looked left and right, scanning the length of the beach.

She raised a weak hand, pointing toward our left. I squinted and finally saw it—right at the other end of the beach. A lone statue rising high into the sky, at least fifty feet.

I tore off my shirt and wrapped it around her leg for extra support. I picked her up again and as soon as I did, I cursed myself for ever touching her leg. I'd managed to smudge her blood on my hands. It was everything I could do to not stop then and there and dig my fangs into her soft neck. Her scent was making me feel nauseous, like a drug taking hold of all my senses.

Biting my lower lip, I continued racing forward, throwing a glance back over my shoulder every ten feet. Rhys was still nowhere in sight. Either he was still talking to Lilith, oblivious of the fact that I'd stolen Rose, or he had just found out and was now chasing after us.

Whatever the case, there was only one thing to do. Run.

I approached the statue—an odd grey structure shaped like an upward-pointing dagger—and circled it. I breathed out in relief as I spotted the crater Rose had spoken of. *So this is another one of the witches' remaining gates.*

I had not the slightest clue what we might find on the other side. But there was no time for thought. I just had to let my instincts and adrenaline keep me running, because the moment I stopped to think, the insanity of what I'd just done would come crashing down on me.

"Hold on tight," I growled, holding Rose closer against my chest as I leapt into the starry abyss.

Chapter 35: Rose

After Rhys had put me to sleep on the boat, I'd come to again once Rhys had already jumped through the crater. The free fall had forced me to consciousness and the next thing I knew, we'd landed on a black pebble beach beneath a tall grey statue. The warlock had refused to answer any questions as he carried me toward the cave, but, despite the agony my leg was causing me, my addled brain managed to come up with some theories.

I thought back to the first time I'd met "Micah". He'd been floating in the ocean calling for help, claiming he'd strayed outside the boundary and needed our assistance in coming back in. That was how the warlock had first entered The Shade. The real Micah must have strayed past the boundary in search of fish, and that was when the warlock had caught him.

I'd seen with my own eyes how Corrine had managed to turn my mother into my father. I doubted it would have been much of an effort for Rhys to turn into a werewolf. I shuddered to think where Micah might be now, if he was still alive.

I remembered how keen he'd been to stray from the boundary that day on Sun Beach. If Saira hadn't swum up to stop him, he would have made off with me then.

And to think I'd been beginning to fall for his act… I thought back to our conversation in the boathouse. Rhys had likely made up everything he'd told me about Micah's tragic past. It had all been designed to evoke sympathy from me and draw me closer. The real Micah likely had a completely different story.

Although I'd managed to piece together some parts of the puzzle, there were still so many questions clouding my mind.

Once Rhys had gained entrance onto the island, why hadn't he taken the opportunity to sneak more witches in and overpower Mona? If he'd done this, it wouldn't have been difficult to take over The Shade and our supply of humans.

And why take me of all people? Why would the witches throw away the chance to take over our island just to have me, a weak human girl, kidnapped again?

Nothing made any sense.

My blood was still boiling at the warlock's deception. I felt almost as angry as I had when I'd believed Caleb too had been a lie. Only in his case, I'd been mistaken.

Now that Caleb had jumped back through the gate with me, I had no idea what was on the other side. I thought we might arrive in Stellan's or perhaps even Caleb's island. But when we reached the end of the tunnel, I landed on a bed of wet soil. I gasped for breath. The air was heavy and humid. A symphony of chirping, hissing and buzzing pierced my eardrums. In the distance was the sound of thundering water.

I opened my eyes, trying to adjust to the darkness. We had landed in the undergrowth of some kind of jungle. Sharp-leaved bushes surrounded us. I stared up at the canopy of trees—so thick it shut out the moonlight but for a few shafts.

Caleb stood a few feet away, casting his eyes around the area. He walked over to me and gripped my arms, helping me up. My leg still useless, I had to lean against him for support.

"Where are we?" I whispered.

Before he had a chance to answer, the bushes rustled to our left. I let out a scream as I came face to face with a wild boar. Caleb grabbed me by the waist and helped me onto his back. Holding my weak legs around him, he began to run.

"We need to get far away from the gate," he said, his chest heaving as we lurched forward with furious speed. I tightened my grip around his shoulders. He was travelling so fast, the jungle was a blur to me and it was a struggle to breathe.

My leg was already causing me agony, but now that it kept bumping against Caleb's hip as he ran, the pain intensified. After what felt like fifteen minutes, I could no longer hold in my groans of pain. He stopped and laid me down on the ground. He crouched down next to me and rolled up the right leg of my jeans. But these jeans were tight and wouldn't roll up high enough for him to reach my injury. To my surprise, he lowered his head to my thigh.

"What are you—?"

The tips of his fangs pierced through the fabric and grazed my skin as he ripped a gash in my jeans. He used his claws to tear the rest of the way around my leg and pulled the fabric away, leaving my skin bare, my injury in full view.

His breath hitched. I dared not look down. The pain was overwhelming enough as it was, I was afraid I might lose consciousness again if I saw how mushy a wound the warlock's sharp boot had caused. I kept my eyes on Caleb's face.

Extending a claw, he slit the center of his palm. Holding the back of my head with one hand, he held his bloody hand to my lips.

"Drink."

I refused to drink my own parents' blood, let alone Caleb's. But my suffering was now so overwhelming, even I wasn't stubborn enough to refuse. I held his forearm and sensed his muscles tense as soon as my mouth touched his skin. I ran my tongue gingerly along his palm, lapping up his blood like a cat would do milk.

I held my nose, trying to avoid experiencing the

taste. But it had such a strong flavor, I tasted it all the same.

Caleb made me keep drinking for several minutes. Finally he let go of my head and allowed me to sit back. But as soon as I did, my stomach began to churn and I felt a burning in my throat. Crouching on all floors, I retched, remnants of the last meal I'd eaten spilling all over the soil. Spinach lasagna laced with vampire blood. *Yum.*

Caleb reached an arm around my waist and forced me to stand. I groaned, pre-empting the pain I'd become accustomed to in my leg, but found I was able to stand straight without even needing to lean on him. I stared down at my knee. It looked quite normal. My skin was grubby and covered in dried blood, but it seemed intact. I ran my hands over my skin over my face and my arms, my lower lip—the cuts seemed to have healed.

I looked up at Caleb, who was looking at me impatiently. I wiped my mouth quickly with the back of my sleeve, realizing I probably still had a bit of puke somewhere there. Not exactly the look I'd imagined sporting when reuniting with Caleb in my fantasies.

"I'm so thirsty," I croaked, realizing how dehydrated I felt for the first time, now that I'd just coughed up the remaining fluids I had.

Wordlessly he bent down and pulled me onto his back again. He began to run again.

"Where are we?" I asked.

"I don't know."

"Who is that warlock? Why did you take me? What was that island? And what were you doing there?" Some of the questions that had been crowding my mind blurted from my parched mouth at once. And Caleb answered exactly none of them. He remained silent as we lurched through the jungle.

When I pressed for answers, he said, "Not now."

My throat was too sore to argue. I had to save my speech for when I really needed it.

It was probably a good thing that it was dark and I had trouble seeing. The disconcerting noises surrounding us—those of predatory animals and tropical insects alike—made me realize that this was a jungle so wild, if I was able to actually see the creatures around me, I'd be screaming. *Sometimes ignorance really is the best course.*

As Caleb ran, the thundering of water got louder and louder, echoing around us. Finally, he stopped again. He set me down on my feet and held my hand, leading me down a slope toward a roaring river. I let go of him and crept toward the edge of the water.

"Careful," he said. "It's slippery."

I tried to heed his advice and go slow, but I was so anxious for water. The sight of it made me even more keenly aware of how much my throat hurt. I lost my footing on a muddy stone. The next thing I knew, I'd slipped into the river. The water submerged me and before I could fight my way back to the bank, a ferocious current sucked me under. By the time I surfaced again, gasping for breath, I was already a good ten feet away from the bank and moving fast. It had all happened so quickly, my body was still in shock.

Caleb had already dived in. His powerful arms sliced through the current as he waded toward me. But this river was so monstrous, it slowed even Caleb down.

He swore.

"Don't look behind you, Rose," he shouted. "Keep your eyes on me. I'm coming for you."

"Wha'd you—" I choked, swallowing a mouthful of

water.

How can he say something like that at a time like this and expect me to actually obey him?

I cast my eyes back over my shoulder. And I immediately wished I'd obeyed him. The moonlight reflected a set of slimy scales, gliding streamlined toward me.

I shrieked. An alligator.

"Look at me," Caleb bellowed. "Look at me, Rose."

I fought to turn myself around and face him again. I forced myself to stare into his intense brown eyes. Eyes that had haunted me for weeks. Eyes that I now believed might be my last vision. I realized I couldn't think of much else that I would rather be looking at. I could look at them all day. I just wished that a giant reptile wasn't creeping up on me from behind, about to swallow me alive. That would have made it much easier to follow his instruction.

"Caleb," I screamed. "Help!"

"I'm coming for you. Just keep your eyes on me. I'm not going to let anything happen to you."

Another current pulled me under water. I was afraid I might resurface right next to the beast, perhaps even underneath it. But I reappeared ten feet away. I fought to turn myself around in the water to look at Caleb again, and breathed out as I saw he too had been swept under by a current and was now only few feet away from me. He closed the distance between us quickly with his broad muscular strokes. And then his strong arm snaked around my waist, guiding me to climb onto his back. I was expecting him to immediately turn round and swim in the other direction. But to my horror, he headed straight for the monster.

"Caleb! What are you—" But it was too late.

The creature quickened its strokes until it arrived within two feet from us. I shut my eyes, burying my face against Caleb's neck.

The alligator bellowed and when I dared open my eyes again a few seconds later, the reptile was bleeding from its eye sockets. Caleb had ripped out its eyeballs, leaving it thrashing in agony. He turned away and began swimming against the current. I felt his whole body tense—pure muscle challenging the might of this terrifying river that was so bent on swallowing us up. Caleb won. It was a slow and steady process, but a few minutes later he was climbing back onto the bank. I rolled off him and lay on the ground, panting.

I stared up at him, then let out a scream. I pointed to his shoulder.

"What's that black thing?"

He glanced down. "A leech," he said. I expected him to immediately pull it off. Instead he crawled over to me and began running his hands over my own arms. I shivered as his hands brushed down my legs, reached up beneath the hem of my ripped jeans and touched my thigh. Then he lifted up my wet shirt to reveal my stomach. I screamed again on seeing a black leech writhing and sucking on my own skin, just above my panty line.

"Lie back," he ordered.

I leaned back, but only enough that I could still keep an eye on what he was doing with the leech. I gasped as he lowered his mouth to my stomach, his mouth enclosing the leech. I shivered as his lips brushed against my abdomen. Then I felt a sharp pain. He sucked the leech from my skin and threw it over his shoulder. He jumped up several feet away from me, wiping his mouth with the back of his hand and spitting on the ground, I assumed to rid himself of any trace of my blood that might have entered his mouth. I couldn't imagine the amount of self control it must have taken him to do that. I knew he craved my blood as it was. If he allowed himself to taste even a drop of my blood, he might not be able to stop himself from sucking me dry.

"You may want to check beneath your clothes," he said, casting me a sideways glance.

This was no time to be worrying about preserving my modesty or being a shy wallflower around him. He turned around while I stripped to my bikini. Thankfully, after a thorough inspection I was able to conclude that there were no bloodsuckers anywhere down there. I slipped my torn jeans back on.

"Okay, there was nothing," I said. "You can turn around."

But he didn't turn around. I walked up to him to see him concentrating on removing a particularly monstrous leech that had attached itself to him just above his navel. He gripped its head and yanked it out, squeezing out the blood from it before tossing it into the bushes.

"How many did you have on you?"

"Just two." He looked down at my stomach,

frowning. "Lift your shirt again."

I lifted it to reveal the wound the black leech had caused, blood flowing freely from it, showing no signs of clotting. His wound flowed similarly. I thought he might bend down to look at it more closely but his jaw tensed and he jolted back several feet away from me again.

This was so difficult for him. I was a walking meal. He turned his back on me, his shoulders heaving, struggling to regain control. Finally he turned around again, his eyes focused on my face, avoiding looking at the blood leaking through my shirt.

"You're going to need to drink my blood again," he said, his breathing still uneven. He extended a claw and poised to slit his right palm again.

"No," I said quickly, not willing to risk vomiting up my guts again. "Don't cut yourself again. My wound will heal."

"Not fast enough. Leeches inject an anticoagulant to stop your blood clotting."

When I still hesitated, he breathed out sharply in irritation. He stood up and began walking away.

"Wait," I said, "Don't leave me!"

"I'm not leaving you," he hissed. "Just stay there. If you won't drink my blood, I need to find something else to help clot the blood, or I'll drink from you myself and there will be no blood left in you to coagulate. Trust me, unlike the leech, there will be no detaching myself from you if I do lose control."

I watched as he disappeared behind a tree, now regretting that I hadn't just forced myself to drink his blood again. I breathed out in relief as he returned a few moments later carrying a handful of long thin leaves. Still keeping his distance from me, he put three of them in his mouth and began chewing.

"What are you—?"

He removed the leaves from his mouth—now crushed to a mushy pulp—and approached me slowly. He swallowed hard as he stood next to me. He lifted my shirt and placed the pulp against my wound.

"Hold it there," he said.

As soon as I held it in place he stepped away, turning his back on me once again.

"It will speed up the clotting," he said.

"Oh, thanks," I said, staring down at the gooey pulp. "And what about you?" I looked back at him, noticing that he was making no attempt to stem his own bleeding shoulder.

"It doesn't matter if I bleed."

"It matters to me," I muttered.

He ignored me. Silence fell between us. He paced up and down in front of me, like a panther protecting its territory. I assumed he was waiting for my blood to stop flowing.

My assumption was correct. A few minutes later, he looked at me again.

"Check the wound."

I peeled back the pulp. The blood had clotted, just as Caleb had predicted.

"It's okay now."

"Then we need to keep moving." He closed the distance between us and bent down in front of me. "Climb back on."

I wrapped my legs around his waist. He stood up and began rushing through the trees again. Still holding the mushy pulp, I reached for his shoulder and placed the plant against it. I looked at his face for a reaction. His jaw twitched, but otherwise he didn't acknowledge my gesture.

I held the pulp there as he raced forward until the blood had stopped flowing freely and began to thicken. Then I threw the pulp away.

I replaced my arm around his shoulder.

"So you still have no idea where we are? Are we even on Earth?"

"Yes, we're in the human realm."

"Where are we going?"

"I don't know," he breathed.

I decided to ask no more questions of him. At least for now. He seemed to be as clueless as me as to our whereabouts, and he needed to concentrate on getting us out of this jungle before day broke. And the sun drained him of all energy.

We passed the next few hours in silence. We didn't stop again. I supposed that was a good thing. The speed at which Caleb was running prevented mosquitoes and other nasty-looking insects from landing on me. I felt their high-pitched buzzing in my ears several times as we ran through particularly thick clouds of them, but thanks to Caleb's swiftness, none were able to land on me.

I didn't know how I did it, but as I rested my head

against Caleb's back, listening to his heavy breathing, feeling the strength of his body so close against mine, exhaustion took over me and I drifted off.

***

Strong hands shaking my shoulders brought me awake with a start. I sat bolt upright, bewildered as to where I was or how I was looking up into Caleb's face. It took a few seconds for the memories to return.

I was lying on the ground, Caleb leaning over me, artificial light casting shadows over his sweaty face. Sounds of civilization surrounded me, just a few meters away. We were in a cluster of bushes, and just a few meters away street lamps lined a concrete road. A little further than that was a market.

I looked up at the sky. The sun was about to break above the horizon.

"Where—?"

"We've reached a town," he whispered.

"Oh… Oh, thank God." I attempted to stand. He pulled me back down.

"I need you to wait here," he said. "Can you do that?"

"For how long?"

"Ten, fifteen minutes. Stay in the shadows of the trees. Make sure you're not seen. All right?"

"O-okay."

I crept further into one of the bushes and peeked through a gap in the leaves to watch Caleb run out onto the road and head in the direction of the market. I stood waiting behind the bush with bated breath, trying to make sense of where on earth we could be. Footsteps sounded on the concrete road a few feet away.

The voices of two men filled my ears. I couldn't understand what they were saying, but at least it sounded like a human language. *We're definitely on Earth, like Caleb said. But where?* I supposed I'd have to wait for Caleb to return.

Although I didn't have a watch, it felt like Caleb had kept his promise to return within fifteen minutes. He crept behind the bushes and dropped down next to me. He had a bulging plastic bag in his hand. He removed the contents one by one, placing some items on my lap, some on his own.

"How did you—?"

"Some early visitors to the market," was all the

explanation he offered.

"So you pickpocketed them," I muttered. He nodded. I guessed it wasn't difficult for vampires to pickpocket, given their superhuman speed and agility.

By the time he was finished, I was holding in my lap a ripe papaya, a liter of water, a toothbrush, toothpaste and a stiff cotton night gown. On his lap was a clear plastic bag filled with fresh fish, a black wallet and another black plastic bag.

He began tearing into the fish, draining all the blood and throwing the rest of it into the bushes. He must have been hungry. I attacked my bottle of water with similar urgency, swallowing half a liter in less than a minute. Then I turned to the papaya.

I wasn't sure how to open it without making a mess of it. I looked at Caleb.

"Could you?"

He extended a claw and sliced the fruit into quarters. I began chewing into the sweet flesh hungrily and I had finished the whole thing in a few minutes. I eyed the toothbrush and the night gown.

"Now what?" I asked once he'd finished his fish blood.

He stood up and brushed himself down. Opening the wallet, he pulled out a wad of cash and began counting it.

I stared at the currency. "We're in—"

"Brazil. On the borders of a city called Manaus."

Brazil. Well, at least that explained the rainforest. The opening of the gate was in the heart of the Amazon.

Caleb's eyes roamed my body.

"Put that dress on over your clothes," he said.

I stared down at my clothes. He had a point. I looked like I'd just walked off the set of a slasher movie. I pulled the dress over my head and did my best to tie back my hair so it didn't look quite so alarming.

I looked at Caleb. He hardly looked presentable. Shirtless, his chest was covered in bloodstains and grime from rushing through the jungle for hours. His hair was a tangled mess and his pants were ripped too. He was in just as bad a state as me.

"And what about you?"

He reached for the unopened black plastic bag and pulled out a pair of shorts and a crisp black shirt. He walked to a cluster of trees nearby and disappeared behind them. When he returned, he was fully dressed in the new clothes.

"All right," he said. "Let's go." He gripped my arm and pulled me forward.

"Wait." I tugged on him, pulling him back. "Bend down."

He raised a brow but did as I'd requested. His head now level with my chest, I ran my fingers through his thick dark hair, attempting to tame it, picking out pieces of leaves and branches. I almost screamed as a small red spider scurried across my finger, burying itself closer to Caleb's scalp. I picked up a stick from the ground and, fishing through his hair to find the creature again, I managed to brush it away.

"Caleb," I whispered, my insides churning, "can you check my hair for spiders?"

He stood up and pulled my head toward him, his strong fingers tugging roughly on my long hair as he sifted through it.

"No spiders. Okay? We need to go."

"Okay," I said in relief.

I slipped my hand in his and, picking up the toothbrush and toothpaste, we left the tree-lined enclosure and walked onto the main road. I was glad that the dress was long enough to cover my feet because I wore no shoes.

Caleb led me directly across the quiet road and headed into the market area. We walked along a line of buildings until we reached a tall one with a sign above a double-doored entrance.

Hostel Amazonas.

Caleb wrapped an arm round my waist and held me close as we ascended the steps and entered into the lobby. There was a small reception desk in one corner where an elderly woman sat reading a paper. She looked up at us through her spectacles as we arrived at the desk.

Caleb picked up a leaflet from the counter and paged through it. He looked up at the woman.

"A private room, please."

"Sala privada? Para dois?" the woman asked, holding up two fingers.

Caleb nodded and placed a few notes down on the counter.

She took the cash and counted it. *"Uma noite,"* she muttered. She handed us a key and pointed to the number engraved on it. *"Vinte."*

Caleb took it from her and pulled me away from the reception desk, up the staircase in the center of the room. We walked up two flights of stairs and found Room 20.

He opened the door and locked it immediately after we'd entered. I found myself standing in a narrow room. It looked much like a basic motel room—a small double bed, a faded chair, an old telephone and an ensuite bathroom. It was basic, but looked clean enough. Most of all, I was thankful to see mosquito nets fixed to the window and also over the bed.

The door clicked as Caleb locked it. He walked about the room, drawing the curtains shut and plunging the room into darkness. He reached for the switch on the wall and flicked on the fluorescent lighting. Then he finally turned to face me. We stood in silence, just staring at each other. It was the first time since our reunion that we'd had time to just look at each other, undistracted by danger. And now it felt awkward. I broke eye contact with him and walked toward the bathroom.

"I need a shower," I muttered.

I locked myself in the small bathroom and undressed.

I placed my torn clothes in the bin in the corner of the room and stepped into the shower.

There was no hot water but it wasn't needed. I was glad to have the cold water spilling down my back after the heat of the jungle. I half expected to find another leech on me but, thankfully, I didn't. I stared at the floor of the shower, amazed at how much dirt was flowing off me.

I soaped myself from top to bottom and washed my hair with the cheap shampoo that had been left on a ledge. I stepped out, dried myself and changed back into the night dress. I wrapped my hair in the small towel, forming a turban, and, after procrastinating a minute longer, stepped back out into the room.

Caleb sat in a chair in the corner of the room, staring down at the leaflet he'd taken from reception. I approached slowly, and soon realized that he was looking at a map. He stood up as I approached and left me alone in the room to take a shower himself. I waited in silence for him, listening to the running water, looking at the map while I waited.

When he finally opened the door, wearing his shorts, his chest bare again, his hair dripping wet, he stopped in the center of the room and looked down at me seriously.

There were so many questions bombarding my mind. I wasn't sure he was ready for them. Hell, I wasn't sure *I* was ready.

"What now?" I asked.

"We stay in this room for a few hours. Get some rest. And then we move on again. This is one of the nearest towns to that gate. It's not safe to stay here."

"But go where?"

"You need to return to The Shade."

I bit my lip.

"Caleb, what were you doing there, on that strange island? And why did you save me again?" He walked over to the window, his back turned to me. "I thought you weren't willing to risk putting anything else on the line for me... for us?"

His back heaved, his muscles rippling beneath his skin.

"I wasn't."

"Then?"

He paused. Then cleared his throat. "We don't have much time here. We should be using it for rest rather than talk."

"You can't keep me in the dark any longer. I can't sleep until I know what's going on."

He threw me a glance, eyeing my bare arms.

"Get under the mosquito net first."

I climbed onto the bed and tucked in the net all around me. I sat cross-legged in the center of the mattress looking at him as he resumed his seat in the chair.

"Firstly, I don't know what that warlock, Rhys, wanted with you. Secondly, I was there because I was paying a visit to that island with Annora."

"What is that island? Why did Rhys take me there, of all places?"

He hesitated. His lips parted then closed.

"It's best you don't know what lies on that island. Just know that it's not pretty. I don't know what they had planned for you or why he stole you away."

"What will happen now? Will Rhys come after us?"

"Oh, yes. You can count on it. That's why we can't stay here for more than a few hours."

"What will he do to you, if he—if they—find out you've betrayed them? And what will you do now?"

Caleb wet his lower lip, his Adam's apple moving as he swallowed. "There's nothing I can do."

I'd seen enough of the witches to know that Caleb wouldn't be spared for such a betrayal.

"Why did you do this for me?" I pressed.

He shifted uncomfortably in his seat. "It was probably another mistake."

"Yet you did it still, with barely a moment's hesitation."

"I did," he said, staring blankly at the opposite wall.

I thought back to the night Mona had burst into our apartment, claiming that she had a sense that my parents were under a spell. I'd found it strange at the time. But now suspicion was beginning to enter my mind. "Caleb, did you warn Mona about my parents?"

His silence was all the answer I needed.

I couldn't restrain myself. I untucked the mosquito next and ran over to him, kneeling down and taking his hands in mine.

"Caleb, you can come back with me. I know Mona will vouch for you. And you returning me a second time... it simply can't be a coincidence. With both myself and Mona standing up for you, there's no way my parents can refuse. They'll just be too relieved to see me again. Why don't you come with me?"

Her refused to look me in the eye.

"If you don't," I said, my voice shaking, "you'll die. You have no choice. Even if you manage to escape Rhys, you only have seven days. Come to The Shade and Mona will be able to rid you of the bond. You can live with us."

Excitement and passion coursed through my body. I reached up to touch his shoulder and finally his eyes fixed on mine.

He stood up, drawing me up with him. He picked me up in his arms and laid me on the bed. Tucking me back under the mosquito net, he remained outside of it, gazing at me.

"Rest now, Rose. We'll talk about this when you wake up."

I reached a hand up to the net, wanting to touch him again, reassure him that it would work out all right, if he'd just come back with us.

But I agreed to his request.

I lay down on the stiff pillow, exhaustion beginning to claim me again. My eyes didn't leave Caleb's still form in the corner of the room until they fell shut.

As I drifted off, I imagined him coming back with me to The Shade. I pictured our arrival at the Port. We'd go straight to my parents. Mona would help me explain that it had all been a misunderstanding. Because Caleb was a good man. A man who deserved more than the life he'd been dealt.

Much more.

CHAPTER 36: CALEB

I moved my chair closer to her once she'd fallen asleep. I wanted to take in her beauty, the gentle flush in her cheeks, the way her lips parted slightly as she breathed.

So much had happened in such a short time, truth be told, I was still in a daze myself.

Rose's suggestion to return with her to The Shade was indeed my only option—if I was to stay alive, of course. Even then, if I agreed, there was no guarantee that we'd make it back in time. I was still bound by Annora's seven-day curse. I studied the map and thought about how we could possibly return. We had no passports. Rose clearly had no special phone on her capable of contacting The Shade. We'd have to find a way to get to the other side of the continent quickly, and then steal a boat to travel the rest of the way to The Shade. I had no idea how long that might take us. Any number of things could go wrong. For one thing, I had the sun to contend with during the daytime. We'd have to do the bulk of our traveling at night and during the day stay out of the sun. All the while traveling with Rose—a frail human girl. And all this was actually the least of our worries. We had Rhys on our tail, I was sure of it. I knew he wouldn't stop until he'd hunted us down. And he was a Channeler, even more powerful than Annora. He might be hurtling through the Amazon rainforest at the speed of light right now, toward us.

Still—detaching myself from the situation—I had to get Rose back to the Shade as quickly as possible. What might happen to me had to be secondary. Of course, if something did happen to me, she wouldn't survive. She was dependent on me now.

Thinking about the odds we were up against sent my mind reeling. I felt overwhelmed. But I realized there was no point worrying about what might happen. Our circumstances were out of our control. We just had to take things one day at a time and do our best to stay alive.

I picked up the map again and continued to study it, trying to decide what our next move should be. Before we set off anywhere, I needed to steal some sort of protection for myself from the sun. Perhaps a long hooded raincoat. We didn't have the luxury of only traveling at night. We simply didn't have that sort of time.

For the next couple of hours, I tried to focus on planning our journey. But thoughts of Annora kept interrupting me. The way I'd left her there, helpless on the ground, so willingly. As though it was just instinct to abandon her for Rose. I wondered what she might be doing now. Whether she might have woken up already, or whether she might still be lying unconscious and alone in that dark tunnel.

As I looked again at Rose, I realized that while I was in her presence, I just didn't care much. I didn't know what would become of Annora, but the fact that I was able to leave her so easily spoke volumes. Although I felt guilty for it, Rose eclipsed Annora so completely, it was hard to feel much for her even as she occupied my mind.

Even if Annora hadn't done all she had, I wondered if Rose might still have eclipsed her. I wondered if trying to fix the witch had been nothing but an attempt to fill the hole Rose had gouged in me. I'd hoped that perhaps if I had Annora back, she'd make me forget the pain I felt in the princess' absence. Perhaps it had all been a big ruse—none of it done for Annora's sake, but for my own.

I looked at the old clock on the wall. It was time.

I untucked the mosquito net. But before I woke Rose, I bent down and gave in to the urge that had consumed me the moment I'd laid eyes on her beautiful face again.

To touch her. Breathe her in.

I caressed her soft forehead with my lips. As much as I wanted that moment to last forever, I allowed my kiss to linger only for three seconds. I didn't want her to realize what I'd done. Because I didn't want this to be another mistake.

I pulled my mouth away and clutched her shoulders,

shaking her awake.

Her green eyes flickered open and she gave me a small smile.

"Caleb." She reached up, her fingers brushing against my cheek.

I closed my eyes, barely breathing. It took all the restraint I had to not bend down and kiss her again, this time on her flushed lips.

I cleared my throat.

"Rose, it's time to go. We have a long journey ahead of us."

CHAPTER 37: ANNORA

My brain was on fire as I sat up. My muscles felt like they'd been put through a shredder and restrung beneath my skin. My bones ached. My vision was blurred and my throat parched. I reached out and felt for the wall. I leant against it as I tried to stand. My eyes slowly came into focus. I was in a dimly lit tunnel. I gripped my head. I felt like I might pass out again from the pain. I could barely think straight.

I placed both forefingers on my temple and muttered an incantation. Nothing happened.

Where are my powers?

I'm supposed to be stronger than ever.

Then the last memory I had before the blackout washed over me. I doubled over.

"Caleb," I gasped.

Pain seared though my chest as I recalled his handsome face, his beautiful brown eyes, the way he'd touched me as Lilith performed the ritual, the way he'd looked at me with concern. As my mind's eye fixed on this man who'd remained by my side all these years, my heart raced. My head felt light. With Caleb in the center of my heart, breathing life into my soul, it felt like I was walking on air. A sudden warmth rushed through me, shooting from my chest and spreading throughout my body. A sensation that was all-consuming. Earth-shattering. A sensation I'd thought I was no longer capable of experiencing.

What is happening?

Tears welled in my eyes and began to stream down my cheeks. I collapsed on the floor. Sharp rocks cut into my knees, drawing blood. But I could barely feel it. The pain in my chest brought about by Caleb's absence and the euphoria coursing through my veins overwhelmed me completely.

What have I done to you all these years, my love? How

could I have let myself lose you?

My body had never felt so weak, so vulnerable. I didn't know what had happened to me. And although I was confused as to why I could summon no magic—I was supposed to have been made into a Channeler, I should be even more powerful—the only thing on my mind was Caleb.

My love. My fiancé. I need to find him.

I managed to stand again. I stumbled through the tunnel toward Lilith's chamber. My hands shaking, I fumbled for the doorknob and swung the door open. "Caleb!" I shouted, casting my eyes around the room.

The chamber was empty. Even Lilith had sunk back into her tomb.

I stumbled back into the tunnel. I ran until I reached the other end. I pushed open the door at the other side, the darkness of the cave enveloping me. I tried to summon light from my palms. Again, I was unable to wield my magic.

"Caleb! Caleb, it's me… Annora… I-I'm back. It's me." My voice broke. I ran to the cave's entrance.

Another pang hit me as I realized Caleb wasn't here. *Did he leave? Where could he have gone without me? Why did he leave me lying on the floor?*

What have I done to him all these years?

It felt like I'd just woken from the dead. I'd forgotten what it was like to breathe. To feel anything other than cold.

"I'm sorry," I gasped, trying to swallow back the tears. "My love, I'm sorry. Forgive me. Please. Come back." I fell to my knees, gusts of ocean wind whipping my skin. I closed my eyes, imagining Caleb standing in front of me. "I made the wrong decision," I breathed. "I should have listened. I never should have given myself up. But I'm back. My love, I'm back. And I promise to love you for the rest of my life. I'll never lose myself again. I swear, I'll be the girl you wanted to marry. We'll run away. Far away from… all this. We'll live our story."

Although my mind was riddled with fear not knowing where he was now or why he'd left me in my vulnerable state, a warm rush of comfort spread through me.

I had found him again in my heart. Now, it was only a matter of time before I found him again in the flesh.

That I knew, because ours was a never-ending story.

Chapter 38: Vivienne

"Eye of snake. Beak of crow. Skin of toad. Blood of Rose."

The chant echoed around the moonlit graveyard.

A tall man with black eyes levitated a few inches off the ground, stirring a black pot. Beside him was a grey tombstone. Smoke erupted from the cauldron, billowing upward, forming a swirling vortex. Within the smoke, another figure appeared, back turned to me. A pure white robe hung against soft curves. She turned slowly in midair, twisting to face me. But she had no face. Where her eyes, nose and mouth should have been was nothing but smooth pale flesh.

An echoing crack pierced the night. Then a hiss.

The tombstone's lid sprang open. A still corpse rose from it into the air. The rotting corpse of a woman, it dwarfed even the man, her bony legs almost twice the size of his. Her ripped clothes revealed more of her moldering body than they covered. Her black eyes glinted in the firelight.

She spoke in ancient tongue, her voice grating like nails.

The man drifted toward her and poured a goblet of boiling liquid into her mouth. She let out a blood-curdling scream. Her jaw expanded and split, the bottom half hanging disjointed.

As the corpse began swirling around in the air, her head snapped back at an almost ninety-degree angle, the faceless woman in white drew closer to me. And a face formed. The face of my young Rose.

Tears of blood spilled from her green eyes.

"Hello, Auntie."

"Vivienne. Wake up!"

I opened my eyes, gasping for breath. Xavier stared down at me, gripping my shoulders and shaking me. I was in our bed. I sat up and leaned against the headboard. Xavier's face was stricken with worry—an expression that everyone on the island had shared since

Rose had been discovered missing again.

I dropped my head in my hands, trying to piece together my jumbled mind. I could barely form a coherent sentence. I was thinking in fragments, thoughts assailing my mind so fast I couldn't keep up with them, much less articulate them.

"They know something."

"What?"

"About the twins. We've been mistaken in thinking there's nothing different about them."

"Vivienne, who's—?"

"We need to discover what the twins have. Before it's too late."

READY FOR THE NEXT PART OF DEREK, SOFIA AND THE TWINS' STORY?

A Shade of Vampire 11: A Chase of Prey is available to order now.

Please visit www.bellaforrest.net for details.

Also, if you'd like to stay up to date about Bella's new releases, please visit: www.forrestbooks.com, enter your email and you'll be the first to know.

A Note About Kiev

Dear Shaddict,

If you're curious about what happened to Kiev during his time away, and how he came upon Anna, I suggest you check out his completed stand-alone trilogy: *A Shade of Kiev*.

Kiev's story will also give you a deeper understanding of the Shade books and the kind of threat Derek and Sofia are now up against.

Please visit my website for more details: www.bellaforrest.net

Best wishes,
Bella

黒鷺死体宅配便
the KUROSAGI corpse delivery service

story
EIJI OTSUKA

art
HOUSUI YAMAZAKI

original cover design
BUNPEI YORIFUJI

translation
TOSHIFUMI YOSHIDA

editor and english adaptation
CARL GUSTAV HORN

lettering and touch-up
IHL

DARK
HORSE
MANGA

contents

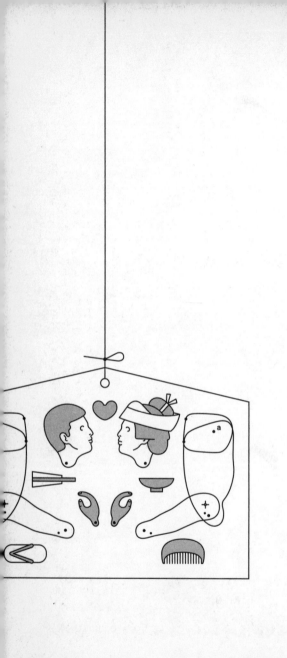

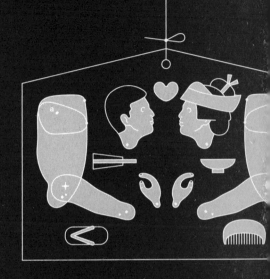

MAN, *HIS* FAMILY'S TEMPLE IS ON 500 *TSUBO* OF LAND *AND* THEY OWN FOUR FUNERAL HOMES! HOW LUCKY IS THAT?

仏教大学信徒会館

WHAT ARE YOU WHINING ABOUT? YOUR FAMILY'S GOT A FAMOUS TEMPLE, TOO.

NOW, *MY* DAD RUNS A PRETTY MODEST MORTUARY...

...BUT THAT STILL PUTS ME AHEAD OF THOSE SORRY FOOLS WHO ENROLL HERE WITHOUT CONNECTIONS... THINKING *ANY* COLLEGE IS BETTER THAN NO COLLEGE.

Chiyoda School of Buddhism Enrollment Ceremony

Doors Open 9:00 AM Ceremony Begins 9:30 AM

OH, RIGHT...IT'S A BUDDHIST SCHOOL...WHY DID I EVEN APPLY TO THIS PLACE...?

HEY, YOU...THE AUDITORIUM IS THE OTHER WAY.

THERE HAVE TO BE OTHER OPTIONS--

WHO ELSE WOULD I BE TALKING TO? YOU'RE A NEW STUDENT HERE, RIGHT? TAKE A FLYER FOR OUR CLUB.

IF YOU FEEL LIKE IT, STOP BY AFTERWARD.

I KNOW THE LAYOUT OF THE SCHOOL'S A LITTLE CONFUSING, BEING THE SIZE IT IS...

UM...ARE YOU TALKING TO ME...?

6

7

1st delivery
学生街の喫茶店
a café in a campus town

HEY, *YOU* THERE...WANNA PLAY TENNIS? OUR CLUB IS PRETTY HAPPENING!

YEAH! WE GO TO KARUIZAWA TWICE A YEAR FOR A TRAINING RETREAT!

Children's Book Club

SEARCH FOR L-O-O-O-V-E IN THE IDOL SINGERS' CL-U-U-U-B...

ESPECIALLY THAT "STUDENT ENTREPRENEUR" GROUP...

YEAH, 'CAUSE THEY DON'T WANT THEM IN THE LIGHT OF DAY.

THERE ARE SOME OTHER CLUBS WITH THEIR TABLES INSIDE, RIGHT?

NOT TO MENTION THOSE SPECIAL CONDITIONS THEY HAVE FOR JOINING...

THE DUDE EVEN TRIED TO GIVE ME A FLYER. WHY WOULD I WANT TO BE AN *ENTREPRENEUR*, ANYWAY? I'M GOING TO INHERIT DAD'S TEMPLE, AND ONCE I DO, MAN, THE KARMA WILL ROLL RIGHT IN.

UM...

"SPECIAL CONDITIONS" ...?!

HOW DO WE KNOW THEY'RE REALLY A CLUB? MAYBE THEY'RE JUST FRONTING FOR SOME CULT. AND WHAT DOES *"CMM"* STAND FOR, ANYWAY?

YEAH, I TOOK ONE LOOK AT THEIR SIGN AND POINTED MY SHOES ELSE-WHERE. THEY'RE KIND OF SCARY, YA KNOW?

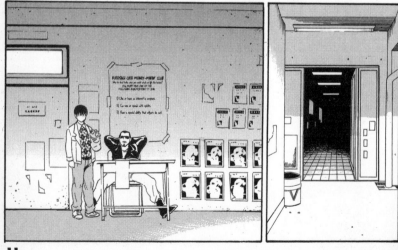

ONLY FOUR SO FAR.

ANYONE YET?

KUROSAGI CASH MONEY-MAKIN' CLUB

Why be dead broke when you could stack up bills like bodies?

YOU **MUST** HAVE ONE OF THE FOLLOWING QUALIFICATIONS TO JOIN:

1) Like or have an interest in corpses.

2) Can see or speak with spirits.

3) Have a special ability that others do not.

Like, THERE'S NO POINT IN *getting* NEW MEMBERS IF THEY CAN'T HELP THE TEAM.

WELL, THE CLUB'S JUST A FRONT SINCE WE FORMED THE DELIVERY BUSINESS, ANYWAY. WE'RE ONLY DOING THIS SO WE DON'T LOSE OUR MEETING SPACE.

I DUNNO, MAYBE OUR CONDITIONS ARE TOO STRICT.

HAVING CHANGED OUR OFFICIAL NAME FROM THE "KURO-SAGI VOLUNTEER SERVICE CLUB" TO THE "KUROSAGI CASH MONEY-MAKIN' CLUB" DOESN'T SEEM TO BE HAVING MUCH EFFECT.

12

13

PLEASE HELP YOURSELVES TO THE WARM SODA AND WASABI-FLAVORED POTATO CHIPS.

DESPITE MY EARLIER USE OF THE TERM "SHIT-FACED," WE REGRET TO ANNOUNCE THAT, DUE TO BUDGETARY RESTRICTIONS, THERE IS NO ACTUAL BEER.

I HEARD THE GOLF CLUB IS HOLDING *THEIR* PARTY UP IN ROPPONGI HILLS...

MAYBE WE SHOULD HAVE TRIED ANOTHER CLUB...?

JUST WHAT KIND OF BUDGET DO THEY *HAVE*...?

LET'S TOAST!

YOU *JEST*, KIND SIR! I SHOULD HAVE GONE THERE INSTEAD.

14

I GUESS WE'LL START WITH HAVING YOU ALL INTRODUCE YOURSELVES... AND TELL US ABOUT YOUR SPECIAL TALENT.

I'M AO SASAKI, THE CHAIRMAN OF THIS CLUB...

KAM-PAIIIIII-IIIIIII!!!

UM... *kampai.*

HUH? ME?

HOW ABOUT *YOU?*

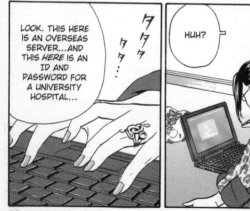

HMM, HE COULD HAVE SOME *potential.*

shhlurrrp WE'LL SEE.

MY NAME IS OKUBO. IT'S MORE LIKE A HOBBY, BUT...I COLLECT PICTURES OF MURDER SCENES AND ACCIDENTS...YOU KNOW, OFF THE NET...

LOOK. THIS HERE IS AN OVERSEAS SERVER...AND THIS *HERE* IS AN ID AND PASSWORD FOR A UNIVERSITY HOSPITAL...

HUH?

THESE IMAGES ARE ONLY SO-SO. ANYONE COULD FIND THESE ONLINE.

LET ME SHOW YOU HOW IT'S DONE.

15

IT'S KIND OF BASIC FOR ME, THOUGH--THE BODY'S STILL IN ONE PIECE. WOULD YOU LIKE TO SEE MORE...?

THIS CALIFORNIA MAN RIGHT *HERE*, FOR EXAMPLE, HAD HIS HEAD CRUSHED BY A TRACTOR WHEEL DURING THE RAISIN HARVEST.

NOW I'M INSIDE A CORONER'S PC. THE FOLDER CONTAINS PICTURES OF BODIES, TAKEN BEFORE AUTOPSY...

Ao Sasaki

Special Talent: Hacking

I... I...th-think it was the w-wasabi chips...

W-W-WELL... P-P-PERHAPS ANOTHER T-TIME...

IS SOMETHING THE MATTER?

YEP.

SCRATCH ONE RECRUIT.

DOWSING?! MY MAN! HOW MANY BODIES HAVE YOU FOUND?

W-WELL... I CAN DO SOME DOWSING.

ALL RIGHT, YOU'RE NEXT. WHAT CAN *YOU* DO?

Makoto Numata
Special Talent: Dowsing (Corpses Only)

NO, IT'S LIKE...I HELP MY FRIENDS FIND LOST JEWELRY OR WALLETS, AND--

BODIES ...?

...TH-THEN I GUESS I WILL.

JEWELRY? *WALLETS?* HOW ARE WE SUPPOSED TO MAKE MONEY FINDING STUFF LIKE *THAT?*

WE NEED SOMEONE WHO CAN FIND BODIES! CORPSES! IF YOU CAN'T DETECT THE DEAD, GET OUT OF HERE!

UM...

MYSELF, KIND SIR? THE SPIRITS; I SEE AND CONVERSE WITH THEM.

WELL, OUR CLUB IS KIND OF...SPECIAL ...SO, WHAT CAN *YOU* DO?

CORPSES? AH, THE DEAD...THEY WHO HASTEN FORTH NOT FROM THEIR CHARNEL CLAY...

who *are* these guys?

REALLY?! YOU'RE JUST THE KIND WE'RE LOOKING FOR!

SEVEN ARE THEY THAT DWELL WITHIN MY BODY...MATTHIAS, IT IS *HE* WHO HAS SPEECH WITH SPIRITS...BELPHEGOR HAS DIALOGUE WITH DEMONS...JULIE LIKES TENNIS AND LONG WALKS ON THE BEACH...

HUH? WHAT DO YOU MEAN?

NOT I *ALONE*, SIR, BUT RATHER, THE VOICES INSIDE.

Kereellis

Special Talent: Puppet (Alien)

CAN'T SPELL GOTH LOLI WITHOUT THE LOLI! HEY, NUTBAR, EACH OF YOUR PERSONALITIES GOT THEIR OWN MYSPACE PAGE? MAYBE YOU BETTER ENROLL IN A *MENTAL HOSPITAL* INSTEAD OF COLLEGE!

Yuji Yata

Special Talent: Channeling

WELL, *REALLY!* ORDINARILY WE GOTHIC LOLITAS STRIVE TO EMULATE THE MANNERS OF A MORE REFINED AGE, BUT *YOU* CAN JUST GO FUCK YOURSELF!

I'M SORRY... THAT WASN'T ME.

Yeah-uh! LIKE, YOU ARE ABOUT TO ENTER THE MOST FASCINATING SPHERE OF UNDERGRADUATE WORK...

Haven't I seen you cosplay as Mumume-tan?

UM...I'M NAKANO. MY SPECIAL TALENT IS MAKING FIGURINES AND MODELS.

WOW! IS THAT A LIFE-SIZE MODEL?

EMBALMING...?

*Hmm...*IF YOU'RE GOOD WITH YOUR *hands,* MAYBE YOU CAN DO SOME EMBALMING.

...DEAD?

AMAZING. THE TRUTH IS, *I* HAVE A LIFE-SIZE ASUKA FIGURE IN MY ROOM, AND...

drool! you even put in hair down--

OH, *yeah.* TAKE A LOOK AT THIS.

PRETTY *good,* HUH? YOU WOULDN'T EVEN THINK SHE WAS *dead.* I EMBALMED HER FOR A LOCAL SURGICAL SCHOOL.

...THE WORLD OF forensic medicine!

FAR AWAY, IS MY GUESS.

NOW, YOU'LL NOTICE SHE'S NOT *gray* LIKE CADAVERS EMBALMED FOR STUDY USUALLY ARE--*that's* BECAUSE I USED A CUSTOM MIX OF 38% FORMALDEHYDE AND RED DYE, WITH A GRAVITY-FEED--WHERE DID HE GO?

SEE, THIS IS THE *"before."* HORRIBLE, ISN'T IT? HER OWN BROTHER CHOPPED HER INTO PIECES.

THIS PART *here* WAS STARTING TO ROT ALREADY, AND I HAD A HARD TIME RESTORING IT...

Keiko Makino

Special Talent: Embalming

WHAT *IS* IT WITH WOMEN AND THEIR MUTILATED CORPSE PICTURES?! DID *YOU* SEE THE GUY TEAR OUT OF HERE? THERE WAS AN ACTUAL PUFF OF SMOKE, LIKE IN THE *ROAD RUNNER* CARTOONS!

UM, WHY ...?

WELL, I KNOW... BUT...

YEAH. IN *various* CONDITIONS.

LOOK, IF THEY'RE GOING TO JOIN OUR GROUP, THEY'RE GOING TO HAVE TO BE OKAY AROUND CORPSES.

YOU *SEE*? NOT A SINGLE NEW MEMBER AGAIN THIS YEAR. HOW ARE WE SUPPOSED TO CONTINUE AT THIS RATE--

...WE LOST THEM ALL IN UNDER TWO MINUTES.

UM...

M-MY NAME IS REI...REI YANAGI. BUT I DON'T REALLY HAVE A SPECIAL TALENT...

--OH, YEAH... SO YOU ARE.

UM...I'M STILL HERE.

OH...WELL... DON'T WORRY ABOUT IT. BESIDES, YOU *ARE* THE ONLY ONE LEFT...

UM, THEN... CAN I JOIN?

WANT ME TO CRUSH YOUR LITTLE FELT HEAD?

NO TALENT? YOU'LL FIT RIGHT IN WITH NUMATA!

...TH-THANK YOU.

...YOU STUCK IT OUT, DIDN'T YOU? SO... WELCOME TO THE CLUB.

22

23

Kuro Karatsu

Special Talent: Itako

...B-BUT WHAT DO YOU GUYS *DO* WITH ALL THESE SKILLS, THOUGH? YOU SAID YOU WERE STUDENT ENTREPRENEURS... HOW DO YOU MAKE *MONEY* THIS WAY...?

UM... INTEREST-ING.

SO WHADDYA THINK?

WE'RE NOT LIKE MOST PEOPLE AT THIS SCHOOL...WHO HAVE A JOB LINED UP AT THE FAMILY TEMPLE AFTER THEY GRADUATE.

DON'T WORRY. THE TRUTH IS, WE ALREADY HAVE A BUSINESS.

WELL, WE KINDA WONDER ABOUT THAT SOMETIMES *ourselves*.

OUR FIRM IS CALLED...
THE KUROSAGI CORPSE DELIVERY SERVICE.

NO INTERN-SHIPS FOR US. WE HAD TO FORM OUR OWN COMPANY.

WE'RE NOT *REALLY* THE KUROSAGI CMM CLUB.

青木ヶ原樹海
AOKIGAHARA FOREST
The Aokigahara Forest covers a 13.5 square-
kilometer area. Between the northern peak of
Mount Fuji, Lake Nishi, Lake Shoji, and Lake
Motosu. Home to several species of flora and
beeches, the depth and darkness of the forest
canopy makes Aokigahara known as the "Wood-
land Sea." Please don't kill yourself here.
Ministry of Health & Welfare,
Yamanashi Prefecture
厚生省 山梨県

STOP!
Suicide Prevention
Message Box
Fuji Yoshida

ブロロ....ン

キ
ッ

YOU WANT TO JOIN US FOR OUR NEXT RUN? WE'LL SHOW YOU HOW THE BUSINESS WORKS. I SUPPOSE WE CAN CALL IT ON-THE-JOB TRAINING.

UM... OKAY.

SO WHAT HAPPENS NOW? ARE YOU GOING TO, LIKE...FIND THEM AND TALK THEM OUT OF IT...?

UMM... ISN'T THIS AOKIGAHARA FOREST? P-PEOPLE KILL THEMSELVES HERE...

ALL RIGHT, WE'RE HERE. COME ON, EVERYONE!

FIND THEM AND TALK THEM **OUT** OF IT?! THEY'RE **ALREADY** OUT OF IT!

チャラン

S-SUICIDE VICTIM...?

WHAT NUMATA IS TRYING TO SAY IS THAT OUR BUSINESS BEGINS WITH FINDING A SUICIDE VICTIM.

THAT'S RIGHT...AND THIS IS WHERE I COME IN.

"AS WELL"? IF YOU CAN FIND SOMETHING ELSE, DON'T YOU THINK YOU SHOULD?

SHUT UP!

ahem! THIS IS CALLED DOWSING. NORMALLY, IT'S USED TO FIND VEINS OF PRECIOUS ORE OR WATER, BUT IN MY CASE, THE PENDULUM IS ABLE TO LOCATE DEAD BODIES AS WELL...

PEOPLE KILL THEMSELVES LIKE THEY'RE HITTING THE RESET BUTTON ON A game.

SPRINGTIME... SEASON OF SUICIDE. A LOT PEOPLE GET TURNED DOWN FOR JOBS OR COLLEGES.

I'M GETTING A READING! CORPSE AHOY!

C'MON! LET'S GO LOOK AT CORPSES!

HEY... WAIT UP, NUMATA!

UM...I DON'T WANT TO LOOK AT--

28

THEY DO...THAT'S WHY YOU'LL FIND THINGS LIKE THIS IN THE FOREST-- WHERE PEOPLE TIED RIBBONS AS MARKERS, OR SPRAY-PAINTED ARROWS ON THE TREES...

UM, I DON'T KNOW ABOUT THIS...DON'T PEOPLE GET LOST HERE ALL THE TIME, TOO?

HE NEVER CHANGES.

...BUT THESE DAYS, YOU CAN DO A *MUCH* BETTER JOB OF FINDING YOUR WAY WITH A GPS UNIT.

10km

COMPASSES HAVE A REPUTATION FOR BEING USELESS HERE--THEY SAY IT'S BECAUSE OF THE MAGNETIC NATURE OF THE LOCAL ROCKS...

WAAHHH!!!

I BOUGHT ONE IN A RARE MOMENT OF SURPLUS.

I DIDN'T KNOW WE HAD ONE OF THOSE.

WELL, HE'S ALWAYS LIKE THAT, SO I'M SURE HE'LL BE FI--

BUT NUMATA RAN OFF ON HIS OWN...

IT'S NOTHING... *NOTHING, I TELL YOU!* JUST SLIPPED ON SOME MOSSY DETRITUS!

YOU ALL RIGHT DOWN THERE, NUMATA?

...*I LOST MY PENDULUM!*

OH, *MAN*...

UM...

YES, EXACTLY.

SO...YOU NEED TO FIND A BODY FIRST...?

WHAT KIND OF A TRAINING SESSION IS THIS GOING TO BE IF WE CAN'T FIND ANY BODIES...?

...KIND OF USELESS, ISN'T HE?

HEYYYY, YOU'RE A QUICK STUDY, NEWBIE!

Huh? HOW DO YOU KNOW?

...DOWN THERE.

...I TH-THINK MAYBE THERE'S ONE THAT WAY.

WELL... UM...

OH. YOU MEAN...

WELL, THAT'S NOT EXACTLY UNCOMMON IN THIS HOTSPOT FOR SUICIDE.

SLEEPING PILL... HALCION.

WHAT IS IT?

HAD TO HAVE BEEN RECENT...IT RAINED A FEW DAYS AGO. MAYBE SOMEONE WAS HAVING SECOND THOUGHTS, AND DROPPED THEM TO MARK A TRAIL...?

...IT'S BEEN KNOWN TO HAPPEN.

...THEY'RE RUNNING IN A SORT OF LINE.

BUT I SEE MORE OF THEM OVER HERE...

HOW MANY SO FAR?

OKAY, I FOUND ANOTHER ONE.

...I COUNT NINETEEN.

OKAY, LET'S GO!

NICE GOING, NEW GIRL!

HEY! DON'T LEAVE ME BEHIND! I CAN STILL DO STUFF LIKE CARRY HEAVY OBJECTS!

ALMOST TWO SHEETS' WORTH...THAT'S ABOUT WHAT YOU CAN GET PRESCRIBED AT A LOCAL CLINIC WITHOUT RAISING SUSPICION.

...oh!

SO THEN, THE BODY SHOULD BE RIGHT AROUND...

...WILD ANIMALS HAVE BEEN AT HER...

AFTER SHE FELL ASLEEP...THERE'S A BLUE TINGE IN THE EXPOSED SKIN. PEOPLE THINK IT ONLY HAPPENS IN COLD WEATHER, BUT LOCAL *conditions* CAN CONTRIBUTE AS WELL.

I THINK SHE *froze* TO DEATH.

NO MORE EMPTY SHEETS...BUT THIS DOESN'T MAKE SENSE. IF SHE ONLY TOOK ONE PILL, HOW DID SHE OVER-DOSE...?

RIGHT...AOKIGA-HARA FOREST IS A THOUSAND METERS ABOVE SEA LEVEL.

YEAH.

ASK HER WHERE SHE WANTS TO GO.

OKAY, WE'VE GOT A CLIENT. NOW WE'LL SHOW YOU THE NEXT STEP IN THE BUSINESS.

THAT'S RIGHT. WHEN WE FIND A BODY, KARATSU USES HIS ABILITY TO SPEAK TO THEM.

WHERE SHE WANTS TO GO...?

AND IF THE BODY IS BADLY *damaged*, I USE MY EMBALMING SKILLS TO RESTORE IT.

IF WE CAN'T GET ENOUGH INFORMATION FROM THE BODY, I RESEARCH IT ON THE NET.

ME? UH...I GET COSMIC ADVICE. AND RUN ERRANDS.

WHAT DO *you* DO, YATA?

WOW. SHE EVEN STUMPED KEREELLIS.

UM...

BUT...CAN YOU *REALLY* MAKE MONEY DOING THIS?

SEE? IT'S A *REVOLU-TIONARY*, *INNOVATIVE* ENTREPRE-NEURIAL APPROACH!

YEAH...WE... UM...STILL NEED TO WORK ON THAT SECTION OF THE BUSINESS PLAN...

SO... HOW'S IT GOING?

36

SOMETIMES, IF IT'S BEEN AWHILE, THE SPIRIT SORT OF FADES AWAY ON ITS OWN...

NO, IT'S JUST LIKE SASAKI SAID EARLIER. SHE HASN'T BEEN DEAD *that* LONG.

WHAT'S THE MATTER, KARATSU? CAN'T CALL THE SPIRIT BACK?

WELL...

LET ME LOOK...

I MAY HAVE TO GET ONLINE FOR THIS. DOES SHE HAVE ANY ID ON HER?

...JUST AN ENVELOPE.

WHAT THE...? THIS IS ON OUR COLLEGE'S LETTERHEAD...

〒102

神奈川県

コーポ春乃荘0

千代田仏教大学

東京都 千代田区 不仁身2-103-3

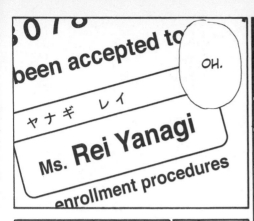

been accepted to

OH.

ヤナギ　レイ
Ms. **Rei Yanagi**

enrollment procedures

I SEE,
THEN...

Yaichi

A spirit attached to Karatsu

...THIS
BODY IS
YOURS.

38

39

...JUST HOW THIRD-RATE IS OUR SCHOOL?

"Backup of a backup"?

...THE ONLY COLLEGE I GOT ACCEPTED TO WAS THE ONE I TOOK...AS A BACKUP OF A BACKUP.

I WAS NEVER VERY GOOD AT STUDYING--BUT STILL, I DIDN'T THINK SO MANY SCHOOLS WOULD TURN ME DOWN...

...AND YOU CAME OUT TO THE WOODS.

BUT YOU *took* THE ONE ACCEPTANCE LETTER WITH YOU...

BUT I'M JUST LIKE YOU GUYS...I DIDN'T HAVE ANY CONNECTIONS TO A TEMPLE OR ANYTHING LIKE THAT...

WHEN I WALKED INTO AOKIGAHARA, I BEGAN TO THINK, MAYBE I SHOULDN'T GIVE UP LIKE THIS...

...I TOOK THE LAST PILL, AND I THOUGHT... WHEN I WAKE UP...I'LL GO THERE AND SEE.

...I COULDN'T FACE MY PARENTS AND TELL THEM WHAT HAD HAPPENED...I JUST PLACED ALL MY REJECTION LETTERS ON THE KITCHEN TABLE...

EVERYONE ELSE JUST IGNORED ME...YOU GUYS WERE THE ONLY ONES WHO NOTICED.

I THOUGHT YOU WERE JUST AN ORDINARY STUDENT.

YOU DID?

...IT'S TOO LATE NOW.

I WISH I *HAD* GONE TO YOUR SCHOOL, BUT LOOK AT ME DOWN THERE...

WE'VE MET A LOT OF DEAD PEOPLE... MAYBE IT RUBS OFF.

I GUESS IT'S BECAUSE I KNEW...

...IT'S JUST A BODY.

...

THESE THINGS CAN BE HORRIBLE, LIKE YOU SAID, MAKINO. I WONDER WHY I *DIDN'T* FREAK OUT BACK IN THE CLUB ROOM...

YOU MUST SEE STUFF LIKE THIS ALL THE TIME.

CAN I...?

LISTEN, I KNOW A WAY TO CLEAR UP THAT REGRET. LET US TAKE YOU TO OUR SCHOOL THE WAY YOU WANTED TO... IN YOUR OLD FLESH.

...YEAH, IT IS.

NEED A LIFT BACK TO CAMPUS?

YOU'RE NOT A CUSTOMER ...YOU'RE A MEMBER OF THE *CLUB!*

I...I'D LIKE THAT VERY MUCH.

42

BAWWLL!!!

NUMATA'S TAKING THIS PRETTY WELL.

...FIVE MINUS FIVE EQUALS *zero*, Y'KNOW.

AT LEAST HER FAMILY WAS GLAD WE FOUND HER.

AS LONG AS THEY DON'T FIND OUT SHE'S ONLY HERE IN SPIRIT.

OH MAN, THAT IS SO NOT FUNNY AS A PUNCH LINE!

AND WE GET TO KEEP OUR ROOM, TOO, 'CAUSE WE ACTUALLY ENROLLED A NEW RECRUIT.

HMM...I WAS GOING TO TELL THEM TO SETTLE DOWN...BUT I GUESS SHE WOULD HAVE HAD TO GET USED TO THOSE IDIOTS, TOO.

ACTUALLY, IT'S SO NOT FUNNY AT *ALL!* COME OVER HERE FOR A *PUPPET BEATING!*

WAIT, NUMATA! DON'T YOU THINK IT'S A *LITTLE* FUNNY?

1st delivery: a café in a campus town—the end

ALWAYS THROWING MONEY AWAY!

giggle! WHAT DID YOU BUY *THIS* TIME?

STEADY... STEADY...

HOW ABOUT HERE?

HMM... A LITTLE MORE TO THE RIGHT.

I DIDN'T THROW IT AWAY...I *NEEDED* ANOTHER REFRIGERATOR-- JUST TO STORE THE CHAMPAGNE. THE ONE WE'VE GOT IS TOO FULL OF CAVIAR.

49

I'M NOT ENVIOUS AT *ALL!* NOT ONE BIT! *NO SIRREE!*

OKAY, I GOT IT. NON-MATERIALISTIC. JUST LIKE THE BUDDHA.

A *real* man uses a *ball-point!* Just like Joe Pesci!

sigh...IT'S ALMOST LIKE THEY LIVE IN ANOTHER WORLD...

DAMNIT, I'M SOOOOOOO ENVIOUS!!

HE WAS RIGHT, YOU KNOW. THAT REFRIGERATOR WAS WORTH 40 MILLION YEN. I MAKE MAYBE A MILLION A YEAR AS A PART-TIMER. SO IT *WOULD* TAKE ME A LIFETIME.

LOOK AT THEM! ROLLING IN DOUGH! *WE* WORK HARD, DON'T WE? "RIGHT EFFORT"-- EIGHTFOLD PATH, ITEM SIX?

DON'T ASK ME. YOU KNOW I HAD TO TAKE THAT CLASS OVER.

UM...SORRY TO SAY GOODBYE ALREADY, BUT...

I SAW THAT GUY LAST WEEK ON TV. HE'S A FAMOUS WEDDING PLANNER. THAT FRIDGE WE DELIVERED? HE WAS ALREADY BOASTING ABOUT IT.

...ARE YOU *SERIOUS?* AND HOW DO YOU KNOW SO MUCH ABOUT IT?

IF THERE'S ANYTHING ELSE YOU NEED, YOU CAN FIND ME IN THE MANGA CAFÉ.

NO, THANK YOU FOR THE WORK.

...HERE'S YOUR SHARE OF THE PAY. THANKS FOR HELPING OUT--ONE OF OUR GUYS CAME DOWN WITH A COLD...

actually, his puppet did...I won't go into details.

IT'S WHERE HE LIVES...

"MANGA CAFÉ"?

SEE YOU...

AT LEAST WE'VE GOT THE CLUB ROOM TO FALL BACK ON...BUT, SITUATION LIKE HIS, WHERE CAN HE AFFORD TO SLEEP, BUT A BOOTH IN A MANGA CAFÉ...?

THE DUDE TOLD ME HE GOT AN ART DEGREE, BUT HE HASN'T BEEN ABLE TO FIND A STEADY JOB SINCE HE GRADUATED... NOTHING BUT PART-TIME WORK. HELL, I CAN RELATE.

ALL-NIGHT DISCOUNT PACKAGE, PLEASE.

...OKAY, TAKE BOOTH #17.

...HOW LONG IS IT GOING TO BE LIKE THIS...?

HUH?

DAMN, YOU'RE MEAN. WHY DIDN'T YOU TELL HIM?

OH, THAT? ONE OF THE DELIVERY BOYS DROPPED IT...

WELL, IT'S JUST A BIT OF TRASH...

HM.

I WOULDN'T CALL IT THAT. IT'S A *BIJIN-GA.* TRADITIONAL GLAMOUR SKETCH. VERY TASTEFUL, ACTUALLY.

...HE'S LOOKING FOR A JOB, ISN'T HE...?

TELL YOU WHAT. ONE OF YOU GO FIND THIS KID, AND BRING HIM HERE.

HUH?

SOMETHING OLD, SOMETHING NEW, GOES THE WEDDING RHYME. AND WE'RE HERE TO LEARN ABOUT AN *OLD* STYLE OF MARRIAGE THAT'S BECOMING THE *NEWEST* TREND IN TOKYO. MR. KANEARI?

103
Kurosagi CMM Club

WE'VE STARTED ARRANGING MEETINGS FOR SOMETHING CALLED THE *MEIKONSHIKI.*

Trendy CHICK

MEIKONSHIKI MEANS "AFTERLIFE MARRIAGE CEREMONY"

THAT'S RIGHT, EIKO. WE'RE BASICALLY BRINGING BACK A CLASSIC TRADITION, INTENDED FOR THOSE WHO'VE PASSED AWAY WITHOUT THE SOLACE OF HAVING FOUND THAT SPECIAL PERSON IN LIFE...

OH, YEAH...THE DAY KEREELLIS HAD THE SPACE SNOT.

...HUH? YOU'RE RIGHT.

SAY, KARATSU, ISN'T THIS THE ITALIAN PEN GUY? THE HILLS TRIBE DUDE?

...WELL, EIKO, THE IDEA IS THAT IF TWO PEOPLE HAVE DIED AT A YOUNG AGE, WE CAN STILL BRING THEM TOGETHER AFTERWARDS.

WHY DON'T YOU TELL US A LITTLE BIT ABOUT IT, MR. KANEARI?

THEY DON'T DO IT FOR THE DEAD...THEY DO IT FOR THEIR PARENTS.

UMMM.. WHAT'S THE POINT OF GETTING MARRIED AFTER YOU *die*?

IT WAS MOST PREVALENT IN CHINA, WHERE A WOMAN'S DEATH EXPENSES ARE THE RESPONSIBILITY OF THE FAMILY SHE'S MARRIED OFF TO. IF YOU DIE SINGLE, THERE'S NO ONE TO BURY OR MOURN FOR YOU. SO, BY MARRYING HER TO SOMEONE'S *SON* WHO DIED SINGLE, THE SON IS HONORED WITH A WIFE...IN EXCHANGE FOR FOOTING THE COST OF HIS NEW BRIDE'S BURIAL.

WHAT HE'S TALKING ABOUT, ANTHROPOLOGISTS CALL *SHIGO KEKKON*. THEY DID IT IN NORTHEASTERN JAPAN. SIMILAR RITES EXISTED IN OKINAWA...CHINA, TAIWAN, AND KOREA, TOO. YOU CAN FIND INSTANCES OF IT THROUGHOUT EAST ASIAN SOCIETY.

YAY, CULTURAL TRADITION.

ARE YOU PUTTING ME ON?

OF COURSE, THERE *HAVE* BEEN CASES WHERE THEY DIDN'T WAIT FOR THE BRIDE TO DIE...WOMEN MURDERED SO THEY COULD BE USED IN THE RITUAL...

EVERYTHING. WE'RE ALL GOING TO ONE OF MR. KANEARI'S EVENTS NEXT WEEK.

WHAT?!

WE'RE BEING MURDERED ON OUR BUDGET, EARTHLING. ANYWAY, WHAT'S IT GOT TO DO WITH US?

BUT...THIS IS MORE LIKE A *funeral* THAN AN ARRANGED MARRIAGE MEETING.

IT'S BOTH... THAT'S THE WHOLE IDEA.

NOT JUST US. I BROUGHT SOMEONE ELSE.

SASAKI, WHAT ARE WE DOING HERE *anyway?*

CLOAK ROOM

YES, AND SHE GIVES ME THE PERFECT EXCUSE.

Oh! THAT'S RIGHT...*um,* YOUR SISTER WAS MURDERED WITH YOUR PARENTS WHEN YOU WERE LITTLE...I'M SORRY, SASAKI, I...

WELL, KEREELLIS WAS RIGHT--PROFITS HAVEN'T BEEN GOOD LATELY. BUT SINCE WE'RE ALREADY USED TO HANDLING DEAD BODIES, I THOUGHT I'D CHECK OUT AN ALTERNATE BUSINESS MODEL.

UM... *excuse* ...?

LIKE, WHEN WILL I LEARN NOT TO SHOW ANY *human emotion* AROUND YOU?

59

DEAR FRIENDS AND GUESTS...WE'D LIKE TO WELCOME YOU ALL TO OUR MEIKONSHIKI MEET-UP THIS AFTERNOON.

PLEASE GET TO KNOW THE OTHER FAMILIES HERE TODAY AS YOU ENJOY OUR FINE FOOD AND DRINK.

...MAY YOU FIND THE PERFECT PARTNER FOR YOUR LOVED ONE IN HEAVEN.

IT'LL BE FINE. SEE? THEY'RE OFFSETTING THE COST OF US BEING HERE.

THIS IS, *um*, KIND OF *extravagant*. WASN'T IT *expensive* TO GET IN HERE?

YES. IT WAS 300,000 YEN PER PARTY.

--*pssh!*

...300,000? I THOUGHT WE'RE REALLY TIGHT ON OUR *budget?*

YES SIR, WE'VE GOT PLENTY.

HEY... MORE *CHAMPAGNE!*

THAT'S RIGHT! OUT OF THAT *FANCY* REFRIGER-ATOR!

Like, YOU BETTER WATCH OUT. EVEN BUDDHA PUNISHED EVIL.

ホーーッホホホホッ

I'VE GOT IT ALL FIGURED OUT. IF THEY WORK HERE FOR THE REST OF THE MONTH, THEIR COMBINED PAY WILL COME TO 300,000 YEN EXACTLY.

DUNNO.

I DON'T GET THIS PLAN. WHY DID SASAKI AND MAKINO COME AS GUESTS, WHILE WE HAD TO SIGN ON AS WAITERS?

OH, HEY...! GUESS WE'RE PART-TIMING NOW, TOO. WHAT HAVE THEY GOT YOU DOING...?

...H-HI.

WELL, IT'S K-KINDA COOL ACTUALLY... THEY HIRED ME AS *MUSAKARI EMA* ARTIST.

MUSAKARI EMA? WHAT'S THAT?

OH...THOSE THINGS YOU WRITE YOUR WISHES ON FOR GETTING INTO SCHOOLS AND SUCH. SORRY, I'M NOT SHINTO.

YOU SEE, WE DO A RENDER-ING OF THE DECEASED COUPLE, AND PLACE THEM ON AN *EMA*...

AH, MY DEAR DELIVERY BOY! *MUSAKARI* IS A QUAINT TERM FOR MARRIAGE, IN THE NORTH-EASTERN DIALECT FROM WHERE WE TAKE THESE RITUALS...

...?...YES... WELL, IN THE *TSUGARU* REGION, THE *EMA* IS USED TO OFFICIALLY REGISTER A POSTHUMOUS MARRIAGE.

WE'RE TAKING A PAGE FROM THEIR TRADITION, AND DOING THE SAME BY PLACING SUCH A DRAWING IN OUR SHRINE AS PART OF THE *MEIKONSHIKI*.

...REALLY, I THINK YOU HAD TOO MUCH EDUCATION FOR A WAITER. WE REGARD AFTER-DEATH UNIONS AS NON-DENOMINA-TIONAL...IT DOESN'T MATTER IF YOU'RE SHINTO OR CATHOLIC.

SHRINE? YOU'RE HOLDING THIS EVENT IN A *CHURCH.*

NOW, YOU DIDN'T SAY ANYTHING TO HIM YOU SHOULDN'T... DID YOU?

N-NO...

O-OKAY ...

MR. SEIJO IS WAITING FOR US IN THE VIP LOUNGE. HE'LL BE EAGER TO SEE YOUR *MUSAKARI EMA* DRAWING.

WHAT MATTERS IS THE PEACE OF MIND FOR GRIEVING FAMILIES.

I KNOW IT'S DIFFICULT TO TALK ABOUT IT. FOR ME, IT WAS MY OLDER BROTHER. A TRAFFIC ACCIDENT, LAST YEAR...

IT...IT WAS MY YOUNGER SISTER...HAD SHE STILL BEEN ALIVE, SHE...SHE WOULD HAVE BEEN ABOUT THE...THE AGE OF MY FRIEND HERE...

...WHO WAS IT THAT YOU LOST?

OH, I'M SORRY. MY SISTER WAS VERY PARTICULAR ABOUT LOOKS.

...UH-HUH.

DID THEY TURN YOU DOWN, TOO...?

I THINK WE SHOULD *leave* SOON.

WELL, I'VE SEEN ENOUGH, ANYWAY.

64

THERE WERE MAYBE A DOZEN FAMILIES THERE, EACH PAYING 300,000 YEN TO GET IN.

WELL, HE DOESN'T SEEM LIKE THE CHARITABLE TYPE TO ME.

THE CATERING, THE VENUE, THE ORCHESTRA...IT'S ALL VERY HIGH CLASS. SO HIGH, I STILL DON'T SEE WHERE THEY'RE MAKING MONEY OFF THIS.

YEAH. SOMETHING IS THE MATTER AROUND HERE.

WHAT DO YOU MEAN?

YEAH, NOT LIKE SOME IDIOTS.

IS SOMETHING THE MATTER, KARATSU...?

65

MY DEAR DEPARTED SON WAS BETROTHED TO HER.

NOT ONLY AN OFFENSE TO YOU, MR. SEIJO. SURELY YOUR SON IS WEEPING IN THE AFTERLIFE.

AFTER MY SON'S SUDDEN PASSING, THEY CAME AROUND TO GIVE THEIR REGRETS THAT IT COULDN'T HAPPEN...CAN YOU *IMAGINE* HOW THAT FELT...?

WE, THE SEIJO FAMILY, ARRANGED IT WITH THE GOTOKUJI FAMILY YEARS AGO, WHEN THEY BOTH WERE CHILDREN.

DON'T CONCERN YOURSELF ANY FURTHER, SIR...WE SHALL MAKE ALL THE ARRANGEMENTS.

MONEY IS NOT AN ISSUE.

...IT'S A MATTER OF FAMILY HONOR, YOU SEE. SOMETHING ALL TOO FEW SEEM TO UNDERSTAND TODAY, MR. KANEARI.

67

GOT HER FACE RIGHT? AND THE NAME?

...Y-YES.

YEAH, I REMEMBER WRITING A WISH ON AN *EMA* TO GET INTO SCHOOL. DIDN'T WORK, OF COURSE...YOU CAN'T COUNT ON GOOD LUCK TO GET BY IN THIS WORLD. BUT I DO BELIEVE IN *BAD* LUCK...

...I'VE SEEN IT HAPPEN WITH THIS SHRINE.

2nd delivery: romance—the end

3rd delivery

僕は死なないだろう

i probably won't die

...MARRY
ME.

MORGUE

73

...WELL...I'M ORGANIZING A YOUTH SOFTBALL LEAGUE TO HELP KEEP WAYWARD LIBERAL ARTS GRADUATES OUT OF TROUBLE.

SO WHAT DO YOU WANT FROM US TODAY, SASAYAMA ...?

HA, HA, BALDY.

BUT THAT'S *NEXT* WEEK. *TODAY,* I NEED YOU TO ID A CORPSE, IDIOT.

THAT'S NOT WHAT I MEANT...

HAVEN'T WE BEEN OVER THIS BEFORE? SHE'S A JANE DOE. OTHER-WISE, THE CITY HAS TO PAY FOR HER FUNERAL.

...I DON'T GET IT. WHY DO YOU NEED OUR HELP TO FIND OUT WHO SHE IS?

NO, I DON'T THINK SHE WAS CARRYING A WALLET IN THE FIRST PLACE. INSTEAD SHE WAS A LITTLE TOO MODERN...USING HER CELL PHONE AS HER ATM CARD AND HER TRAIN PASS. VERY CONVENIENT...BUT NOT ANY MORE, AS YOU CAN SEE.

NOT A HOMELESS PERSON WHO DIED IN THE STREET...DIDN'T SHE HAVE ANY IDENTIFICATION ON HER? WAS SHE ROBBED, OR SOMETHING...?

LOOK AT HER. I'D GUESS SHE WAS AN OFFICE WORKER.

DON'T GIVE ME ONE, AND I'LL DO IT.

SO, I JUST NEED YOU TO DO YOUR THING LIKE USUAL.

C'mon, I'll give you a back rub...

WHO ARE YOU...? TELL ME.

76

TELL ME, OLD MAN...

...WERE THOSE MARKS VISIBLE *BEFORE* ...?

...THIS IS COLD, EVEN FOR YOU. AREN'T YOU CONCERNED THAT SHE WAS KILLED BY A SPIRIT FROM BEYOND THIS WORLD...?

NOPE. OUT OF MY JURISDIC-TION, FRIEND.

BY A *GHOST* ...?

...SO IT WAS MURDER?

I DON'T CARE IF IT WAS A GHOST, A GHAST, OR A *GHOULIE!* JUST FIND OUT WHO SHE *IS*, OKAY?

THAT, I DON'T KNOW...

DOESN'T QUITE ADD UP, THOUGH. THE GUY DIED OVER A YEAR AGO. IF HIS GHOST *WANTED* TO TAKE HER WITH HIM...WHY'D HE WAIT SO LONG TO DO IT?

TAKE A LOOK... IT'S HER.

...C'MON, KID, WHAT'S WITH THE LONG FACE? YOU WERE A NET CAFÉ REFUGEE! SLEEPING IN CHAIRS, EATIN' SANDWICHES FOR DINNER! *THIS* MUST BE LIKE GETTING REBORN IN PARADISE!

WHAT DO YOU THINK OF OUR BOSS'S *CONNECTIONS*, HUH? THAT GIRL OVER THERE IS THE NEW ANNOUNCER FROM TV KADOKAWA. AND *THAT* GIRL OVER *THERE* IS A SWIMSUIT MODEL! HEH HEH HEH! AREN'T YOU GLAD YOU JOINED US?

...

'COURSE, MAYBE YOU JUST DON'T GET THIS IS *REAL* YET. SEE THOSE AV STARS OVER THERE? BET YOU JACKED OFF TO THEM ON SCREEN...

NO...I, UM...

HEY! ARE YOU DRUNK *ALREADY*?

WAAA!

...TIME TO GO 3-D!

YES, HELLO ...?

!

81

YES...WELL... IT'S A SYMBOLIC RITUAL, YOU KNOW. SO YES, WE COULD DO IT THAT WAY, TOO. THERE'S A HIGHER FEE...

UMMM...I HEARD ABOUT YOUR MEIKONSHIKI CEREMONY... IS IT TRUE...THE OTHER PERSON DOESN'T HAVE TO BE...DEAD YET...?

ALL RIGHT, SIR. WE CAN ARRANGE AN APPOINT-MENT...

REALLY? AS LONG...AS LONG AS MY BROTHER CAN BE HAPPY, IT'S NOT A PROBLEM...

...A MUSAKARI EMA... JUST LIKE BEFORE.

I NEED YOU TO DRAW AGAIN...

...BACK TO WORK, KID.

WHO IS THE OTHER PARTY, SIR?

AND YOU SAY HE NEVER EVEN KNEW HER NAME? IT'S A HEARTFELT TRAGEDY, SIR. BUT YOU SEE, WE NEED A NAME FOR THE RITUAL...

WELL...THE TRUTH IS...MY BROTHER WAS IN LOVE WITH HER FOR A LONG TIME. BUT HE NEVER HAD THE CHANCE TO TELL HER HOW HE FELT...

...I JUST HAPPENED TO RUN INTO HER AT YOUR GET-TOGETHER.

THAT'S ALL RIGHT. THE THING IS...

MY BROTHER HAD A TELEPHOTO CAMERA, YOU SEE...HE WAS KIND OF SHY, BUT HE BELIEVED ONE DAY THEY'D BE TOGETHER... FOREVER...

SHE'S THE ONE HE'D TALK ABOUT.

...SHE WAS THERE.

YES, Y-YOU'RE RIGHT...

TH-THANK YOU SO MUCH...B-BUT ARE YOU *SURE* THIS ISN'T ILLEGAL...?

I THINK THIS SHOULD BE SUFFICIENT, SIR...WE'LL JUST CHECK THE REGISTRATION FORMS. AND THEN WE'LL SEE TO IT THAT SHE'S BY YOUR BROTHER'S SIDE.

ABSOLUTELY CERTAIN, SIR. AS I SAID, OUR RITE IS SYMBOLIC...WE DO NO MORE THAN PLACE A PICTURE INSIDE A SHRINE.

84

85

HEY, PART-TIMER. PERFECT! I WAS THINKING ABOUT CALLING YOU.

HELLO?

...HUH? WHAT WAS THAT YOU SAID?

I DIDN'T WANT TO DO IT, BUT...

I'M SO SORRY...I... I DREW A PICTURE OF A FRIEND OF YOURS...

THE...YOU KNOW...THE *EMA.* I DREW HER ON ONE. LIKE KANEARI TALKED ABOUT AT THE GET-TOGETHER...

WHAT DO YOU MEAN, YOU DREW A PICTURE...?

HUH? YOU MEAN SASAKI'S SISTER? SHE SAID SHE DIDN'T FIND ANYONE...

87

88

...ACCIDENTAL DEATH... SUICIDE...DIED SUDDENLY IN HER SLEEP...

--WHO'S THERE?!

MARRY ME...

WHAT THE HELL?! WHO *ARE* YOU--

I KNOW THE BRIDE'S NAME. DON'T YOU WANT TO KNOW MINE...?

3rd delivery: i probably won't die——the end

4th delivery

ラブソングはいらない

no need for a love song

チッカ

チッカ

HEY! WHAT'S WRONG? WHAT'S GOING ON, PART-TIMER?!

I DON'T KNOW...IT CUT OFF ALL OF A SUDDEN. LISTEN, I THINK SASAKI MAY BE IN DANGER...I'M GOING TO GO CHECK ON HER.

WHAT'S THE MATTER, KARATSU?

UH... GOT IT.

NO, SASAKI'S IN DANGER... BUT I THINK THE PART-TIMER'S IN TROUBLE. YOU GUYS GO AROUND KANEARI'S OPERA-TION, AND SEE IF YOU CAN FIND HIM.

WELL, GET IN THE CAR, MAN!

...BUT WHY?

YAKUZA, MAN, YAKUZA. THEY LIKE TO DIVERSIFY THEIR PORTFOLIO...AND THESE DAYS, THERE'S EVEN MORE MONEY IN MARRIED BLISS THAN PROSTITUTION. WISE UP AND RELAX, KID--YOU'RE WITH A WINNING CREW NOW...AND YOU'RE GOING TO *STAY* WITH THEM.

THOUGHT POOR PEOPLE WERE SUPPOSED TO KNOW HOW THE WORLD WORKS. MAN, WHERE DO YOU *THINK* THE CAPITAL IS COMING FROM...TO PAY FOR ALL THOSE FANCY RENTS IN ROPPONGI HILLS?

WHERE'D YOU G-GET THAT...? WHAT'S A WEDDING PLANNER DOING WITH A *GUN*...?

I'M GOING STRAIGHT TO THE POLICE AND TELL THEM EVERYTHING, AND THEN-- I WON'T HELP YOU MURDER ANY MORE PEOPLE!

...

NO...

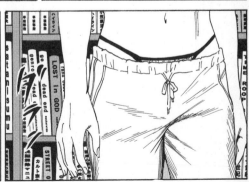

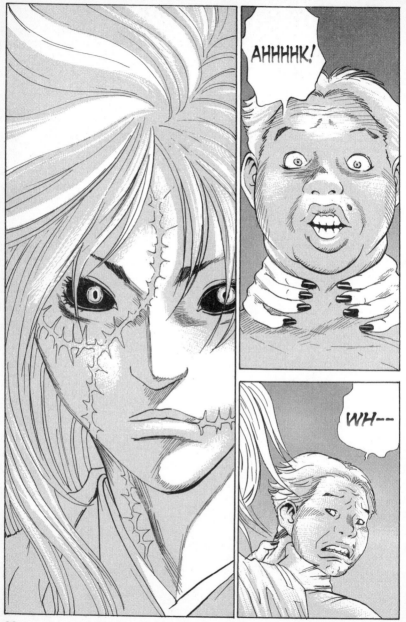

101

H-HEY... I MEAN... ARE YOU ALL RIGHT...?

...YES?

YES. IT SEEMS YOU SAVED ME AGAIN. THANK YOU. SO, WHAT'S GOING ON?

"saved"? "thank you"...?

UM... WELL, ACTUALLY...

UM

...WHAT DO YOU THINK?

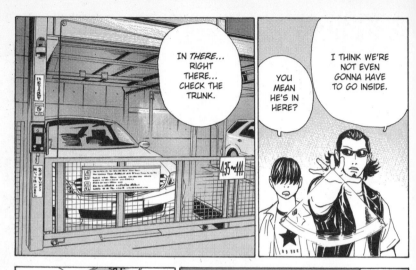

103

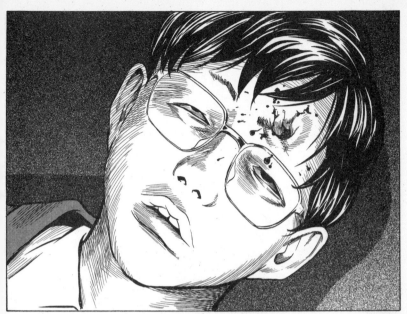

EVEN WITH THE CAR, WE GOT THERE TOO LATE.

I THINK WE'RE ALL A LITTLE LATE...FIGURING OUT WHAT KIND OF PEOPLE WE'RE DEALING WITH.

GOOD THING I STUDIED IN AMERICA, 'CAUSE YOU DON'T COME ACROSS *this* MUCH IN JAPAN. HE WAS SHOT AT CLOSE RANGE. LOOKS LIKE A 9mm SLUG.

FORTUNATELY...

THIS KIND OF KILLING MEANS ONLY ONE THING...ORGANIZED CRIME. AND THE FACT THEY WERE *WILLING* TO DO IT MEANS THEY'D DO THE SAME TO US...IF THEY CATCH ON TO WHO WE ARE.

US AGAINST THE MOB, THOUGH? MAYBE WE SHOULD GO BACK TO THE OLD MAN...

WHAT NOW? THEY'RE GOING TO KEEP ON DOING WHAT THEY'RE DOING...

WHAT'S THIS?

...WE *ARE* WHO WE ARE.

AH-HA...

BLANK. MY GUESS, IT WOULD NEED SOMEONE WITH SKILL TO MAKE IT WORK.

IT'S AN *EMA*...

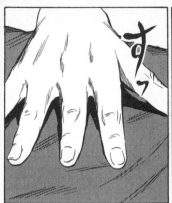

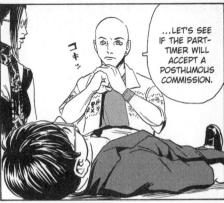

...LET'S SEE IF THE PART-TIMER WILL ACCEPT A POSTHUMOUS COMMISSION.

BOTH HIS PARENTS ARE DEAD...KID DIDN'T SEEM TO HAVE ANYONE. NO WONDER HE WAS A HALF STEP FROM THE STREETS.

SPEAKING OF *TALENT,* I'VE CALLED FOR A FEW EXTRA GIRLS TONIGHT FROM THE AGENCY, BOSS...WHAT DO YOU SAY WE CELEBRATE BEING THE TWO BEST THINGS IN THIS WORLD...?

I'LL DUMP HIM TOMOR-ROW.

TOO BAD...HE HAD TALENT. BUT THERE'S BOUND TO BE ANOTHER ART STUDENT OUT THERE WITH BOTH TALENT *AND* SENSE.

...AND SINGLE.

AND WHAT WOULD THOSE BE...?

ピンポーン
ピンポーン

ALIVE...

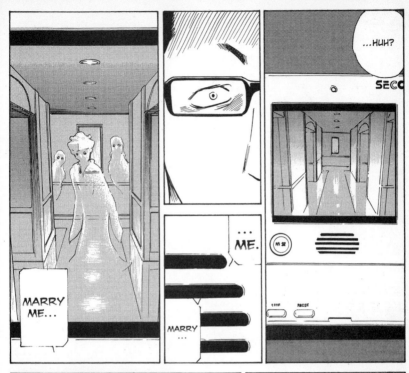

...HUH?

SEC

...
ME.

MARRY
ME...

MARRY
...

HUH? WHAT'S THE MATTER?

TH-THE W-WOMEN ...TH-TH- THEY...

SCARED OF PUSSY IS FOR *PART-TIMERS*...

!

WHA ...?!

WHAT THE...

110

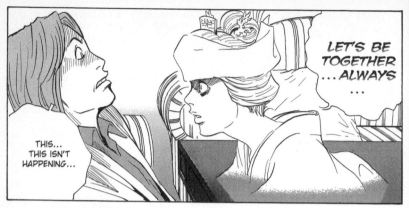

111

あ
あ
あ

I JUST THOUGHT OF SOMETHING. THEY GOT POLYGAMY IN THE AFTERLIFE?

MAYBE AT FIRST THEY JUST USED IT FOR SHOW...THEN THEY DISCOVERED IT HAD POWER...

THIS SHRINE COMES FROM THE NORTH-EAST, WHERE THE *SHIGO KEKKON* TRADITION IS STRONGEST. IT WAS MOVED TO TOKYO DURING THE WAR...SO THAT THE SONS WHO DIED IN BATTLE COULD BE MARRIED IN THE AFTERLIFE.

BUT, *like*, WHAT IS THIS PLACE ANYWAY...?

SASAKI SAYS THE TECHNICAL TERM IS *POLYGYNY*.

115

THEY FOUND
OUT ABOUT
THIS PLACE
SOMEHOW...

...SOMEHOW
NOW, I WISH
I COULD
FORGET IT.

4th delivery: no need for a love song——the end

--LAST ONE THERE HAS TO PAY, OKAY?

WHAT?

HEY! WAIT UP!

117

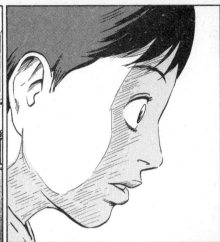

119

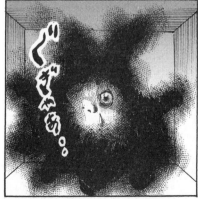

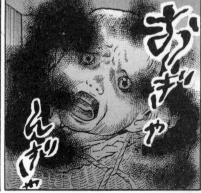

NAMU
AMIDA
BUTSU...
NAMU
AMIDA
BUTSU...

WAAA-
AAH!

助
産
婦

LICENSED
MIDWIFE

5th delivery
二人だけの昼下り
an afternoon with just the two of us

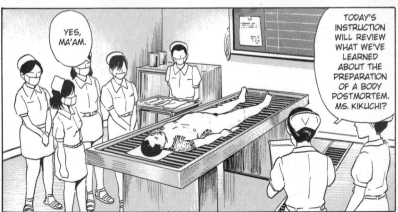

YES, MA'AM.

TODAY'S INSTRUCTION WILL REVIEW WHAT WE'VE LEARNED ABOUT THE PREPARATION OF A BODY POSTMORTEM. MS. KIKUCHI?

LASTLY, THE BODY IS CLEANED WITH COLD WATER, MIXED WITH HOT...

COTTON IS PLACED IN THE MOUTH, EAR, AND NOSE, BEFORE TURNING THE BODY FACE UP TO REMOVE FECES AND URINE THROUGH PRESSURE TO THE LOWER ABDOMEN.

THE PROCEDURE BEGINS BY TURNING THE BODY ONTO ITS LEFT SIDE. PRESSURE IS APPLIED TO THE UPPER ABDOMEN TO EXPEL THE CONTENTS OF THE STOMACH.

NO, NOT WHEN YOU'RE MAKING *SAKASA-MIZU*.

AND COLD WATER, MIXED WITH HOT? SURELY, IF THE WATER IS TOO HOT, YOU ADD *COLD* WATER TO IT...

MS. KIKUCHI? YOU MEAN WITH A STERILIZATION SOLUTION, DON'T YOU?

THIS IS THE ORIGIN OF THE CUSTOM TO WRAP THE KIMONO OF THE DECEASED IN REVERSE ORDER. LIKEWISE, THE WATER FOR WASHING THE BODY IS...

IT MEANS *REVERSE WATER*, MA'AM... IN JAPAN, SINCE ANCIENT DAYS, IT HAS BEEN BELIEVED THAT THE AFTERLIFE IS A MIRROR OF THIS WORLD.

...*SAKA-SA-MIZU?* THAT WASN'T IN THE LESSON PLAN...

125

...THEY STILL HAVE SOULS, YOU KNOW...

I'M SURE THERE ARE CERTAIN CULTURAL TRADITIONS, BUT OUR PURPOSE HERE IS TO CLEAN THE BODY SUFFICIENTLY FOR PRESENTATION...

AHEM. MS. KIKUCHI. NOW, WE'RE REALLY GOING OUTSIDE THE PROCEDURE, AREN'T WE?

NOW, WHY DON'T WE START OVER, MS. KIKUCHI? EXPEL THE CONTENTS OF THE STOMACH, PLEASE.

DON'T MIX MEDICAL PRACTICE WITH SUPERSTITIONS.

THEY--MS. KIKUCHI, PLEASE. THAT'S A MATTER FOR A PRIEST. WE'RE NURSES.

ゴロリ

グッ

...YES, MA'AM.

126

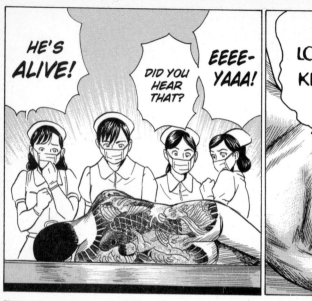

HE'S ALIVE!

DID YOU HEAR THAT?

EEEE-YAAA!

LOC... KER...

IT TALKED.

BUT... DIDN'T YOU HEAR..

WHAT YOU JUST HEARD WAS AIR EXPELLED FROM THE STOMACH, VIBRATING THE VOCAL CORDS...

CALM DOWN!

UH...

UM...

THE DEAD *BELCH*, ALL RIGHT? THAT'S WHY WE PUT COTTON IN THEIR MOUTHS, IF ONE OF YOU CAN BE *TROUBLED* TO...

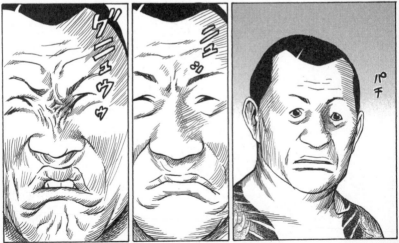

128

129

M-MS. KIKUCHI...?!

MATERNITY WARD

H-HE CAME BACK TO LIFE!

WHAT'S HAPPENING?!

SOMEONE GET THE DOCTOR!

DOCTOR, IT'S THE ALARM FOR THE BABY DROP...

...BOY, THAT'S ONE ENERGETIC BABY...I CAN HEAR HIM ALL THE WAY IN HERE.

FINALLY FINISHED THE ROUNDS FOR THE DAY... HUH?

REALLY...

ダタタタ…

ガチャ

 AREN'T YOU...?

YES, SIR. KIKUCHI. I HEARD THE ALARM...

AND THE BABY...?

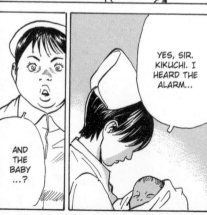

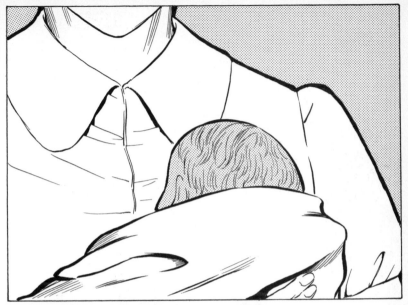

...AGAIN.

132

sigh DON'T YOU KNOW ABOUT THIS, NUMATA?

Watch some more TV...

BABY? DROPPED IT OFF?

YEAH, BUT WHY'D YOU BRING IT HERE...?

SOMEONE DROPPED OFF A BABY?

OH, YEAH, YEAH, YEAH, RIGHT. DIDN'T PEOPLE SAY IT WAS GONNA ENCOURAGE PEOPLE TO DUMP THEIR KIDS?

IT'S SO PEOPLE DON'T JUST ABANDON UNWANTED BABIES TO THE ELEMENTS. HOSPITALS SET UP AN ANONYMOUS DROP-BOX FOR THEM, AND THEY GET CARED FOR.

THIS YEAR ALONE, THEY'VE HAD 67 CASES OF ABAN-DONED CHILDREN AND OVER 200 CASES OF FAMILIES ASKING TO PUT THEIR BABIES UP FOR ADOPTION. AND THEN...WE HAVE CASES LIKE THESE.

YEAH...AND THERE *WAS* AN INCIDENT WHERE A DAD PUT HIS THREE YEAR-OLD IN ONE.

MORGUE

THERE AREN'T TOO MANY RESOURCES IN JAPAN TO ASSIST WITH UNWANTED PREGNANCIES. THAT'S WHY THE HOSPITAL'S NEW DROP BOX SYSTEM HAS BEEN OVERWHELMED... PEOPLE EVEN COME FROM OUTSIDE THE PREFECTURE TO USE IT.

PEOPLE KEEP THEIR PREGNANCIES A SECRET...OR THEY CARRY THEM TO TERM BECAUSE THEY DON'T HAVE THE MONEY FOR AN ABORTION...OR THEY JUST PANIC.

OR BALANCE SHEET... SAME THING.

THAT'S WHY I LIKE YOU, KARATSU. YOU CAN SEE SO DEEP INTO MY HEART.

...WHICH MEANS WHEN THE BABY IS *DEAD*, IT BECOMES YOUR PROBLEM.

EVEN AN IMAGE OF THE PARENT MIGHT HELP ME TRACK THEM DOWN FOR THE FUNERAL COSTS...SEE IF THEY CAN AFFORD FOR DEATH...WHAT THEY COULDN'T FOR LIFE.

ANYTHING WILL HELP. THE DROP BOX SYSTEM WAS DESIGNED FOR PRIVACY...SO I'VE GOT NOTHING AT ALL RIGHT NOW.

Well, actually, it wasn't really the mom, was it...?

WAIT....THE *LAST* TIME YOU TRIED THIS WITH A BABY, ALL WE GOT WAS A SPIRIT PHOTO OF THE BABY'S MOTHER....

...NUMATA, WILL YOU TAKE THE PICTURE FOR ME?

OKAY.

YOU READY, KARATSU ...?

.....

NO FLASH?

WHAT'S WRONG?

スッ

...HUH?

...I CAN'T GET IT TO COME BACK TO THE BODY.

THIS SOUNDS STRANGE, BUT...EVEN THOUGH I CAN FEEL THE SPIRIT STILL CLOSE BY...

I NEED TO PREPARE THE BODY...AND WHO ARE YOU PEOPLE?

THAT'S ODD...IT HASN'T BEEN VERY LONG SINCE THIS BABY DIED...

UM...

SASAYAMA, PUBLIC WELFARE OFFICE... AND THESE ARE... UH...

...JUST SOME ORDINARY GUYS. PLEASE DON'T MIND US.

136

NURSES CALL IT *ANGEL CARE*...BEFORE IT WAS NORMAL FOR PEOPLE TO PASS AWAY IN HOSPITALS, FAMILY MEMBERS USED TO DO THESE KINDS OF TASKS...THESE DAYS, MANY FAMILIES DON'T WANT TO SEE THEIR DEAD...LET ALONE TOUCH THEM.

...MY DEPARTMENT RECEIVES A LOT OF BODIES, BUT I HAVEN'T SEEN ONE PREPARED...

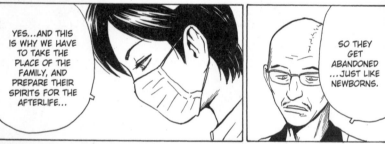

YES...AND THIS IS WHY WE HAVE TO TAKE THE PLACE OF THE FAMILY, AND PREPARE THEIR SPIRITS FOR THE AFTERLIFE...

SO THEY GET ABANDONED ...JUST LIKE NEWBORNS.

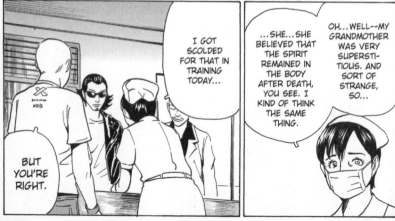

I GOT SCOLDED FOR THAT IN TRAINING TODAY...

...SHE...SHE BELIEVED THAT THE SPIRIT REMAINED IN THE BODY AFTER DEATH, YOU SEE. I KIND OF THINK THE SAME THING.

OH...WELL--MY GRANDMOTHER WAS VERY SUPERSTITIOUS. AND SORT OF STRANGE, SO...

BUT YOU'RE RIGHT.

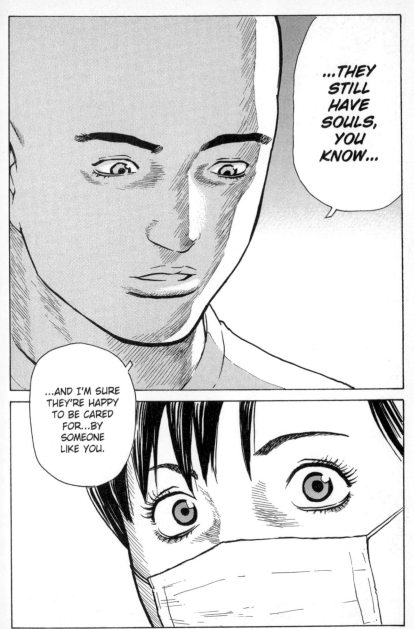

138

LEAVE THEM ALONE...AND COME WITH ME, NUMATA. I NEED YOUR HELP WITH SOMETHING.

B-BUT WE CAN'T LET THIS GO ON!

Are we turning into a love comedy?!

WHAT'S WITH THIS TURN OF EVENTS?!

HE'S STILL YOUNG...LET HIM DO AS HE WANTS.

...WHY AM I DOWSING TOWARDS A WALL...?

チャラン

SO...

BECAUSE ON THE OTHER SIDE OF THIS WALL IS THE BABY DROP-OFF. THEIR ALARM DOESN'T DETECT IF IT'S ALIVE OR DEAD...BUT YOURS WILL.

140

HUH? WHY DON'T WE JUST WATCH IT FROM THE OUTSIDE?

AND IT'S NOT LIKE PEOPLE DROP OFF DEAD BABIES EVERY *DAY*, RIGHT?

WHACK OF THE CANE, *ONE*--IF WE KEEP WATCH OUTSIDE, NOBODY'S GOING TO GO *NEAR* THAT DROP BOX...

OW...

OW...! INTENTION-ALLY? WHAT DO YOU MEAN?

...SUSPECTS THEY'RE BEING LEFT INTENTION-ALLY.

WHACK OF THE CANE, *TWO*-- OLD STITCH-DOME HERE... YEAH, I *KNOW* YOU CALL ME THAT...

赤ちゃんのゆりかご

WHAT BETTER WAY TO DISCREDIT THE PROJECT, WHAT BETTER WAY TO SHOCK...THAN BY LEAVING *DEAD* BABIES IN A LOCKER DESIGNED TO SAVE THEIR LIVES...?

PEOPLE PROTESTED THE INTRODUCTION OF THESE BABY DROP-BOXES. TALKING HEADS ON TV...EDITORIALS... PEOPLE SAYING IT JUST ENCOURAGES PARENTS TO IGNORE THEIR RESPONSIBILITIES.

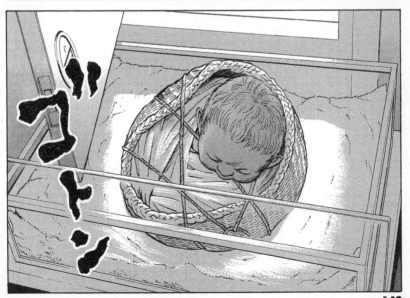

143

5th delivery: an afternoon with just the two of us—the end

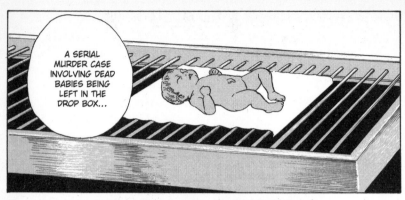

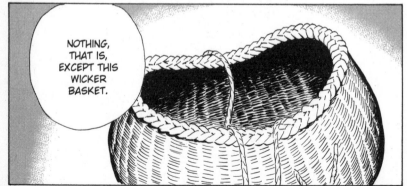

145

IT'S CALLED A *SANTOGARA*. IT MEANS "NEWBORN'S SHELL." IN THE TOHOKU REGION, THEY WERE ONCE USED BY IMPOVERISHED FAMILIES FOR *MABIKI*...INFANTICIDE.

IT'S THE SAME TERM RICE FARMERS USE WHEN THEY THIN OUT THEIR SEEDLINGS. ABORTED BABIES AND NEWBORNS ALIKE WOULD BE PLACED INSIDE...DOWN A RIVER TO FLOAT AWAY.

YEAH. *WELL?*

SYMBOL-ISM OF WHAT?!

IT'S NOT EXACTLY A *MODERN* PRACTICE... BUT IT COULD HAVE BEEN ADOPTED FOR ITS SYMBOLISM.

DO YOU THINK THE CULPRIT'S FROM THERE...?

WHAT ARE YOU EVEN *TALKING* ABOUT?! THE SYSTEM IS DESIGNED TO *SAVE* THE LIVES OF ABANDONED BABIES! IT'S NOTHING LIKE INFANTICIDE!

FOUR DEAD BABIES HAVE BEEN LEFT IN YOUR DROP BOX ALREADY. CAN YOU RULE OUT PROTEST AS A MOTIVE...?

SEEING HOW THINGS HAVE TRANSPIRED, IT'S OBVIOUS THAT REALITY AND IDEALS ARE SOMEWHAT DIFFERENT THINGS.

HMM...SO YOU'RE MISS KIKUCHI.

...I–I KNOW SOME PEOPLE DON'T LIKE IT... I JUST CAN'T BELIEVE THEY'RE THAT *CALLOUS.*

YOU CAN INTERPRET IT HOWEVER YOU WANT...

DON'T *BELIEVE?* WHAT DOES THE *EVIDENCE* SUGGEST?

...MAN, ONE GIRL DIGGING HIM IS BAD ENOUGH...BUT TWO IS *REALLY* UNACCEPTABLE.

um, WHEN I MENTIONED WHAT YOU SAID ABOUT KARATSU AND THE NURSE SEEMING TO HIT IT OFF, SHE INSISTED ON COMING *along.*

HEY, WHAT'S SASAKI DOING HERE ANYWAY, WITH ROUGH LABORER TYPES LIKE OURSELVES?

HUH? WELL... UH...I, UMM...

YES, WHAT DO YOU THINK?

WHAT DO *YOU* THINK, KARATSU?

HE'S GOT A CERTAIN POWER...LIKE AN *ITAKO*, YOU MIGHT SAY.

DON'T ASK THAT BOY TO DO ANY THINKING. KARATSU, AS LONG AS THIS BABY DIDN'T DIE AT BIRTH, IT MIGHT HAVE SEEN SOMETHING...

S-SEEN SOMETHING...?

ITAKO...?

OF COURSE, IN THE CASE OF INFANTS WHO CAN'T SPEAK, I GET MORE OF AN IMAGE THAN A VOICE...

...D-DON'T GET FREAKED OUT...BUT WHEN I TOUCH A CORPSE, I CAN TRY AND SPEAK WITH THEIR SPIRIT.

...UM ...OKAY.

KIZUMONO KIB'S

UM, LET ME DEMONSTRATE ...NUMATA, WILL YOU GET READY WITH THE CELL PHONE CAMERA?

RIGHT.

YEAH, THE SOUL IS STILL HERE...BUT IT FEELS... UNSTABLE, FOR SOME REASON...

"UNSTABLE"?

OKAY... YOU GETTING SOMETHING?

BUT IT'S ALL RIGHT. I CAN SEE A...OKAY, TAKE THE PICTURE.

GOT IT.

HUH? WHAT IS THAT? A BUILDING?... NO, IT LOOKS MORE LIKE A LOCKER..

カシャッ

DOMOCO L7021D

WHAT DOES THAT MEAN? THE CULPRIT PICKED UP A DEAD BABY FROM THIS LOCKER, AND THEN TOOK IT TO THE DROP BOX...?

like, WHY NOT JUST TAKE IT *directly* TO THE DROP BOX...?

SO YOU'RE SAYING THE LAST THING THE BABY SAW WAS THIS...?

A LOCKER ...?

THE SOUL...IT'S SUDDENLY GONE.

WELL, THIS DOESN'T TELL US WHAT THEY LOOKED LIKE. KARATSU, YOU'D BETTER TRY AGAIN...

...WHAT'S THE MATTER?

GONE...?

ゴトン
ゴト
ゴッ
ゴト

I-I DON'T KNOW...

NURSE, WHAT'S THAT NOISE?

ド
ゴッ
ゴト
ドン
ゴ

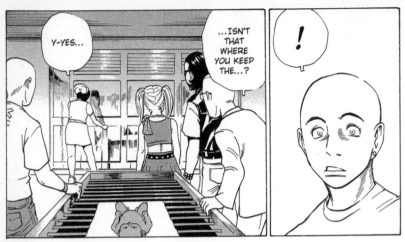

154

IT WASN'T THE *DEAD* MAN WHO WAS REBORN...

...IT WAS THE *BABY*... ENTERING INTO THE CORPSE... AND REANIMATING THE BODY.

AND YOU'RE SAYING THIS HAS HAPPENED *BEFORE?*

Bro, snap out of it!

gaa, gaa.

YES, AND IN THE SAME FASHION. BOTH TIMES IT WAS RIGHT WHEN A DEAD BABY HAD BEEN LEFT IN THE BOX. THE FIRST WAS A GANGSTER, THE SECOND HAD DIED OF OLD AGE...

...BUT IN BOTH CASES, WHEN THEY ROSE AGAIN, THEY WERE LIKE INFANTS.

WAIT A MINUTE...YOU HEARD THE VOICE OF THE DEAD...?

JUST WHO ARE YOU...?

LOC... KER...

JUST BEFORE THE FIRST MAN CAME BACK TO LIFE, I HEARD THE CORPSE SAY...

YOU SAY YOU CAN *TALK* TO THEM...I CAN'T. I CAN *HEAR* A LAST MESSAGE FROM THE DEAD...ALWAYS JUST A FEW WORDS, NO MORE.

...MOST OF THE TIME, I HAVE NO IDEA WHAT IT EVEN *MEANS*-- THAT MAKES IT EVEN MORE HORRIBLE.

...I MEAN, WHAT IF IT WAS SOMETHING IMPORTANT TO THEM? WHAT IF IT WAS THEIR FINAL WISH...?

...YOU MIGHT SAY, IT WAS THE RESULT OF AN ACCIDENT.

NO...

WERE YOU BORN WITH THAT POWER?

...MAYBE THEY ARE MEANT FOR EACH OTHER.

as much as I hate to admit it...

YOU'RE YUI KIKUCHI...THE MIRACLE OF FLIGHT 109.

I KNOW YOU. WHEN YOU WERE A KID, YOU WERE ALL OVER THE NEWS.

THE PLANE CRASH? THAT WAS *YOU?* TWO HUNDRED PEOPLE DIED IN THAT CRASH...SHE WAS THE ONLY ONE TO SURVIVE...

THAT'S A COMMON MISTAKE...

SEVEN PEOPLE SURVIVED THE *CRASH*...I WAS THE ONLY ONE TO LIVE THROUGH THE NIGHT.

OUR SECTION OF THE PLANE HAD BEEN THROWN CLEAR...THAT'S WHY WE DIDN'T BURN WITH THE REST.

BECAUSE OF THE SMOKE, THE SEARCH COPTERS COULDN'T SEE US. IT WAS COLD, WE WERE INJURED...

...

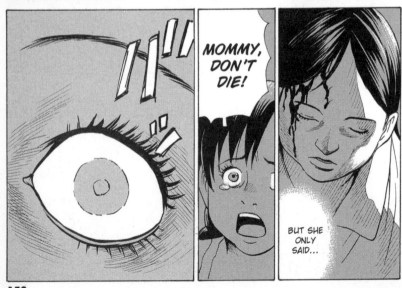

PA...TH
...

"PATH"
...?

MAYBE WE'LL FIND OUT.

IT WASN'T MY IMAGINATION. I KNOW THAT MUCH...

...BUT I DON'T KNOW WHAT IT MEANS.

160

...JUST THAT. I'M SORRY.

IT CAN'T BE *coincidence*... THE BABY SEEING IT, AND THE MAN SAYING IT. IS THAT ALL HE SAID...?

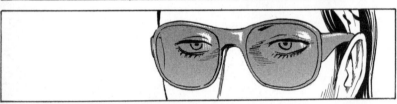

...

HEY, YUI! I'VE BEEN LOOKING FOR YOU ALL OVER! SOMETHING'S HAPPENED...

UH...NO PROBLEM.

I HAVE TO SAY GOODBYE FOR NOW...IT'S MY GRANDMOTHER. I'VE BEEN TAKING CARE OF HER AT HOME.

HMM...

ISN'T THERE ANYTHING ELSE TO GO ON IN THIS PICTURE ...?

...THIS WHOLE BUSINESS JUST KEEPS BOUNCING BACK AND FORTH LIKE PACHINKO.

川中央

NOW THAT ONE'S NEW TO ME...

I THINK IT'S AN AKAGO-ZUKA.

WHAT'S THAT? LOOKS LIKE A STONE MONUMENT ...

UM...WELL... SINCE WE'RE STILL HANGING AROUND CAMPUS...I THOUGHT I'D TAKE SOME MORE COURSES.

SURPRISED *YOU* KNOW SOMETHING THAT DIDN'T COME OUT OF A BLISTER PACK.

THE MOST FAMOUS ONE INVOLVES THE CANDY SELLER IN NAGASAKI, AND THEN THERE'S THAT ONE IN TONO, BUT TRADITIONALLY THEY'RE FOUND ALL OVER THE COUNTRY... WHEREVER THREE ROADS MEET.

YOU KNOW, A BABY'S HEADSTONE. THEY'RE ASSOCIATED WITH THE LEGEND OF THE GHOST THAT RAISES A CHILD.

162

TELL ME, CAN THAT PENDULUM DETECT BRAINS?

HA! THE "N" IN NUMATA *STANDS* FOR KNOWLEDGE!

FUNNY HOW WE ALL WENT TO THE SAME SCHOOL, AND YET SOME OF US CAN'T EVEN SPELL "KNOWLEDGE."

HEY YOU GUYS, SHUT UP A MINUTE!

NO, JUST DEAD PUPPETS!

HOW ARE WE SUPPOSED TO FIND JUST THAT SINGLE ONE...?

WHAT? UM, THEY'RE ALL OVER JAPAN, LIKE I SAID.

LOOK... DOESN'T THAT MEAN THAT IF WE FIND THIS *AKAGO-ZUKA*, WE'LL FIND THE LOCKER?

--WE'RE GOING TO HANDLE THIS LIKE *MEN*!

--HEY, WHERE'D SHE GO...?

MAYBE SASAKI CAN RESEARCH--

...JUST WHEN WE NEED HER. ALL RIGHT--

SHE DISAPPEARED RIGHT AFTER MS. KIKUCHI WENT HOME.

163

SHOULDN'T WE STOP AND ASK DIRECTIONS ...?

...OKAY, I CAN'T THINK OF ANYTHING BETTER, EITHER.

WELL, WE COULD ...

AS MANY AS IT TAKES FOR US TO COME UP WITH A BETTER IDEA!

...LOOK...HOW MANY MORE THREE-WAY INTERSECTIONS ARE WE GOING TO *CHECK*?

NO, NEVER.

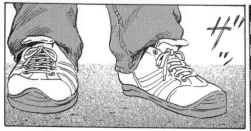

6th delivery: princess's mirror—the end

167

7th delivery

i'll go alone 一人で行くさ

...WE FOUND THE CULPRIT.

UM...HEY... IS THAT...

WHAT?

...

WHAT A SURPRISE... THE LOCKERS WE WERE LOOKING FOR ARE RIGHT OUTSIDE HER DOOR.

I HEARD A CERTAIN LACK OF CONVICTION IN MISS KIKUCHI'S VOICE BACK AT THE HOSPITAL, SO I FOLLOWED HER HOME.

SO... YOU'RE REALLY ...?

YEAH. *TORIAGERU,* "DELIVER," AND *OBAA,* "GRAND-MOTHER."

WHAT'S THAT MEAN... LIKE, "DELIVERY GRANDMA" ..?

SHE RAISED ME AFTER THE CRASH. THEY USED TO CALL PEOPLE LIKE HER *TORIAGEBAA...*

THERE ARE TRADITIONALLY TWO KINDS OF MIDWIVES IN JAPAN--*SANBA* AND *JOSANBU.* THE MAIN DIFFERENCE BETWEEN THE TWO...

...IS THAT *JOSANBU...*

WERE PREPARED TO COMMIT INFANTICIDE.

WE DIDN'T HAVE TO. THE LOCKER IS THE PATHWAY.

NEITHER OF US DROPPED THEM OFF.

WAIT A MINUTE, SHE WAS THERE AT THE HOSPITAL-- HOW COULD *SHE* HAVE DROPPED IT OFF?

THEN YOUR GRANDMOTHER WOULD... KILL THE BABY...AND YOU WOULD DROP IT OFF...?

THE TRADITIONAL METHOD TO SEND THE BABY AWAY WAS TO COVER THE FACE WITH DAMP PAPER, INDUCING DEATH THROUGH SUFFOCATION.

THE LOCKER?

SHE WOULD PUT THE BABY INTO THE LOCKERS, PLACED AT THE *AKAGO-ZUKA* WHERE THREE ROADS MEET...AND THEN WITH A PRAYER SHE WAS ABLE TO SEND THE BABY BACK...BOTH BODY AND SOUL.

MY GRAND-MOTHER USED A DIFFERENT METHOD...

THE *AKAGO-ZUKA* WERE BUILT IN PLACES THAT HAVE A CONNECTION TO THE SPIRIT REALM--LIKE AN UMBILICAL IN REVERSE... RETRACTING INTO DARKNESS.

BUT THERE WAS ONCE ANOTHER *AKAGO-ZUKA* IN THIS TOWN--RAZED YEARS AGO, WHEN THEY CONSTRUCTED THE NEW HOSPITAL.

IT WAS MORE OR LESS WHERE THE BABY DROP BOX IS NOW.

THEY PUT IT THERE AT MY SUGGESTION.

IT'S THE HOSPITAL'S FAULT FOR PUTTING IT IN THAT LOCATION.

...WELL, IT'S NOT *YOUR* FAULT, IS IT...?

...YOU KNEW ...?

...BUT WHY'D YOU REALLY DO IT...?

WHEN THE HOSPITAL LET THE PRESS KNOW THAT THE MIRACLE CHILD WHO SURVIVED THE PLANE CRASH WAS BECOMING A STUDENT NURSE TO SAVE *OTHER* CHILDREN...IT WAS JUST THE RIGHT PR TO COUNTERACT THE PROTESTS.

MISS KIKUCHI'S A BIT OF AN ODDBALL AS AN *EMPLOYEE*... BUT SHE ALSO HELPED SELL THE LOCAL GOVERNMENT ON THE BABY BOX.

IF YOU DON'T MIND WAITING, I CAN TELL YOU.

I NEED TO PREPARE MY GRAND-MOTHER'S BODY.

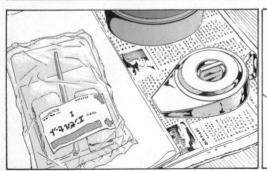

...DO YOU WANT US TO STAY...?

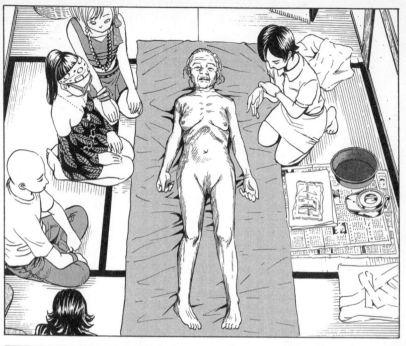

A WOMAN WHO WANTS A BABY... GOES TO SEE AN OBSTETRICIAN, IF SHE CAN. MAYBE A TRADITIONAL MIDWIFE.

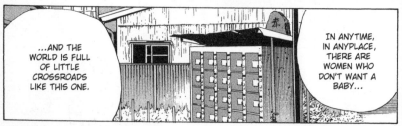

...AND THE WORLD IS FULL OF LITTLE CROSSROADS LIKE THIS ONE.

IN ANYTIME, IN ANYPLACE, THERE ARE WOMEN WHO DON'T WANT A BABY...

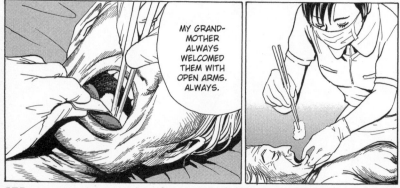

MY GRAND- MOTHER ALWAYS WELCOMED THEM WITH OPEN ARMS. ALWAYS.

175

...AND THAT IS WHY YOU SUGGESTED THE BABY DROP?

SHE WOULD NEVER GO TO A HOSPITAL, EVEN FOR HERSELF...EVEN WHEN I TOLD HER I WOULD START WORKING THERE. SHE SAID A MOTHER IN NEED MIGHT COME BY AT ANY TIME...

THAT'S... PART OF IT...

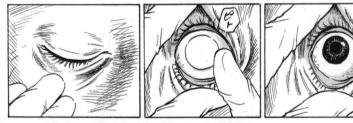

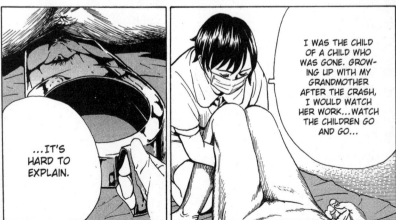

...IT'S HARD TO EXPLAIN.

I WAS THE CHILD OF A CHILD WHO WAS GONE. GROW-ING UP WITH MY GRANDMOTHER AFTER THE CRASH, I WOULD WATCH HER WORK...WATCH THE CHILDREN GO AND GO...

YOU SEE, *I* THOUGHT THE BABIES WOULD REAPPEAR IN THE BOX...ALIVE.

ONE DAY GRANDMA TOLD ME ABOUT THE OLD *AKAGO-ZUKA* WHERE THE HOSPITAL IS NOW. IT TOOK ME A LONG TIME TO WORK UP THE IDEA.

...A CORPSE IS A CORPSE.

BUT IT SEEMS...

178

...ARE YOU SURE YOU DON'T NEED TO SPEAK TO HER?

THE LAST THING IS TO SEAL THE MOUTH.

LIKE I TOLD YOU, I CAN'T SPEAK TO THEM. I CAN ONLY HEAR A FEW WORDS, IF *THEY* CHOOSE TO SPEAK...AND I ALREADY DECIDED TO CARRY ON HER WORK.

CARRY ON...?

EVEN IF I CLOSE THIS PLACE DOWN...

...MABIKI.

KARATSU...

THINNING OUT THE SEEDLINGS...

...COME AND HOLD HER HAND.

IF YOU WANT...

IT'S ALL RIGHT.

BUT...

YOU BOTH SHOULD HAVE A TALK.

WH-
WHAT
THE...

YU...I...GO...
DO...WN...TH...E...
PA...TH...THA...T...
YO...U...BE...LIEVE...
IN.

...IT WOULD SEEM YOUR GRANDMOTHER IS GOING TO WATCH OVER THEM FOR NOW.

SOME CULTURES SEE IT AS A RIVERBANK.

WAS THAT...?

SOME-THING'S BANGING OUTSIDE!

IT'S THE LOCKERS--

…

THE LOCKERS WERE NOTHING… EVEN THE STONE IS NOTHING…

…ONLY THE PLACE WHERE THEY MEET.

THANK YOU FOR DRIVING ME BACK.

UM...ARE YOU GOING TO BE ALL RIGHT?

HOW TO FACE DEATH, I MEAN. IT'S SOMETHING A NURSE *SHOULD* KNOW...DON'T YOU THINK...?

...I KEEP TRYING, BUT I STILL DON'T REALLY KNOW.

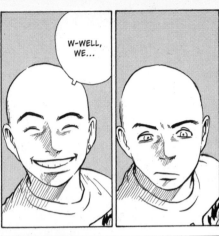

W-WELL, WE...

THANK YOU FOR EVERYTHING.

...WE GOTTA GET GOING.

YEAH...?

KARATSU...

BESIDES... WHAT?

WHY DIDN'T YOU JUST COME OUT AND ASK HER TO JOIN US?

...BESIDES...

THAT'S NOT WHAT I WAS THINKING...

I HAVE A FEELING I'LL BE SEEING HER AGAIN.

OH. IN *THAT* CASE, I'LL HAVE TO TELL SASAKI ON YOU.

HUH? WHAT ARE YOU TALKING ABOUT?!

7th delivery: i'll go alone—the end
continued in *the kurosagi corpse delivery service* vol. 9

the KUROSAGI corpse delivery service

黒鷺死体宅配便

eiji otsuka 大塚英志 housui yamazaki 山崎峰水

designer **HEIDI WHITCOMB**
editorial assistant **ANNIE GULLION**
art director **LIA RIBACCHI**
publisher **MIKE RICHARDSON**

English-language version
produced by Dark Horse Comics

Published by
Dark Horse Manga
A division of Dark Horse Comics, Inc.
10956 SE Main Street
Milwaukie, OR 97222
www.darkhorse.com

To find a comics shop in your area,
call the Comic Shop Locator Service
toll-free at 1-888-266-4226

First edition: January 2009
ISBN 978-1-59582-235-2

1 3 5 7 9 10 8 6 4 2

PRINTED IN CANADA

DISJECTA MEMBRA

SOUND FX GLOSSARY AND NOTES ON KUROSAGI VOL. 8 BY TOSHIFUMI YOSHIDA
Introduction and additional comments by the editor

TO INCREASE YOUR ENJOYMENT of the distinctive Japanese visual style of this manga, we've included a guide to the sound effects (or "FX") used in this manga. It is suggested the reader *not* constantly consult this glossary as they read through, but regard it as supplemental information, in the manner of footnotes, or perhaps one of those nutritional supplements, the kind that's long and difficult to swallow. If you want to imagine it being read aloud by Osaka, after the manner of her lecture to Sakaki on hemorrhoids in episode five of *Azumanga Daioh*, please go right ahead. In either Yuki Matsuoka or Kira Vincent-Davis's voice—I like them both.

Japanese, like English, did not independently invent its own writing system, but instead borrowed and modified the system used by the then-dominant cultural power in its part of the world. We still call the letters we use to write English today the "Roman" alphabet, for the simple reason that about 1,600 years ago, the earliest English speakers, living on the frontier of the Roman Empire, began to use the same letters the Romans used for their Latin language to write out English.

Around that very same time, on the other side of the planet, Japan, like England, was another example of an island civilization lying across the sea from a great empire—in this case, that of China. Likewise, the Japanese borrowed from the Chinese writing system, which then, as now, consisted of thousands of complex symbols—today in China officially referred to in the Roman alphabet as *hanzi*, but which the Japanese

pronounce as *kanji*. For example, all the Japanese characters you see on the front cover of *The Kurosagi Corpse Delivery Service*—the seven which make up the original title and the four each which make up the creators' names—are examples of kanji. Of course, all of them were hanzi first—although the Japanese did also invent some original kanji of their own, just as new hanzi have been created over the centuries as Chinese evolved.

(Note that whereas both "kanji" and "hanzi" are examples of foreign words written in Roman letters, "kanji" gives English speakers a fairly good idea of how the Japanese word is really pronounced—*khan-gee*—whereas "hanzi" does not—in Mandarin Chinese it sounds something like *n-tsuh*. The reason is fairly simple: whereas the most commonly used method of writing Japanese in Roman letters, the Hepburn system, was developed by a native English speaker, the most commonly used method of writing Chinese in Roman letters, called the Pinyin system, was developed by native Mandarin speakers. In fact, Pinyin was developed to help teach Mandarin pronunciation to speakers of other Chinese dialects; unlike Hepburn, it was not intended as a learning tool for English speakers per se, and hence has no particular obligation to "make sense" to English speakers or, indeed, to users of the many other languages spelled with the Roman alphabet.)

Whereas the various dialects of Chinese are written entirely in hanzi, it is impractical to render the Japanese language entirely in them. To compare once more, English

is a notoriously difficult language in which to spell properly, and this is in part because it uses an alphabet designed for another language, Latin, whose sounds are different (this is, of course, putting aside the fact the sounds of both languages experienced change over time). The challenges the Japanese faced in using the Chinese writing system for their own language were even greater, for whereas spoken English and Latin are at least from a common language family, spoken Japanese is unrelated to any of the various dialects of spoken Chinese. The complicated writing system the Japanese evolved represents an adjustment to these great differences.

When the Japanese borrowed hanzi to become kanji, what they were getting was a way to write out (remember, they already had ways to *say*) their vocabulary. Nouns, verbs, many adjectives, the names of places and people—that's what kanji are used for, the fundamental data of the written language. The practical use and processing of that "data"—its grammar and pronunciation—is another matter entirely. Because spoken Japanese neither sounds nor functions like Chinese, the first work-around tried was a system called *manyogana*, where individual kanji were picked to represent certain syllables in Japanese. A similar method is still used in Chinese today to spell out foreign names; companies and individuals often try to choose hanzi for this purpose that have an auspicious, or at least not insulting, meaning. As you will also observe in *Kurosagi* and elsewhere, the meaning behind the characters that make up a personal name are an important literary element of Japanese as well.

The commentary in Katsuya Terada's *The Monkey King* (also available from Dark Horse, and also translated by Toshifumi Yoshida) notes the importance that not only Chinese, but also Indian culture had on Japan at this time in history—particularly, through Buddhism. Just as in Western history at this time, religious communities in Asia were associated with learning, as priests and monks were more likely to be literate than other groups in society. It is believed the Northeast Indian *Siddham* script studied by Kukai (died 835 AD), founder of the Shingon sect of Japanese Buddhism, inspired him to create the solution for writing Japanese still used today. Kukai is credited with the idea of taking the manyogana and making shorthand versions of them—which are now known simply as *kana*. The improvement in efficiency was dramatic: a kanji previously used to represent a sound, that might have taken a dozen strokes to draw, was now replaced by a kana that took three or four.

Unlike the original kanji they were based on, the new kana had *only* a sound meaning. And unlike the thousands of kanji, there are only forty-six kana, which can be used to spell out any word in the Japanese language, including the many ordinarily written with kanji (Japanese keyboards work on this principle). The same set of forty-six kana is written two different ways depending on its intended use: cursive style, *hiragana*, and block style, *katakana*. Naturally, sound FX in manga are almost always written out using kana.

Kana works somewhat differently than the Roman alphabet. For example, while there are separate kana for each of the five vowels (the Japanese order is not A-E-I-O-U as in English, but A-I-U-E-O), there are, except for *n*, no separate kana for consonants (the middle *n* in the word *ninja* illustrates this exception). Instead, kana work by grouping together consonants with vowels: for example, there are five kana for sounds starting with *k*, depending on which vowel follows it—in Japanese

vowel order, they go KA, KI, KU, KE, KO. The next set of kana begins with *s* sounds, so SA, SHI, SU, SE, SO, and so on. You will observe this kind of consonant-vowel pattern in the FX listings for *Kurosagi* Vol. 8 below.

Katakana are generally used for manga sound FX, but on occasion hiragana are used instead. This is commonly done when the sound is one associated with a human body, but can be a subtler aesthetic choice by the artist as well. In *Kurosagi* Vol. 8 you can see an example on 32.7, with the SA of Rei turning her head away, which in hiragana style is written さつ. Note its more cursive appearance compared to the other FX. If it had been written in katakana style, it would look like サツ.

To see how to use this glossary, take an example from page 6: "6.4 FX: KYORO KYORO—looking around sound." 6.4 means the FX is the one on page 6, in panel 4. KYORO KYORO is the sound these kana—キョロキョロ—literally stand for. After the dash comes an explanation of what the sound represents (in some cases, like this, it will be less obvious than others). Note that in cases where there are two or more different sounds in a single panel, an extra number is used to differentiate them from right to left; or, in cases where right and left are less clear, in clockwise order.

The use of kana in these FX also illustrates another aspect of written Japanese—its flexible reading order. For example, the way you're reading the pages and panels of this book in general—going from right to left, and from top to bottom—is similar to the order in which Japanese is also written in most forms of print: books, magazines, and newspapers. However, some of the FX in *Kurosagi* (and manga in general) read left to right. This kind of flexibility is also to be found on Japanese web pages, which usually also read left to right. In other

words, Japanese doesn't simply read "the other way" from English; the Japanese themselves are used to reading it in several different directions.

As might be expected, some FX "sound" short, and others "sound" long. Manga represent this in different ways. One of many instances of "short sounds" in *Kurosagi* Vol. 8 is 6.2's SU—スツ. Note the small ツ mark it has at the end, which stands for the sound "tsu"—in hiragana, such as 32.7, it looks like つ. The half-size "tsu" seen at the end of FX like this means the sound is the kind which stops or cuts off suddenly; that's why 6.2 and 32.7 are written as SU and SA, and not SUTSU and SATSU—you don't pronounce the "tsu" when used this way. Note the small "tsu" has another occasional use *inside*, rather than at the end, of a particular FX, where it indicates a doubling of the consonant sound that follows it.

There are three different ways you may see "long sounds"—where a vowel sound is extended—written out as FX. One is with an ellipsis, as in 105.4's KOTO. Another is with an extended line, as in 61.6's HOOO HO HO HO HO. Still another is by simply repeating a vowel several times, as in 70.1's GOOOOO. You will note that the HOOO in 61.6's HOOO HO HO HO HO has a "tsu" at its end, suggesting an elongated sound that's suddenly cut off; the methods may be combined within a single FX. As a visual element in manga, FX are an art rather than a science, and are used in a less rigorous fashion than kana are in standard written Japanese.

The explanation of what the sound represents may sometimes be surprising, but every culture "hears" sounds differently. Note that manga FX do not even necessarily represent literal sounds. Such "mimetic" words, which represent an imagined sound,

or even a state of mind, are called *gitaigo* in Japanese. Like the onomatopoeic *giseigo* (the words used to represent literal sounds— i.e., most FX in this glossary are classed as giseigo), they are also used in colloquial speech and writing. A Japanese, for example, might say that something bounced by saying PURIN, or talk about eating by saying MUGU MUGU. It's something like describing chatter in English by saying "yadda yadda yadda" instead.

One important last note: all these spelled-out kana vowels should be pronounced as they are in Japanese: *A* as *ah*, *I* as *eee*, *U* as *ooh*, *E* as *eh*, and *O* as *oh*.

2 All of the titles are once again song names. For this volume, the songs are by the folk rock group GARO. The band was made up of three members: Mamoru "Mark" Horiuchi, Tomiaki "Tommy" Hidaka and Masumi "Vocal" Ono. With a sound sometimes compared to Crosby, Stills, Nash & Young, they had a million-selling #1 hit with 1973's *Daigakuseigai no Kissaten* (which means "A Café in a Campus Town") and were an emblem of Japanese rock for the next two years, but broke up at the end of 1975.

5.2 The *tsubo* is a traditional Japanese measure of area—still in use even though Japan is metric—equal to 3.05785 sq. meters. The translator notes that if his math is correct, 500 tsubo is only 2/5 of an acre, but bear in mind that's impressive by Japanese land prices. Come to think of it, a lot that size (17,790 sq. feet) is nothing to sneeze at in America, either. In the immortal words of Harvey Korman (peace be upon him), "Land…'Land: see *snatch*.'"

6.2 **FX: SU**—starting to step away

6.4 **FX: KYORO KYORO**—looking around sound

10.1 There are certain stations of the cross a school manga must traverse: among these are the beach episode, the hot-springs episode, and this, the first for *Kurosagi*, the campus-festival episode. The scene at the post office–owned spa resort in Vol. 6 might have counted as a hot-springs episode, but (and this is a qualification for all such episodes) it would have needed the main female and male characters present to allow full cast interaction—see *Genshiken* Vol. 8. *Campus* festivals in manga tend to be of three main types: the "culture fest," (usually an excuse to set up a themed café in one's homeroom), a track and field day, or this, the big student club sign-up. *Kurosagi*'s version is pretty mild; the master of campus-festival scenes in manga is doubtless Kosuke Fujishima in *Oh My Goddess!*, especially in those early volumes, with all the teeny-tiny signs that needed to be retouched in such detail.

12.1 The editor himself might have patronized the rough tape-trade to be found in certain off-campus anime clubs, but he had no intention of introducing these beastly practices to the ivy-covered halls (actually, only Harwood had ivy on it; that's why it was used for the dorm scenes in *Real Genius*) of Pomona College, anno MCMLXXXVII. Instead he was part of the Laissez-Faire Club at Pomona

College, whose purpose was to "smoke cigars, drink Cognac, and discuss the virtues of a free economy." The first two were a bit ahead of the curve; the cigar boom wouldn't hit for another ten years, and hip-hop hadn't yet discovered "yak"; its most lavish ads were still in *The Far Eastern Economic Review* rather than *Vibe* (not after I cut them out of the magazine, however, and pasted them to the wall, together with any coverage of Amy Yip. And I know there weren't no *Vibe* magazine in '87, but please allow me the rhetorical indulgence). As for the third, there was a feeling among some students in 1987 that the Democrats were becoming the enemies of freedom rather than the Republicans. One could respect P. J. O'Rourke, denouncing drug tests and Ollie North in his writing for *Rolling Stone*; one could have no respect whatsoever for Tipper Gore, pursuing the menace of Prince and Twisted Sister. The problem, of course, was that Republicans like P. J. O'Rourke weren't the kind gaining political power, whereas Democrats like Tipper Gore would continue to do so. In retrospect, the idea that tacking right would promote liberty wasn't the most well-considered opinion, but it was driven in part by the leisurely (as we did all things) contempt Gen-X had for the baby boomers in power. Not so much for their era, the terrible and glorious 1960s, but for their shame and resentment of it, for the pathetic spectacle of their culture war over who was on what side, that they maintained

(and still maintain) even as the country's real problems changed with the decades—bearing out once and for all, whether liberal or conservative, the charges laid against them when they were young: that their generation cared only about itself, and could not grow up.

13.5 **FX: GATA**—getting up out of chair

15.4 **FX: KATA**—opening laptop

15.7 **FX: TATATA TATA**—keyboard sounds

16.4 **FX: BA**—grabbing computer back

16.5 **FX/balloon: GACHA**—door opening

18.1 Even as we enjoy a few cheap laughs (for what other sort could the Kurosagi gang afford?), we do not wish to show disrespect to our esteemed comrades in the gothic-lolita community. Patrick Macias invited me to sit in on his "Japanese Schoolgirl Inferno" panel at AWA (I'm not sure why he invited *me* to sit in—I'm more *Collezioni* than *Emporio*). The panel was named for the book he wrote with coauthor Izumi Evers (the woman who created the look of *PULP* magazine) and illustrator Kazumi Nonaka—*Japanese Schoolgirl Inferno*, fun and wild, details the last forty years of Japanese schoolgirl fashion trends, from creation, to co-opting, to rejection, and then to reincarnation. Most importantly, it rejects the idea that fashion is necessarily superficial or something only purchased, but shows how it can be made from the ground up (sometimes, from the gutter up) to reflect a chosen meaning. Ephemeral—like all things. A major

asset to the panel was an elegantly actual goth loli in the front row, who discussed what the scene was like in Atlanta, GA, and the reaction to it, often unhip, but not always unkind (one old lady told her it was wonderful that young girls were starting to dress more modestly). The *New York Times*, ever alert to breaking news, picked up on the existence of goth loli recently (admittedly, I'm counting on them more to keep an eye on things like Iraq and the financial crisis). Initial comments on the Jezebel blog in reaction to the article included such remarks as: "What are they rebelling against?" "Messed up." "Makes me uncomfortable." "All this says to me is 'I want attention.'" "There is no point at which I do not find this subculture absolutely ridiculous." In other words, the exact same comments that have been made about every youth style since cavekids started wearing those stupid deer hides, instead of respectable bearskins like their dads.

18.6   **FX: PAKU PAKU**—sound of the mouth flapping

19.3   This suggests he saw her "performance" at the fanboy's funeral in Vol. 5.

19.6   There's gotta be a name for that ponytail Nakano (*vide* Vol. 7, notes for 22.1) is sporting; only otaku have that ponytail. It goes back at least to Hino in *Otaku no Video*. Let's give it a name. *O-tail*, or *opptaku*, or maybe *otaku no suisei*. Japanese speakers are invited to weigh in on whether those last two sound clever.

20.2   Probably Asuka from *Neon Genesis Evangelion*. This is the point where

I might have attempted a smart remark about his life-size figure and those awful otaku, but as I'm the awful otaku editing the fan-service-filled *Neon Genesis Evangelion: The Shinji Ikari Raising Project*, first volume out in June, it wouldn't sound quite right.

20.4   **FX: SU**—passing over a photo

23.4   **FX: SU**—touching body sound

23.5   **FX: KATA KATA KATATA**—body shaking

24.1   **FX/balloon: PIKU PIKU**—fingers twitching

24.2.1   **FX: SU**—removing hand

24.2.2   **FX/balloon: PITA**—body suddenly stopping

26.4   **FX/balloon: BURORORORO**—car sound

27.5   **FX: GURI**—pushing on the ring for his pendulum

27.6   **FX: CHARAN**—sound of metal chain dangling

28.3   **FX: HYUN HYUN HYUN**—sound of the pendulum swinging

29.6   **FX: BAKI BAKI GASASA**—breaking branches and sliding sound

32.7   **FX: SA**—turning head away

35.2   **FX: SU**—placing hand on body

44.4   There is an actual term, *yurei buin*, "ghost club members," used for the not-uncommon practice of campus clubs inflating their membership to claim more funding from their schools. It's done through the simple expedient of getting students to sign the club register, even if they have no intention of ever attending a meeting.

45.1 This is Mori Tower, the iconic building associated with Tokyo's trendy, expensive Roppongi Hills complex. Opening in 2003, it was first sighted in *Kurosagi* on page 70 of Vol. 5, and has served to literally hang over the heads of its main cast ever since, reminding them of just how nonmaterialistic their status is. Nakano back in 14.4 even mentioned that the campus golf club was having *their* new-member party in Roppongi Hills, putting Kurosagi's basement meeting room in rather sharp contrast.

45.2.1 FX/balloon: BURORORO—engine sound

45.2.2 FX/balloon: KII—sound of brakes

45.3 FX: SHA SHA—scribbling sound

46-47 What's so wonderful about this chapter title page is that it puts me in mind of those 1970s "mystery" comics (as Howard Chaykin points out, the Comics Code wouldn't allow them to say "horror") where people were always getting married to ghosts, ghouls, and skeletons. Check out Dave Merrill and Shaindle Minuk's Stupid Comics blog for some choice examples at http://www.misterkitty.org/extras/stupidcovers/stupidcomics92.html. Well, come to think of it, this story puts me a little in mind of them, too.

48.2 Note that the two kanji that spell Kaneari's name mean "money" and "have."

49.1 FX: GURU—sound of the fridge toppling

49.5 The one vanity the editor has never been able to comprehend is designer pens. It might come from taking an early interest in cartooning (and calligraphy, which was big in the late '70s), which taught, as Thulsa Doom would say, what is the nib, compared to the hand that wields it?

50.1.1 FX: SU—taking out towel

50.1.2 FX/balloon: HIRA—sheet of paper falling out

50.2 FX: PASA—sheet of paper landing on floor

52.2 FX/balloon: SHUUU—sound of an automatic door opening

52.3 The phenomenon of people using manga cafés (*mankissa* in Japanese, after *kissaten*, "café"—basically, private manga libraries where one pays by the hour) to spend the night is known even outside Japan, thanks to Hiroko Tabuchi's widely syndicated piece for the Associated Press in May of 2007, which also discussed its relation to those who survive on part-time work arranged by cell phone. Tabuchi mentioned a net café (they are often also manga cafés) where cubicles rented for 82 cents an hour, showing that the 700-yen all-night package here is quite realistic.

52.4 FX/balloon: GISHI—chair creaking

52.5 FX: PATA—putting down pad of paper

53.1 FX/balloon: MOGU MOGU—eating sound

53.2 FX: SHA SHA—sketching sound

54.1 The translator notes that *bijin-ga* often refers to such glamour pictures of Japan's *ukiyo-e*—the famous, frequently colorful woodblock prints that influenced the

Impressionists when Europe discovered them in the nineteenth century. However, the term can be applied to works in other media, even modern ones such as photography, as long as the subject remains a Japanese woman in traditional dress.

55.2 The traditional word for a wedding in Japanese is *kekkonshiki*, which combines three kanji by themselves pronounced *ketsu*, "union," *kon*, "marriage," and *shiki*, "ceremony" (the rules of Japanese pronunciation make the first two combine to be read *kekkon* instead of *ketsukon*). Kaneari changes this to the near-rhyming *meikonshiki* by making the first kanji *mei*, "afterlife," instead.

55.3 Note the Mumume-tan figurine, no doubt left by the fleeing Nakano.

59.2 **FX: KATA**—rattle of the picture frame

59.3 As seen in Vol. 2. In the Silver Age, there would have been a big ol' box in the panel to remind you of this, but such primitive methods have been replaced with *Disjecta Membra*.

61.6 **FX: HOOO HO HO HO HO**— chuckles. I'm not sure Makino is aware she's quoting *The 36th Chamber of Shaolin*, AKA *Master Killer*.

62.3 *Ema* means "horse picture," meaning that it is symbolic of the literal offering of a horse that used to be made (by those who could afford it) in exchange for a blessing at a Shinto shrine. Even today, some shrines maintain a stable for a *goshinme*, a horse kept by the priests for the gods to ride.

Excel, for whom there is no god but Il Palazzo, blasphemously stole the steed from one such temple in Vol. 1 of the *Excel Saga* manga.

62.6 Karatsu is making himself a little arch here (*get it?*); most Japanese don't stress too much about performing the rites of more than one religion—it should also be noted that, just as in America, performing the rites isn't necessarily a sign of deep personal belief, but may be done simply for tradition's sake, social obligation, or (especially with Shinto rites) having fun with friends. And just as we see here, many Japanese aren't adverse to Christian rites either, or at least, the appearance of them; some get married at places made up to look like churches, with an actor portraying a priest (as seems to be the case on page 78). There have, of course, been actual Japanese Christians for centuries (the new prime minister of Japan, Taro Aso, is Catholic), and there are also some Japanese of whatever faith who truly consider themselves "religious" in the American sense—but faith, or anything else for that matter, is rarely allowed to trump social harmony in Japan.

66.1 **FX: SU**—putting a photograph down

67.3 **FX: SU**—paintbrush touching *ema*

67.5 **FX: HYUOOOO**—sound of gusting wind

68.1 **FX: HYUUU**—sound of wind

68.4 **FX: KATA KATA GATA**—sound of the *ema* rattling. The *ema* says, by the way, "Dedication: New Bride

Kurara Gotokuji, Died 2007; New Groom Zatou Seijo, Died June 7, 2006. After Death Marriage." The 2007 date is taken from the fact this particular chapter of *Kurosagi* appeared in the June 5, 2007, issue of its current home magazine, *Comic Charge*.

70.1   **FX: GOOOOO**—sound of train pulling away

70.3.1   **FX/balloon: PI**—hanging up cell

70.3.2   **FX/balloon: KAN KO**—footstep on stairs

72.2   **FX: GUI**—tugging sound

72.4.1   **FX/black: GA DOKA**—impact sounds

72.4.2   **FX/white: BAKI BOKI**—breaking bone sounds

73.1   **FX: GO**—sound of head hitting floor

73.2   **FX/balloon: PIIPOO PIIPOO PIIPOO**—ambulance siren

74.4   As you might expect, Sasayama didn't say "Jane Doe" in the original, but *kooryo-shinahito*, "traveler deceased," a technical term for an unidentified body. Although Japan does sometimes use the name "Taro Yamada" to signify a generic Japanese (a little like the way you might use "John Smith" in America), there is no custom of assigning a standard pseudonym to the unidentified dead.

75.2   The editor doesn't even *have* a cell phone, not being what you'd call an early adopter (he *did* finally buy an iPod a few months ago— used, from his sempai, Toren Smith), but he doesn't think you can perform all these functions yet on an American cell phone. But the rest of the world has always been a bit ahead of the cell curve. I remember some years ago Hiroyuki Yamaga (most recently, coproducer of *Gurren Lagann*, and director of its recap episode) showing off his 3G phone at Fanime Con, before such things were available in the U.S. But of course, nothing would show up on its screen, as it used a Japan-only service. It felt like that scene in *Spinal Tap* where Nigel Tufnel says, "You would, though, if it were playing."

75.3   **FX: MOMI MOMI**—massaging shoulder

75.4   **FX: SU**—placing hand on body

77.1   **FX: SU**—pointing sound

77.2   **FX: SA**—lifting sheet

79.1   **FX: PA**—sound of spotlight turning on

79.2   **FX: PACHI PACHI PACHI PACHI**—clapping sounds

81.3   Not as in high school A/V, refuge of the chaste, but AV as in "adult video"—the Japan porno industry uses the English-language term.

81.5   **FX/balloon: VUU VUU VUU**—cell phone vibrating

81.6   **FX: CHA**—putting phone to ear

82.3   **FX: TA**—putting glass down

84.1   **FX: BASA**—sound of photos being dumped on table

85.2   This time, the *musakari ema* reads "New Bride Ao Sasaki, Died 2007; New Groom Yaro Nozaki, Died 2005. After Death Marriage."

85.4   **FX: KATAN**—hanging *ema*

85.5   **FX: GARA PATAN**—closing shrine door

a suggestion of the bullet's spin. I wonder whether in *Kurosagi*'s Housui Yamazaki and *MPD-Psycho*'s Sho-u Tajima, author Eiji Otsuka found the kind of artists whose relatively clean, clinical style supports an idea Philip Simon and I sense in Otsuka's work—not simply voyeurism, but the consciousness of voyeurism. Perhaps due to his anthropologist's training, he seems to take as a given that many of us humans (including, of course, himself) are inclined to stare at and perhaps even like the lurid, the extreme, or the taboo. Rather than say "don't look," or "you shouldn't look," or "oh, what a terrible thing it is to look at this," Otsuka is interested in what might be learned if on such occasions we decided to look *at* our looking. The immediate inspiration for *MPD-Psycho*, which premiered in 1997, was not only the Aum Shinrikyo cult terrorist attacks two years before, but also the media frenzy surrounding them, which famously led *Akira*'s Katsuhiro Otomo to declare that the reporters came off as crazier than the cult—but of course, presumably, it earned ratings.

105.1 Imagine a country where someone's dead of a pistol wound, and you can immediately assume it was organized crime. Most handgun deaths here are hardly that colorful. See also the notes for Vol. 1's 51.3 for how *Kurosagi* illustrates the difference between Japan's gun culture and our own.

105.4 FX: KOTO—putting a board down on the table

106.1 FX: KOKI—cracking knuckles

106.2 FX: SU—placing hand on body

107.4 FX/balloons: PINPOON PINPOON—doorbell sound

107.5 FX/balloon: PI—pressing button

109.1 FX: KATA—putting glass down

109.2 FX: GATAN—falling down sound

109.5.1 FX: ZU ZU—being pulled down sound

109.5.2 FX/balloon: KACHI KACHI—bottles rattling

109.5.3 FX/balloon: KATA—rattling sound

109.5.4 FX/balloon: KATAN—glass falling over

110.1-2 FX: NU NUUUUU—sound of head coming through table. The ghost is wearing the *tsunokakushi*, the traditional bridal headdress of a Shinto wedding (seen earlier, of course, on several of the *ema*). Japanese tradition says it is to hide the "horns" of evil impulses held by the bride—selfishness and jealousy (often meaning "jealousness" towards the mistresses it is assumed her husband will take!). It has been claimed that the move towards Christian-style weddings (not necessarily Christian weddings; see the note for 62.6) represents a wish by some Japanese women to reject the symbolism of the *tsunokakushi*, but it's the editor's impression that it's more a decision of style than symbolism. Weddings in Japan, as they are in many places, are often an occasion for deeply traditional *gestures*, not necessarily deeply held attitudes; in particular, no one expects a marriage in 2007 Japan to be like that of 1957, or even 1987 (the country having gone through

something of a quiet sexual revolution in the 1990s—the upside of its long recession being a loosening of social restrictions, as old institutions and attitudes lost respect). One of Otsuka's constant themes as a writer, though, is the *latent* power of folklore, and the idea that every society lives in both its present and past.

111.4 **FX: FU**—sound of the lights going out

112-
113.1 **FX: WAAAAAA**—final scream

115.1 **FX: KATA**—picking up broken *ema*

115.3 **FX/balloon: BO**—*ema* catching fire

115.4 **FX: PACHI PACHI**—crackling fire sound

115.6 **FX: HYUOOO**—sound of the wind gusting

116.1 **FX: KATA KATA**—*ema* rattling

116.2 **FX: KATA KATA**—*ema* rattling

117.1 **FX: MIIIN MIIIN**—sound of cicadas

118.2 **FX/balloon: KII**—bike brake sound

118.3 **FX: KIII**—locker creaking closed

118.4 **FX: PATA**—locker door closing

118.6 **FX: KARARA**—sound of bike rolling

119.1 **FX: KIII**—bike brakes

119.3 Roadside coin lockers, like roadside vending machines (see notes for Vol. 2, 105.1), or ads that hang from subway ceilings without being snatched down, are all testament to Japan's lingering sense of social restraint. Of course, as Haruki Murakami wrote in *Underground*, his study of the Aum Shinrikyo terror attacks, that restraint

extended to its victims writhing poisoned beneath those very same subway ads, receiving no help from their fellow passengers—not so much out of callousness, but out of a wish to wait until a station was reached, and the matter could be dealt with by the authorities. This, incidentally, is also what enables one to enjoy the most shocking manga on a train without fear of offending others (it's not like all Japanese are into sex and violence, or manga for that matter), for what would be truly impolite would be to *notice*.

119.4.1 **FX/balloon: GOTOTO**—sound of something moving inside

119.4.2 **FX/balloon: GOSO**—sound of something shifting inside

119.7 **FX: KIII**—locker door creaking

120.1 **FX: OGYAAAA ONGYAAAA OGYAAA GYAAA GYAA**—baby wailing

120.2 **FX: OGYAA NGYAAA**—more wailing

120.3 **FX: GUGYAAA**—wailing starting to fade

121.1 **FX: GYAAA**—small waning wail

121.2 **FX: BAAAAN**—locker slamming shut

121.3 **FX: SHAAAA**—sound of bikes speeding away

121.6 *Namu amida butsu* is a traditional chant associated with Pure Land Buddhism (see notes for Vol. 7's 6.2.2), although Karatsu's *nanmaida* way back in Vol. 1's 11.4 was a variation on it. *Amida butsu* refers to the Buddha Amida, or Amitabha, whereas *namu* derives from the Sanskrit *namaste*; often translated

hail," "praise," or "amen," and a part of many longer prayers.

122-123 The editor was talking over Vol. 8 with his pal, Director of Asian Licensing Michael Gombos, when Gombos gave a discourse on the shoes in this scene. It seems these sorts of sandals—two Velcro straps over the toe and one over the ankle—are the type commonly worn by nurses and teachers in Japan. Japanese teachers do a bit more walking than American ones, as, in Japan, it's the teachers who move from class to class each period, while the students stay put in a homeroom. When teachers get to school, they take off the shoes they arrived in, and switch to these sandals in the *shokuin-shitsu*, the teachers' room. Now, what Gombos found interesting is that even though this footwear is as cheap as the 1,000 yen *oyajigutsu* that old men wear— the slip-ons with the faux patent leather and the fake gold chains— that they are, in short, as he put it, "the least boner-iffic imaginable," they nevertheless become a fetish to those lads who find themselves with strange and wonderful feelings towards a certain teacher, or, presumably, health-care professional. At this point I invoked Rule 34, but Gombos riposted this was an Internet rule. We wondered whether an appropriate corollary for reality might not be called Rule 34A, for "actual," or perhaps 34', for "prime," sort of like the E' that designates Kereellis on the back cover of this book. Gombos pointed out this might imply reality has now become the puppet of the Internet,

but I said that was more a plot point for Vol. 10. Anyway, it seemed we were starting to digress a little from the shoes, so I mentioned it seemed odd, this thing about nurses wearing open-toed sandals, since wouldn't there be a hygiene issue? But Gombos pointed out this is Japan, where you're allowed to smoke in the hospital. And that pretty much put paid to all Japanese ways we might consider strange, because before we tut-tut, let us reflect that as of 2007, the average Japanese lived to 82, whereas the average American made it no further than 78.

124.1 Once again, this is the Kadokawa Central Hospital, evidently just another part of the publisher's inescapable empire.

126.6 FX: GU—grasping body

126.7 FX: GORORI—turning body over

128.2 FX: PACHI—eyes opening

128.3 FX: NYU—starting to frown

128.4 FX: GUNYU—scrunching face

129.1 FX: ONGYAAAAA GYAAA HONGYAAAAAA—wailing like a baby

130.1 FX: NGYAAA AAAA GYAAA ONGYAAA—wailing

130.3 FX: TATATATA—running off

130.5 FX: OGYAAAA OGYAAA NGYAAA—wailing

130.6 FX: PIII PIII PIII—alarm sound

131.1 FX: DADADADA—running sound

131.2 FX: GACHA—door opening

133.4 There was, of course, the incident last September in Omaha (which

sounds Japanese, but it's in Nebraska) where a widower, who said he was unable to care for them any longer, left *nine* of his children at a hospital under a similar law. Although it seemed outrageous, there was a surprising amount of sympathy for the father's decision, with those supporting him saying it reflected a lack of government assistance to families, and pointing out it's not unknown for parents overwhelmed by stress to abuse or even kill their children. In the words of Bushwick Bill, "It's a fucked-up situation, I feel sorry for the families, but this song was inspired by the truth."

133.5 FX: **KIII**—door creaking open

134.2 Japan has a national health-care plan, but unlike those in many Western European countries, it doesn't pay for abortion (or contraception, for that matter). Many people are surprised to hear the birth-control pill was only legalized there in 1999, and condoms and the "rhythm method" remain the most common forms of contraception—which means that abortion remains a common default method of "birth control" as well.

135.4 FX: **SU**—placing hand on baby

136.1 FX: **SU**—lifting hand

137.2 "Angel Care" is the actual term used in Japanese nursing, pronounced *enzerukea* ("en-zeh-roo-keh-ah") and the procedure is in fact as shown here and in more detail later on in "7th Delivery." It should be emphasized that its intent is to make the body temporarily presentable, as opposed to embalming, which seeks to slow its decay over the longer term.

140.4 FX: **CHARA**—pendulum dangling

141.2 FX: **KON**—hitting with cane

142.3 FX: **KIII**—door opening

142.4 FX: **GOTON**—baby being dropped off

143.1 FX: **PIII PIII PIII**—alarm sound

143.2 FX: **PIII PIII**—alarm sound

143.6 FX: **ZA**—footsteps

150.2 FX: **SU**—placing hand on baby

151.1 FX: **KASHA**—shutter sound

152.4 FX: **GOTO GOTO GOTON GO GOTO**—sound of something moving around loudly

152.5 FX: **DON GOTO DOKO GON**—sound of pounding on the little door

153.3 FX: **GAAAA**—sound of the drawer being slid out

153.4 FX: **MOGO GOSO MOGOGO GOSO GUMO**—sound of struggling and muffled groans

154.1.1 FX/white: **BARI**—body bag opening up

154.1.2 FX/black: **OGYAAA GYAAA AAAA OGYAAA ONGYAAAA**—baby wails

154.2 FX: **ONGYAAA ONGYAAA ONGYAAAA**—baby wails

155.1 FX: **PATATATA**—sound of a distant helicopter

157.6 FX: **PATATATA PATATATA**—distant helicopter sound

158 This is almost certainly inspired by the infamous JAL Flight 123, which crashed into Japan's Mount Osutaka in the early evening of August 12, 1985, killing 520 people—still the deadliest single aircraft disaster in history. Four

were found alive (including a mother and her eight-year-old daughter) when rescue crews landed in the remote area the next morning, although Yumi Ochiai, a flight attendant who was one of the four, later said that she could see the search helicopters during the night (its pilot had originally reported no sign of survivors) and could hear screams and moans that gradually weakened.

158.1 FX: BATATATA—helicopter sound

159.7 FX: BA—eyes opening suddenly

162.5 Yata is making reference to the legend of the *Ko Sodate Yurei*; please see the notes in Vol. 4 for 147.4 for more details.

164.1 FX: GWOOOO—sound of a speeding car

164.3 FX/balloon: GYUKYUKYUO—tires squealing

164.5 FX: DON—sound of the tires hitting the road

165.1 FX/balloon: JANKA JAKA CHARAN—ring tone

165.5 FX/balloon: PI—hanging up

166.1 FX/balloon: KIII—car braking

166.2 FX: ZA—footstep

167.7 FX: GARARA—sound of a sliding door opening

170.6 Carl Djerassi, one of the original developers of oral contraceptives in the 1950s, wrote in his 2003 memoir *This Man's Pill* that abortions in Japan can be very expensive—as much as $2,000 (in the United States, they tend to range between $300 and $1,000), and suggests lobbying by doctors eager to keep this revenue was a factor behind the great delay in birth-control pills becoming legal in Japan. By contrast, Djerassi notes, Viagra was made legal in Japan less than a year after it came on the market in the U.S. (there are stories of foreigners during those few months paying for an entire trip in Japan by bringing a Viagra prescription to sell off at $200 a pill). A *josanbu*'s "services" would presumably be much less; nor would such a traditional midwife report the "procedure," as a doctor is required to by law in Japan for an abortion.

172.3 FX/inset: GOTON—sound of a baby dropping into the post

175.1 FX: GORORI—body being rolled over

175.2 FX: GUGU—pressure being applied to stomach

175.3 FX/balloon: DORORI—fluid oozing out

175.5 Infanticide is in no way legal in Japan (abortions are permitted only through the twenty-second week of pregnancy), nor is it an act a typical Japanese woman would commit without feeling personal guilt and remorse; the story "Maternal Instinct" in Vol. 3 of Housui Yamazaki's *Mail* deals with a variation on this theme. But with the greater acceptance of abortion in general, there has been more willingness to accept "stillbirths" when the only ones in the know are the *josanbu* and the pregnant woman herself. Sasayama alludes to such attitudes in Vol. 6's 143.1. As with the mysterious "crying woman"

of Volumes 5 and 6, Otsuka uses a crone (in an archetypal and not pejorative sense) to embody acts that once had a ritualistic conception, but today are often just acts.

176.2 FX/balloon: PI—peeling off sound

176.3 FX/balloon: KUPA—eyelid being spread open

176.4 FX/balloon: PITO—eye cover/sticker being applied

177.1.1 FX: GUUUU—pressure being applied to lower abdomen

177.1.2 FX/balloon: BUPI—bowels evacuating

177.2 FX: KACHA—putting on metal cover

177.3 FX: NURU—spreading lubricant

177.4 FX/balloon: GURI—pushing in funnel-like instrument

177.5.1 FX/balloon: ZUBU—sound of cotton being pushed in

177.5.2 FX/balloon: ZUBUBU—more cotton being inserted

184.2.1 FX/balloon: KACHI—sound of stone being stacked

184.2.2 FX/balloon: KACHA—more stones

184.3 FX/balloon: KOTO—stone being placed on top

185.1 FX: MIIIN MIIIN—sound of cicadas

185.3 Kikuchi's grandmother is seen acting in the role of Jizo, the incarnation of the Buddha who took a vow to save the souls of those trapped in the realms of hell. William R. LaFleur's *Liquid Life: Abortion and Buddhism in Japan* (the title refers to *mizuko*, "water baby"; i.e., miscarriages and abortions) speaks of the folk belief that such souls end up on a deserted riverbank known as Saino-kawara in Meido, the realm of the dead. There, they play by stacking stones, an act that earns grace for their families on Earth. But at night, they are frightened by demons who come to knock down the stones. Jizo is said to wander the riverbank as a guardian, protecting the *mizuko* and praying for their eventual salvation. LaFleur notes that although this belief is comforting to women who have had such experiences, Buddhist temples make a good business of it, too, by selling personal Jizo figurines that can be decorated with children's clothing or toys; the author saw literally thousands of them lining the courtyards and walkways of a temple in Kamakura.

185.5 FX/balloon: BATAN BATAN BAKON—sound of wooden locker doors opening and slamming shut

185.6 FX: BAN BATAN BAN—slamming/banging sounds

186.1 FX/balloon: BATAN BATAAN BAGON—sound of wooden locker doors opening and slamming shut

186.2.1 FX/balloon: BAN BAN BAN—sound of wooden locker doors opening and slamming shut

186.2.2 FX/small: OGYAA OGYAA—faint sound of a wailing baby

186.3.1 FX/small: OGYAA OGYAA OGYAA OGYAA—faint sound of a wailing baby

186.3.2 FX/balloon: MEKI—sound of wood cracking

186.3.3 FX/balloon: BEKI—sound of wood breaking

wood breaking

186.4.2 FX/balloon: BEKI—sound of wood breaking

186.4.3 FX/balloon: BEKI—sound of wood breaking

186.5 FX: GOGOGOGO—rumbling

186.6 FX: GOFU—small imploding sound

189.4 FX: BURORO—car sound

189.5 FX: GOTOTOTOTO—sound of car rattling

189-190 The editor can't help but wonder if the staging of the last scene is meant to be reminiscent of the end of Hayao Miyazaki's 1979 classic *Lupin III: The Castle of Cagliostro*. Numata, with his grin, goatee, and most especially, bent cigarette, seems to conjure Jigen. *Cagliostro*, made a decade before Miyazaki broke out to the wider public with *Kiki's Delivery Service* (his first box-office smash), was actually his directorial debut in film, although he had directed TV anime beforehand. It's probably the greatest pure adventure film anime has produced, comparable in speed, wit, and excitement to its near-contemporary, *Raiders of the Lost Ark* (incidentally, the Spielberg praise-quote on the Special Edition DVD for *Cagliostro* has never, to my knowledge, actually been confirmed, but is simply based on a fan rumor dating back to the early '80s that he *did* like the movie!). It is true that Miyazaki's knight-errant take on Lupin reformed the reprobate seen in the original *Lupin III* manga (published by Tokyopop), but in Miyazaki's hands, it was magic.

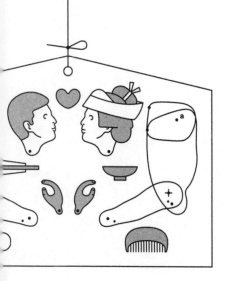

CPSIA information can be obtained at www.ICGtesting.com
Printed in the USA
LVOW11s1354300516

490437LV00014B/1031/P